# THE FINAL CHAPTER FOR ANASTASIA DeMARS

## A Novel

Jan Rosman

BookLocker

*For my Girls*

# CHAPTER 1

On the day of my sentencing I wore a simple black suit. It was Armani, but still, the Carolina Herrera jacket with the bell sleeves would have made a much bigger statement. My attorney, Clayton Fairhope, had issued strict instructions regarding my wardrobe and I would not have gotten past the front door in that magnificent ensemble. Clayton is a bit of a buzz kill, but I must say he takes his job seriously. He appeared in my hotel suite dressing room just as I slipped black pumps on my freshly pedicured feet. This seemed to be taking his job a bit too seriously.

"Clayton, what are you doing in here! Where is Maria? I told you not to worry. I have everything under control."

Clayton frowned. He has a deep crease between his eyebrows so I think frowning might be his usual face, even when he is not with me. I tried to lighten the mood. "A little Botox would take care of that furrow on your brow. I can ask Dr. Silverman for the name of a good plastic surgeon – if there ARE any good ones around here. My treat!"

"Anastasia, I am a lawyer. I do not do Botox. In fact, I like my face just as it is; we are used to each other. So thank you, but no. And those shoes are not exactly what I specified in my email."

"They are black! And if you can give fashion advice, you can get a wee bit of Botox to fix those trenches in your forehead."

Clayton sighed. "Those black shoes are Louboutin (Clayton pronounced it La-boo-teen) stilettos with tell tale red soles. And this is not fashion advice – clearly I am in over my head on that topic. But I do know we are going to your sentencing, not a photo shoot. You smacked a law enforcement officer in the head with your purse because he accidently stepped on your Jimmy Choos. Let's not rub the Judge's nose in it by wearing another pair of over priced shoes."

"Why Clayton Fairhope, look at you rattling off designer names like a stylist! Did Maria give you a short course in fashion branding? Surely you haven't been pricing ladies' shoes, unless there is something you need to tell us? Have a secret stash of fashion magazines under your mattress, do you?"

Clayton was not amused. As a good old Texas boy, he'd probably be less embarrassed by a hidden stack of *Playboy*s than a collection of *InStyle*s. I got the distinct impression my teasing was trying his patience. I did not care, and returned to my last minute touch-ups. I caught his eye in the mirror.

"Besides, you are wrong, Clayton. Every public appearance is a potential photo shoot. Representing a cosmetics empire is a lot of responsibility! I must always look my best."

"Keeping my client out of jail is also a big responsibility. Let me do my job. Maria?"

My assistant sheepishly poked her head around the door, making me think she had been there all along. She passed a box to Clayton. Traitor! He dropped the lid to reveal a pair of low heeled, sensible pumps. I had seen my dentist wear a pair just like them last week.

"Clayton, I did not assault the officer! That man would not let me explain why I had to run the red light, and he was clearly prejudiced against well dressed women driving expensive foreign cars. There was no reason to make me stand in the puddle; I could have given him a satisfactory explanation from inside my car. Unfortunately, my Marni bag got in between us when I tried to leap the mud. And he didn't just step on my shoes – he RUINED my new Jimmy Choos!" Maria slunk away backwards, one slow step at a time. The louder I got, the more soothing Clayton became, like he was asking a toddler to hand over a sticky lollipop.

"Now now, let's not lose sight of what happened, Anastasia. You were arrested because you hit him with your oversized tote. I've seen the video, remember? And so has the Judge. He understands, in your own words, how expensive those sparkly shoes cost. But we are past that part of these proceedings, so let's get through sentencing with the least amount of drama. And that begins with nondescript shoes and no handbag. You can leave your belongings in the car with Maria."

Whose side was he on? "That officer is a wimp! Confident females often intimidate average men. I should not have to pay a price for his insecurity. And obviously that bystander who filmed our encounter had no idea what was at stake. My shoes aren't even in the video! His editing made me look like a crazy person flinging my bag around for no good reason."

Clayton took a deep breath. True, we had been over this before, but ugly shoes bring out the irritable in me. That video, that 8 second cell phone movie, haunted me. What happened to respecting peoples' privacy? They say a picture is worth a thousand words, but a picture does not fill in the back story. Anyone in my position would have been frustrated.

It's not like I pulled a weapon on the cop. I simply tried to move him out of my way so I could stand on dry ground. It's not my fault he outweighed me by 200 pounds.

"Anastasia, listen to me. You will not try to explain ANYTHING to the Judge. You will be respectful and polite. You will listen. You will say 'Yes, Sir' and nod. It shouldn't take long. You can do it."

This is hard for me, I admit. Clayton had every reason to be concerned. During my preliminary hearing I was scolded for rolling my eyes, scoffing when the charge was read, and interrupting the Judge. Apparently this is frowned upon in Texas. At home in Los Angeles surely the court system is more accommodating to the temperaments of models and actors. Sterling Garrett, my retained attorney, is not licensed to practice law in Texas; that's how I got stuck with grandpa Clayton. I was still miffed that despite how much he's paid, Sterling couldn't stop that video from going viral. Our last conversation was heated, but how was an attorney to learn without feedback from his clients? He should thank me. My expectations were clear and Sterling failed to protect me when it mattered.

Clayton is nothing like Sterling. In a TV movie of my life, Brad Pitt could play Sterling (the *Ocean's*

*11* Brad, not the scruffy unwashed one), and Fred Thompson could play Clayton (if only Fred were still with us and wore a tired brown suit.) Sterling assured me Clayton came highly recommended. He said I needed a local attorney who was familiar with the county courts, one who could translate my profound remorse into a slap on the wrist. Let's hope Sterling is right and not just getting even for being reprimanded. LA types can become spiteful when they are held accountable.

The average person wouldn't be suffering such public scrutiny for trying to protect a $1500 shoe investment. My high profile profession made me a target for losers hoping to sell photos to the tabloids. Without that video it would be my word against the police officer's, and I'm sure the Judge would have been sympathetic to my side of the story. But once it went viral, and I became the laughingstock of middle America, the Judge had no choice but to adopt a stern tone. People love to hate the privileged.

I surrendered my pretty Louboutins and promised to be a good girl. Poor Clayton looked tired. "Good. Now remove that lipstick and let's go for something a bit less eye catching." What? My Warrior Red lipstick was armor against being washed out in pictures! It was my trademark, my signature. The headlines announced ANASTASIA

DeMARS GOES TO BATTLE AND THE OFFICER SEES WARRIOR RED when they released that damning video. Clayton widened his stance in the door. I relented.

"OK, OK, but it's on you to explain to my agent why I was caught wearing Barely There lips in public when they pay me to be the face of Warrior Red."

Clayton attempted a smile. "I think she will understand. Let's go. I've arranged a decoy car and look alike model to leave from the hotel garage. Once the press parade tails her we can slip out the back. I think you will get a kick out of your chariot."

Clayton had learned a lot since our first meeting. The paparazzi snapped him wearing cowboy boots with his suit that day and dubbed him my legal John Wayne. He was now fluent in upscale shoe brands and decoy strategies. Behind his slow drawl lurked a whip smart mind that moved much faster than he spoke. The lipstick came off. Today I needed John Wayne to save me, mostly from myself.

Maria, Clayton, and I headed down the service elevator to the basement garage. I couldn't help but notice Clayton's grin as I struggled to climb into the backseat of a giant Chevy pickup in my slim pencil skirt. My chariot indeed. He offered his hand and practically launched me into the seat. I was surprised to see TV screens built in for our viewing pleasure. Who knew a truck could be so luxurious? Our young chauffeur greeted me with enthusiasm a bit too eager for a trip to the courthouse.

"Good morning Miss DeMars. You are even prettier in person than on TV! I'm sorry to hear about your troubles." Clayton handed me a bottle of water.

"Anastasia, this in my grandson Cody. He helps me out on occasion. I trust him and so can you. Cody will get us to the courthouse incognito." He pronounced it in 4 distinct syllables, in-cog- NEE-toe.

Maria chimed in from the front seat. "Nice truck!" Cody beamed at the compliment.

Clayton tuned in for the day's headlines. And there I was, closing out the hour with the dig of the day.

"Anastasia DeMars will be sentenced today for the assault of a police officer after a traffic stop earlier this year in the Houston area. The incident was recorded on a cell phone and the video went viral, giving late night talk show hosts plenty of fodder. This caps off a difficult year for DeMars, whose break-up from movie star Grant Adams caught her off guard while they were promoting his latest adventure film *Warrior in Red*. Looks like being a super model is more dangerous than previously thought!"

The anchors all shared a laugh as the video played in the corner of the screen. The officer was a statue, calmly repeating his request that I exit the car and undergo a breathalyzer test. I had not been drinking, but if I took an objective look at the video I did look a little crazed. I was shouting "Don't you know who I am? You are going to be in trouble for this, mister!" I got out of the car with my bag in hand and tried to step over the mud, but tripped. In an effort to regain my balance, and avoid the puddle, I swung the bag and hit the guy on the side of the head. That's my story and I'm sticking to it. From the video, it looks like I tried to hit him – camera angles can distort all kinds of things, just ask a football referee- but what captured the media's attention was me screaming "MY JIMMY CHOOS! YOU DROWNED MY $1500 JIMMY CHOOS!" As a side note, my Warrior Red lipstick remained flawless. Score? Me one, guy with the cell phone, several million hits.

"Terrorists are planning attacks around the world and cable news has time to show that stupid video? OK Clayton, turn it off. You look like such a nice guy, but I am beginning to wonder."

"Well, Anastasia, I don't want you to forget what you are up against. This is Texas, not LA. The rules are different here. You will nod, say 'Yes Sir', and be polite."

I felt 2 feet tall. "Houston is not some outpost, Clayton. Plenty of women here wear Jimmy Choos, and not one of them would appreciate having their shoes ruined by an officer ignorant to the cost of fashion." I wasn't one to give in easily. Neither, it turns out, was Clayton.

"Well, you were not arrested in Houston," Clayton drawled. "You were arrested in Pleasant County, 50 miles and light years away from Neiman Marcus. Do not forget that. Texans outside the city are remarkably old school. They expect their children to use good manners, their bankers to be fair, and their traditions to be observed. One of those time-honored traditions is a respect for the law. Sheriffs are considered public servants; they get a nice watch and a party when they retire. You are considered a foreigner; antics that play in LA don't translate here. The Judge does not care about your shoes. He cares that esteemed customs remain intact so his grandchildren inherit a world grounded in strong values, not celebrity tomfoolery. So you will play by his rules." He patted my hand as he chastised me. I retreated into the corner of the seat, silent. Tomfoolery?

We passed a billboard that warned DON'T MESS WITH TEXAS. They weren't kidding. I heard this slogan began as an anti-littering campaign, but it pretty much summed up Clayton's rule book. Fine. Let's just get this over with so I could go back to LA, where people understand that a bad day might lead to a hissy fit. Hey, some people get paid for broadcasting that fit on TV. Why do the Housewives get rewarded for behaving badly, and I got arrested? Life is not fair.

The Pleasant County courthouse anchors a town square that resembles a set on the back lot at Warner Bros. Studios. Mayberry does exist and Opie drives a tricked out pickup. The local theater – stage, not movie – faces the courthouse across the green, a smaller rendition of the courthouse's stately 20th century architecture. Its white marquis advertised the upcoming revival of *GREATER TUNA.*

"*Greater Tuna*? Is that a play?" Maria emerged from her cocoon in the front seat. She'd gone radio silent since I glared at her in the great shoe exchange. We were stopped at the red light and she pointed to a poster depicting two old ladies behind a microphone. "Does that say 'Starring Clayton Fairhope as Pearl?'"

I shot out of my corner and opened the window to get a closer look. Clayton tapped Cody on the shoulder. "Light's green, son. Let's go."

I'd bet a dollar Clayton blushed. He refused to look me in the eye. For a moment I forgot my embarrassment over Jimmy ChooGate. "Wait just a minute! Are there two Clayton Fairhopes in Pleasant County, Texas, or did I just see you featured on a life sized poster dressed in drag? At a public theater? Does Judge Goodman know about this? Or wait – maybe the Judge is his co-star!" I could not stop laughing. "Cody, go back! I need to get a picture of this! My day just got a whole lot better!"

Clayton caught Cody's eye in the rear-view mirror. "We need to get to the courthouse. Anastasia, let's get through sentencing without a detour through my community theater resume. Suffice it to say we value local around here – local beef, local theater, and yes, local attorneys. That's why Sterling recommended me. You, however, are not local. So mind your ps and qs young lady." Clayton's tone was stern but the spell was broken. I could not dislodge the visual of him in a white wig and jeweled cat glasses. If laughter is good medicine I was fortified by a hefty dose as we rounded the square.

In other good news, the decoy worked. We passed the black Mercedes idling a block away; several photographers hovered near the parking garage waiting for "my" entrance. Our pickup blended in with all the other trucks and SUVs. Cody maneuvered around a construction barrier on the opposite side of the building and stopped in front of a spot blocked by orange cones. He hopped out, moved the cones, and pulled right in. I got the impression he had done this before. Clayton cleared his throat, straightened his tie, and offered his hand to climb out of the vehicle.

We entered the courthouse through the employee door, proceeded through the metal detector, and made our way up the stairs to Judge Goodman's third floor courtroom. It was early and we were the first ones on his docket to arrive. A large sign at the door clarified who was in charge.

ALL PEOPLE WHO ENTER JUDGE GOODMAN'S COURTROOM WILL OBSERVE THESE COURTESIES:

NO GUM
NO T-SHIRTS WITH SLOGANS
NO EXPOSED MIDRIFFS
NO UNTUCKED SHIRTS
NO BAGGY PANTS
NO PHOTOS, VIDEO, OR RECORDING OF ANY KIND
NO TALKING ON CELL PHONES, SILENCE THEM

IF YOU NEED ASSISTANCE COMPLYING WITH THESE COURTESIES, PLEASE SEE THE BAILIFF. IF YOU REFUSE TO COMPLY, THE BAILIFF WILL SEE YOU OUT.

I elbowed Clayton in the ribs. "Lucky for you Judge Goodman's list does not include NO DRESSING IN DRAG."

Clayton eyed me straight faced. "OK, that is enough."

I was familiar with Judge Goodman's decrees. The day I plead no contest the bailiff kindly pointed to the 7 commandments posted on the wall, handed me a tissue for my gum, then resumed his post as sentry. Today he nodded and opened the door, following us in to the empty tribunal. If he noticed my barely contained amusement, he didn't let on.

"Good morning. Judge Goodman has elected to see Miss DeMars and counsel in his chambers. Please wait here and I will come back to escort you when the Judge is ready."

I wondered if Bailiff Meecham had considered a career as a character actor. With crime shows all the rage he would be in high demand. How old was he? Hard to tell. Somewhere between 25 and 45. His shiny bald head, Popeye stature, and authoritative saunter begged to be in a courtroom drama. A low riding belt supported his ample belly while his gun bounced gently against his hip. He disappeared behind the raised altar of the Judge's bench.

I plopped into a wooden chair behind the spectator rail. Things were looking up. The sense of dread that woke me at 5:00 am had lifted. I took a deep breath. "That is so nice of Judge Goodman. Southerners really are gentlemen. The last thing I wanted was to stand here in front of a crowd to get sentenced. That was very thoughtful of him."

Clayton frowned. "Anastasia, he has not invited you to tea. It is to protect his courtroom from turning into a circus. Judge Goodman is the star of this show, not you. Please do not forget that. The same rules apply in chambers as in an open courtroom. Don't speak unless spoken to. Be polite. And try to wipe that smirk off your face. He might assume you are laughing at him instead of laughing at me."

"Clayton, I am not laughing at you! You just surprise me. I didn't expect to see Mr. Country Lawyer dressed in drag to play a woman named Pearl. I am beginning to think there is more to this little town than meets the eye. The paparazzi is confused – I'm not the story, you are!"

Bailiff Meecham interrupted our exchange, much to Clayton's relief. "Please follow me. Do not sit until after Judge Goodman sits." We entered a small office, devoid of the pomp that decorated the courtroom. Judge Goodman's diplomas hung behind his desk, announcing dual degrees in Law and Social Work from the University of Texas at Austin. I hadn't finished college. I was discovered during my sophomore year at University of Illinois when I made the front page of the *Daily Illini* for winning the annual Dance Marathon. My dance partner (assigned to me by my sorority) was 5'8", and I was 6'4" in heels, so we made for a good story when we won. A scout from Fame Cosmetics figured if I looked good in a candid college photo (after dancing for 24 hours), I had potential to look good in a professionally produced ad campaign. It didn't hurt that I was wearing Warrior Red lipstick, still vibrant, at the end of the marathon.

My 'True Story' testimonial hit the pages of *Seventeen* and *Marie Claire* in full color, this time with a 6'6" model named Enrico as my dance partner. I thanked my beautiful mother for the inheritance of a voluptuous kisser – all the better to model lipstick with – and she said you're welcome, please finish college. I signed a contract with Fame and promptly moved to LA.

Judge Goodman snapped me back to the present with a flutter of his black robe. With a nod he excused us to sit, and the butterflies that had flown away earlier landed right back in my gut. He reviewed my file while I tried not to fidget in the uncomfortable wooden chair. You'd think he would have done his research before arriving. Clayton gently stepped on my foot – message received. I sat up straight, tried to arrange my face in a calm repose, and waited. I am not usually good at waiting. Judge Goodman seemed in no hurry.

"Good Morning Miss DeMars. Mr. Fairhope. Miss DeMars, it has been several months since you pleaded no contest to charges you assaulted a police officer during a routine traffic stop. Your attorney Mr. Fairhope has delayed sentencing several times, presumably to convince me you are an upstanding citizen and this incident was an aberration in your usual demeanor. Am I to assume you have been on good behavior?"

"Yes Sir."

"I'm curious Miss DeMars, since it's just us here in these chambers (and a bailiff and a court reporter, but who was I to correct him.) Why did you hit the officer with your bag? It seems a bit out of character for a young woman dressed in fancy high heels. Your sobriety test revealed no alcohol, so your judgement was not impaired. Did something happen involving the officer before the camera began to roll? I like to be certain I have all the facts before I sentence offenders, and since you opted out of a trial I am in the dark as to what happened that night. I believe justice is best served when the facts are on the table."

I glanced at Clayton, not sure how to respond. We had only discussed me saying "Yes, sir". Clayton raised his eyebrows and nodded.

"Well, sir, I was very frustrated. The officer refused to listen to me. When he first pulled me over, and I gave him my license, he asked if I knew I'd run a red light. Of course I knew! I'd just witnessed my boyfriend kissing another woman in a short skirt. I had to follow them! I came all this way to Texas to surprise Grant at his sister's wedding, and caught him running around with the flavor of the week. Grant should have been the one humiliated in the press, not me!" With that the tears started flowing. Clayton slowly shook his head and stared at his lap.

Judge Goodman stared at me. The court reporter stared. Bailiff Meecham stared. I am not a pretty crier, I know. My nose gets all runny and I have this hiccupping thing that takes over. Once unleashed, it's difficult to put the genie back in the bottle. They all waited until I pulled myself together.

"Miss DeMars, perhaps I need to make myself more clear. Did the OFFICER do anything to upset you, besides pulling you over for running a red light?"

"He made me get out of a perfectly dry car and stand in the mud! Was that necessary?" Clayton not so gently stepped on my foot. I realized I was shouting. This was off script.

It was Judge Goodman's turn to sigh. "He was following protocol Miss DeMars, especially since you appeared to be agitated. Under the circumstances, I think he demonstrated remarkable restraint. Let's proceed with sentencing. You are clearly suffering ill effects from exposure to the press. That seems an occupational hazard for a model dating a film star, but nonetheless I am not insensitive to your position. I am sentencing you to a fine of $500 and 100 hours of community service. You will serve those 100 hours assisting a local non-profit, The Joy Chorus. The Director, Duke Valentine, will be your supervisor. He will report your progress to your Probation Officer. Mr. Valentine can be trusted to put you to work without courting media attention. Once you have successfully fulfilled your service, your record will be expunged provided you have no further run-ins with the law. My clerk will provide Mr. Fairhope with all further instructions."

"But Your Honor, Sir, I live in LA. Can't I just pay a bigger fine, or give money to this non-profit instead? I have my work to consider."

Judge Goodman stood up. Bailiff Meecham announced, "All rise!" I felt the tears beginning to flow again. Can a judge do that? Can he impose a sentence that handcuffs me to a small town in Texas when I have an important life in LA? Yes, yes he can.

"Miss DeMars, this is not a negotiation. Your offense happened in Texas, and your sentence will be fulfilled in Texas. My decision is final. I suggest you embrace the experience, you just might learn something."

Clayton glared at me to remain silent. Bailiff Meecham escorted us out of chambers. He kindly showed us through the side door so we could escape through the back stairway. I said nothing until we emerged into the hot Texas sunlight. "Clayton! Do something! I..."

"Let's just get out of here without making a scene, Anastasia. Don't forget, someone is always watching and they usually have a camera in hand."

I zipped it and struggled into the back seat of the truck. Cody and Maria wisely kept eyes forward without asking how things went. This was awful. How was I supposed to do community service in Texas? So much for Southern gentlemen! And sensitive to my position? Ha! These people had no idea how difficult my situation was. I regretted coming to Texas. I regretted hitting the officer with my bag. But mostly I regretted ever meeting Grant Adams.

# CHAPTER 2

A year ago, women across the country would have traded their Louis Vuitton luggage to be in my designer shoes. I met Grant on a photo shoot. Fame Cosmetics partnered with a movie studio to promote his latest adventure film, *Warrior in Red.* Since I was the face of Fame's Warrior Red lipstick, they did a clever ad campaign featuring me with a sword crafted from a huge tube of lipstick. In the ad I am lunging to pierce his red armor in the heart. The slogan read "NOTHING TESTS A WARRIOR LIKE A WOMAN IN RED." The plot of the movie had Grant (sexy Warrior) almost taken down by a woman in a slinky red evening gown (wearing Warrior Red lipstick) before he realizes she is the evil force trying to conquer the world. Think James Bond meets Star Wars. In the end the Warrior prevails, the evil woman is exiled into a life of servitude (devoid of red evening gowns or a bath, apparently), and the hero finds true love with a meek woman in white. Men with dominance fantasies clearly write these scripts.

I was under contract with Fame Cosmetics to be the face of Warrior Red lipstick, so I went to the shoot without asking for a back story (models are paid to follow directions, not weigh in on the set up of an ad). After a long day of fake swashbuckling, Grant suggested sharing a drink at the Chateau

Marmont. Saving the world, even in choreographed ad stills, makes a man bold; he sealed the invitation with a steamy kiss. The paparazzi snapped photos of us at the entrance to the hotel and the next day's tabloids exposed our "secret" romance. My mom called from the check out at her local Publix. "Hello sweetie. How's everything in Hollywood?" Classic Ginger. She has yet to recover from my quick exit from college, but never resorts to nagging. She learned from her own mother's meddling that it's best to simply offer warm cookies and an open door when I make it back to Chicago.

"Hollywood is great! I shot a movie promotion campaign yesterday with Grant Adams, and I have a guest spot on *So You Think You Can Model* later this week. What's new there?"

She paused. "Nothing new here. Just checking in. Have you seen the headlines at the grocery store? Thought maybe you had a new beau, but sounds like you were just working with that Grant Adams guy." The relief in her voice was palpable, even through the phone.

"Mom, you can't believe those rags. We grabbed a drink after our shoot, that's all. But I'll admit, he's cute. You should see him dressed in red armor wielding a sword!"

Silence. My mom knows I am a sucker for cute. She was too. That's how she married my gorgeous, cheating, good for nothing father. No doubt she had witnessed the parade of Grant's models and actresses march across the tabloids. This is where her no meddling policy gets tricky. Her mother, my crazy one eyed grandma Edna, was a young (and forever) widow. She berated the hordes of young men fawning over my enchanting mother. Edna, whether from jealousy or caution, criticized my mother's beauty constantly. 'Makeup is for tarts, put your hair in a bun, your skirt is too short.' In her very public opinion, beautiful women always married cads and suffered for it. Maybe she wanted to protect her daughter from that fate, maybe she was just mean, but words have power and my mother did just as Edna predicted. With me, my mom swung the pendulum to the other side, rejecting criticism in favor of encouragement. Since I became an adult she resisted the temptation to tell me what to do. But I could feel her concern travel from Chicago to LA over the airways.

After a few moments, she took a deep breath. "You are a smart, talented woman Anna, destined for great things. Just remember that. "

"Thanks Mom. You're the best. I hope to get home in the next few weeks. Let's talk soon. Love you."

It only took a few dates with Grant to forget I was destined for great things. He was so charming, and funny, and handsome. Every girl in Hollywood was jealous of me. We were on top of the world, running from premier to red carpet. Our time together was snatched between modeling gigs and his interview schedule; promoting a movie is more demanding than you'd think. Grant and I made the cover of *Celebrity* magazine the week *Warrior in Red* premiered. And that's when things began to unwind.

The *Celebrity* piece was a nightmare from the beginning. Grant wanted to do the interview alone, but his fans were more interested in our relationship than the movie. The reporter, Kelly Roberts, showed up an hour early (claiming we got the time wrong), so I wasn't ready. Grant didn't like the outfit I chose because in heels I was taller than him. He insisted I stay in jeans and go barefoot, claiming a 'casual' look was more 'authentic.' The chit chat started without me; I could hear them through the open bedroom door. Kelly asked Grant if he ever made it back home to Texas now that he was Hollywood's hotshot. Grant laughed. "Well, my baby sister is getting married next week, so I'll be home for her wedding. I try to get back for holidays but my schedule is grueling. And there's not much happening in Pleasant County, Texas!" I had not heard about his sister getting married. I tried to remember her name. Christy? Chrissie?

Kelly elbowed her way right through that open door. "Speaking of love, is your romance with Anastasia the real thing? Any big plans you'd like to announce? You two certainly make a gorgeous couple!"

That's when I heard Grant scoff. "It's only been a few months. And what's the real thing anyway? I'm having fun, she's having fun, everybody is happy. You want true love? Watch a movie! Besides, I'm young."

Watch a movie? What about last night when he told me I was the most fascinating woman he'd ever known? And he wasn't that young. 35 is middle aged for a man in Hollywood. I was young! 24 is still fresh in LA, even for a woman. But I was having fun, right? My career had enjoyed a boost since we started dating. Guest spots on modeling shows had progressed to an interview on *After Dark*.

Grant yelled from the living room. "Anastasia! Come on – I'm hungry! Let's get started so I can get something to eat!" I was hungry too, did he think about that? His flippant response about true love was a shot to my gut. This was not the best frame of mind for an interview with a snoopy reporter, and clearly the interview had already begun whether Grant knew it or not. I plastered a smile on my face. Kelly Rogers stood to greet me.

"Anastasia, Grant and I were just chatting. I hear you two met on a photo shoot promoting the movie. You have become quite the IT girl since then! Are you more like the woman in red, feisty and battle ready, or the woman in white, sweet and wholesome?"

Grant fidgeted on the couch. I wasn't even in the movie and this conversation was already off track. I was unprepared for Kelly's line of questioning; my agent tried to warn me, but I had been too busy with dress fittings to sit down for a role-playing game. Grant had instructed me to field all questions about our relationship to him, but I ran with his advice to be 'authentic' instead.

"Well, since the woman in red is an evil manipulator, and the woman in white is a doormat, let's go with neither, Kelly."

Again, I was hungry and my feelings were hurt. I may have lost sight of the objective at hand. My experience prepared me for looking glamorous, not responding to a snarky magazine reporter. It was a set up for disaster and I blindly walked into a carefully laid booby trap. Kelly smelled blood.

"That sounds like you aren't a fan of the movie at all! Grant, are you a fan of Anastasia's work? Or are you two an evolved couple, comfortable living in a house divided?" Kelly was practically drooling at the gift I just handed her.

Grant paused. "That is not what she meant. Anastasia is a huge fan of the movie. What's not to love about an adventure where good triumphs over evil and the characters look great while saving the world? And we don't live together." He attempted a weak laugh. I moved toward the middle of the couch, away from Grant. Kelly Roberts took notes. She leaned closer to me with sympathetic eyes.

"Anastasia, I understand your concerns about the portrayal of women in movies like these. Why can't an intelligent woman be the hero for once?"

I took the bait. Don't judge, you would have too. "Exactly! Even the ad campaign reinforces the notion that women's only weapons are sexual. Have you seen it? I have a sword make of lipstick! No need for a brain, just take a macho man down with alluring lips and a red dress. Ridiculous!"

It seems I have more of my mother downloaded in me than I realized. I remembered a similar tirade from her when I was 15 and wanted to rent the movie *Pretty Woman*. My mother looked me in the eye and said "We do not need men to rescue us. Make your own way in life, and the right man will appreciate it." Lessons learned the hard way, after she left my dad.

Grant didn't appreciate my opinion at that moment; he probably loved *Pretty Woman*. "Kelly, would you give us a minute?" And with that he grabbed my hand and practically dragged me out onto the patio.

"What are you doing?" Grant whispered, seething. "This interview is supposed to be about promoting a movie – my movie – not some feminist rant from you!"

"When were you going to tell me about your sister's wedding? Am I even invited? And she set me up for that rant! The movie IS ridiculous!"

Grant stepped back. "That's not the point! What is wrong with you? You are messing with my career! You are not going back in there. I'll tell Kelly you had to leave. Do not answer the phone if she calls you. It will be hard enough for me to fix this without your intellectual perspective. Ha! You model lipstick for a living!" Grant had gone from whispering to almost shouting. I took the volume up a notch.

"You are kicking me out? Because I stated the obvious about your stupid adventure fantasy? Fine! Tell her anything you want." I stalked into the bedroom from the patio, grabbed my shoes, and left through the back yard.

Guess what - Kelly Roberts is no dummy. Remember, people love to hate the privileged, especially when you are prettier than they are. The story headline screamed "GRANT ADAMS NO HERO TO ANASTASIA DeMARS." The movie was mentioned, but only in the context of my disdain for it. Kelly pronounced my early exit from the interview evidence of an impending breakup (speculation on Kelly's part, but a pretty safe gamble). She praised me as a champion for women in Hollywood while throwing my career under the proverbial bus. Kelly made it clear I viewed the ad campaign as sexist, while casting Grant as a misogynist. As soon as the story hit the stands I got a call from my agent, Diane Feldman. She predictably direct.

"Anastasia, I'll cut right to the chase. Fame Cosmetics has put you on probation. They are citing the clause requiring you to represent their products with dignity. I've already talked to Sterling, and we both agree that your best strategy is to lay low. They may have reason to terminate, but for now you won't be working on any new shoots and the ad campaign for the movie is on ice. Maybe take some time off. Don't give any interviews! It will just backfire, you aren't trained in this side of the business. Let us handle it."

So giving me a "sword" shaped as a tube of lipstick in an overtly sexual ad passed the dignity test, but stating the obvious (that the movie it promoted was stupid) justified suspension? Fame executives were so out of touch! The public had to be on my side in this. I had a mind to set the record straight. Maybe Ellen DeGeneres would invite me on her show to expose this ugly side of Hollywood.

Diane had a mind to set ME straight. "Anastasia, I mean it. No talking to anyone about the situation; it could trigger immediate termination. Your success as a model is currently tied to sales of Warrior Red lipstick. Repeat after me; 'I am taking some time off.' That's it. Then go underground for a while."

I was being silenced by my own agent, and she worked for me. My threshold for bad news was diminishing. Photographers stalked me, Grant wouldn't answer my calls. I went from red carpet appearances to binge watching *Gilmore Girls* alone in one sharp thrust of the press. How was I going to fix this? If I could only explain face to face that I meant no harm. I'm young and naïve, remember? You used to like that about me?

That's when I decided to surprise Grant in Texas. It's easy to unearth information when you play the damsel in distress. Southerners can be so helpful. I called the nicest hotel in Pleasant County (there weren't too many, believe me) and pretended to be a flighty guest who forgot the important wedding details. "Hello, I am coming to Chrissie Adam's wedding this weekend and lost my itinerary! Can you help me? I am traveling there tomorrow and don't want to bother Chrissie since she is busy with preparations."

A perky young man named Justin jumped at the chance to demonstrate his establishment's excellent customer service. "Hello! I would be happy to assist you. We have gift boxes for all the guests here at the front desk – surely there is a schedule tucked inside. Just let me break one open. Here we go. Ooooo, there are some nice goodies in this box! Looks like dinner for out of town guests- that's you! - is at 6:00 at La Fontaine on Friday– very nice! If you're lucky they will serve their signature chocolate mousse for dessert. The wedding on Saturday is at 6:30 at Plantation Manor. I went to an event there last year and the venue is stunning. Is it an outdoor ceremony? The live oak is spectacular, but you might consider wearing flats. I saw women's heels sink in the grass and we have had some rain this week. Does that help?"

"Yes, yes, thank you. Happily my schedule cleared and I am able to attend. Do you still have rooms available?"

Justin was sympathetic. "We are technically sold out, but I do have a few rooms set aside for emergencies like this. It happens all the time with big weddings! Guests are so rude these days, showing up with no RSVP. I'm sorry, I didn't mean to imply you are rude. You are clearly very nice. Who is the room for? I will need to guarantee it with a credit card."

I pulled out my wallet and reached into the back zippered pocket. "Anna Martin. You can reserve it for Anna Martin."

Operation Get Grant Back was in motion. I would arrive Friday afternoon and surprise him for the Rehearsal dinner at La Fontaine (thank you, Justin). That would give us time to make up before the festivities on Saturday. I would apologize, bat my big brown eyes, and promise never to give another interview again.

The only glitch? I hadn't considered Grant might have planned festivities of his own. Just as I pulled under the hotel canopy, Grant jumped into the back seat of a black limo. A leggy blond in a very short pink skirt draped herself over him before the door closed. Through the rear window I could see them kissing. They sped off, me in hot pursuit. You know the rest. That's how I ended up in the back seat of a pickup truck contemplating 100 hours of community service, pathetic and embarrassed.

The day after my arrest video went viral, Grant appeared in the tabloids wearing the leggy blond on his arm. The headline announced SUPERHERO GRANT ADAMS MOVES ON WITH A WOMAN IN PINK. To the left of their picture was a slightly blurry photo of me bemoaning my shoes' drowning death. Since then, Grant had been photographed with a woman in black, one in yellow, and the last one in a vivid floral print. I hoped not be photographed in low heeled nondescript pumps.

Right after my arrest, while I was waiting for Sterling to secure legal counsel, I sat in a gray room on a wooden chair and called my mom. She answered with her usual good spirits. "Hi sweetie, what's new in Hollywood?" Between sobs I told her about following Grant to Texas, my high speed chase, and hysterical arrest. "I should have listened to you! I never should have come here!"

"Anna, you never told me you were going to Texas."

"I know, but I heard you anyway! In my head you said 'Anna, don't be that girl who chases a guy just to be kicked in the teeth!' You said 'Anna, you deserve better than Grant Adams!' So go ahead and get it over with. I know what you are thinking!"

Silence. My mom is good with pauses. She gently asked, "What exactly am I thinking, Anna?"

"You are thinking 'what did you expect from a pretty boy with a terrible reputation? Did you think you could change his stripes? Did you consider listening to your mom once in a while?'" With that I lost it, heaving through the tears and searching the room for tissues.

"Anna, that is what YOU were thinking. Because I was thinking good, it's over. You are embarrassed. So what? Nobody ever died of being humiliated. Short term pain is better than suffering long term with a man who cares more about his image than he cares about you. This is just a detour! Quit feeling sorry for yourself. Face the music for this incident and move on. Why don't you come home for a visit to regroup? Walk the dogs, eat home cooked meals, leave Anastasia DeMars behind for a few days. We will boycott all tabloids and social media. We will flog anyone who utters the name

Grant Adams! We will spit in Hollywood's eye, one mani pedi at a time! Plus there is a new Anne of Green Gables movie I've been waiting to watch with you."

The image of my mother spitting in anyone's eye stopped the waterworks. She is too polite to spit out a bad piece of chicken in a restaurant. "Thanks mom. I'll let you know what happens. I'll be OK."

"I know. You are a smart girl Anna, destined for great things. I love you." Clayton introduced himself as I hung up. Fast forward three months; my career had stalled, my shoes were frumpy, and I lay at the mercy of the Texas Justice System. This was not what I had in mind when I was proudly voted "Most Likely to be in the News" in high school.

# CHAPTER 3

Judge Goodman made his point - he did not care about the woes of a heartbroken model. As soon as the pickup door closed after my sentencing, I erupted. "Clayton, why didn't you do something! Community service? In Texas? Really? You couldn't arrange a deal with a bigger fine instead? I have the money! I would be happy to pay a big fine! Wouldn't that help this choir more than me hanging around punching Judge Goodman's clock? You are local! You were supposed to fix this for me!"

Clayton seemed fascinated by something out the window. Cody and Maria slid down in their seats up front. "Clayton! I'm talking to you! I paid you to fix this!"

"Anastasia, I think you are missing the point. There are guidelines the Judge must follow as to the fine he imposes. Second, community service gives the defendant an opportunity to give something back. Optimists believe that by doing so, the defendant might learn to appreciate the benefits society offers and make better choices in the future. Judge Goodman is an optimist. Besides, the deal is done. Be thankful this will all go away once your community service hours are completed."

Clayton resumed patting my hand. He reminded me of my stepfather Frank, kind and solid, but unbending in his principles. My mother hit the lottery when she met Frank. My birth father was like a colorful kite, observable from the ground out of the corner of my eye. But Frank had been shelter. Short and balding, he and my statuesque mother were Mutt and Jeff. He was a prince among men, and my parents had enjoyed 18 happy years together. I should call Frank more often. And probably be nicer to Clayton.

"Anastasia, I will get the service specifics from Judge Goodman later today. Maybe we go meet Duke tomorrow? Then you can work with Maria to get your hours scheduled between work commitments."

"Well, that shouldn't be too difficult since I have no work commitments. One stupid interview, one nasty reporter who uses me to make a point, and now I am kryptonite."

Clayton ignored my theatrics. "Alrighty then, that will make this easier. I'll contact Duke." Cody turned up the radio. Some crooner named George "Stopped Lovin' Her Today". Even the radio knew I got dumped and was rubbing my nose in it.

Maria's phone rang. She silenced it immediately, which made me suspicious. "Maria, who is calling? Maria!"

"It's Diane Feldman."

"Did she leave a message?"

Maria flinched. "Yes."

"Ok, let's hear it. Put it on speaker. Maybe we will get some good news."

Maria complied. "Maria, have Anastasia call me as soon as possible. Fame just terminated her contract."

Great.

Maria declined my dinner invitation in the hotel bar. She didn't say it, but I guessed a movie and room service was preferable to keeping company with me. I agreed. Two martinis in I gave up on dinner and surrendered to the comfort of sleep.

*** 

Clayton picked me up at 3:00 on Tuesday. He eyed me up and down like I examine a dress on the hanger. I eyed him back. "What. Are you the fashion police again today?" I was grumpy, and who was Clayton to judge? He was in faded jeans and a pair of ancient cowboy boots.

He just shook his head. I think he muttered something about natural consequences being the best teacher, but it's hard to say, and I did not ask for clarification. I was ready for battle, dressed to the nines in case a photo op presented itself. A model cannot afford to find herself looking down in the dumps in the tabloids. Especially a model who is out of work. Once you made the CELEBRITIES WITH CELLULITE list, or the YOU'LL NEVER BELIEVE WHAT SHE LOOKS LIKE WITH NO MAKEUP club, those pictures were forever available online. I vowed to avoid all future PR traps. Every girl looks her best in stilettos with lipstick in place. I was still mad at Fame, but hadn't broken the Warrior Red habit; they couldn't dictate my lip color. It had become my signature, not the other way around. They would come to regret their hasty decision to can Anastasia DeMars.

We pulled up behind a big barn just off the highway feeder road. This was bizarre. Right between an IHOP and a strip mall sat The Watering Hole. Its marquis advertised local talent Bubba James on Saturday night, event SOLD OUT. Last night's rain had formed puddles in the gravel parking lot all the way from the car to the back door. I'd seen a paved walkway in the front, but I didn't want to give Clayton the satisfaction of seeing me sweat. I could navigate a few puddles, contrary to popular opinion. My tight leather skirt and Carolina Herrera jacket with the bell sleeves suddenly felt a bit much. There was not a photographer in sight. True, nobody knew I was coming here – the specifics of my community service weren't in the news so far – but you never know. Best to be prepared. I felt most confident dressed for all contingencies, which included everything except a flooded parking lot.

Once I picked my way carefully around the puddles, Clayton held the barn door open. My eyes adjusted to the interior, and to my surprise the inside looked like a real barn. The walls were dark aged vertical planks, the floors scuffed hardwood. Split rails separated the balcony from the stage below. Massive beams supported the roof. Vintage signs advertising Coke-a-Cola and Esso gasoline decorated the walls. The room was filled with long farm tables covered in red and white checkered cloths.

A man in jeans and boots was adjusting the lighting on stage. His white ponytail lay against a blue button down shirt, starched but untucked. Clayton greeted him with enthusiasm. "Duke! Good to see you! It's been too long. This is Anastasia DeMars, at your service."

I stepped forward to shake his extended hand. A large tattoo covered his right forearm; it said JOY, with Galatians 5:22 under it. He was very tall. In heels I stand well over six feet, and he towered above me. "Miss DeMars, welcome to The Watering Hole. Duke Valentine. I understand we are your purgatory. Hopefully we err on the side of heaven when it's all said and done. Do you sing?" His voice was a booming baritone.

"Sing? Not really. I had a part in my high school production of *Damn Yankees*. Does that count?"

"As long as you agree with the sentiment, sure. You'll fit right in."

It took me a moment to connect the dots. Yes, we were in Texas, the South. Got it.

"The show isn't about Northerners, it's about baseball. I played a woman whose husband trades his wife and soul to the devil so his team can finally beat the Yankees." Geez, I was rehearsing for my future in high school before I even knew Grant Adams.

Duke smiled. "Yes, I know. I've seen the play. We are Astros fans around here, not Yankee fans. Guessing from your accent you are not from these parts."

Wow, nothing like miscommunication right off the bat. He was talking about baseball while I was resurrecting the Civil War. We were off to a bad start. "No, I'm from LA – Chicago originally. I'm a model."

Duke resumed his work with the lights. "So I hear. What brings you to our humble barn? Robert - Judge Goodman - didn't fill in the gaps."

I looked at Clayton. His raised eyebrows said go ahead. "Um, well, I'm sure you've seen the video. In addition to being humiliated the world over, I was sentenced to 100 hours of community service. Judge Goodman specified I serve it with the Joy Chorus. Is that you?"

"100 hours –that must be some video. Can't say I've seen it, but I'm not one for the 24 hour news cycle. Did the Judge say what you were supposed to do here?"

"No. He just mentioned you would keep the media at bay. That's why he picked it. You. The choir."

"Is that what he told you? Funny. Here I am courting press for my barn and he sends me a model with instructions to lock them out. Sounds like he is punishing me, not you. Don't worry, a model won't get much attention around here – if you could sing or play the guitar, that might be a different story, but for now let's hear what you can do. Are you a good short order cook? How are your math skills? Ever driven a school bus?"

I couldn't tell if he was teasing me again or not.

"What does math have to do with singing?"

Duke threw his head back and laughed. "You are about to find out! Clayton, didn't you tell your client anything about what goes on here? That's a dirty trick, my friend! Miss DeMars, you might want to dress for comfort in the future; think tennis shoes and an apron."

Clayton piped in. "Some things are best learned hands on. Don't scare the girl, Duke. We haven't worked out a schedule yet; today is just her introduction. She lives in LA, so we have some logistics to work out. When do you want her?"

"We gather here every Wednesday from 3:00 to 5:00 pm, and Saturdays from 10:00 – 12:00."

This was NOT going to work for me. I couldn't travel to Texas every week, 4 community service hours at a time. "That's it? What do you do here when you aren't singing? Seems like a lot of space for 4 hours a week."

Duke paid no attention to the panic in my voice. "The Watering Hole is a music venue; it's my business. The Joy Chorus is a labor of love – or labor of torture, depending on the day. We are all volunteers. We meet here because the acoustics can't be beat. Helps with the members who have your level of talent. Kind of like singing in the shower; everyone sounds good."

"So it's not a professional choir?"

Duke pointed to a photo of kids on the wall. "The Joy Chorus is an outreach to high school kids. Crazy? Messy? All consuming? Yes. Professional? No. Anyone can join if they stay in school and commit to regular practice."

This was a disaster. "I am a model, not a music teacher. How do you expect me to teach teenagers to sing? I didn't like high school kids when I was in high school! I can't imagine I'd like them any better now." Duke was right – the acoustics were great. It sounded like I was shouting. Clayton frowned.

Duke nodded as if pondering this information. "Good to know. I don't want you teaching kids to sing. Your *Damn Yankees* experience hardly qualifies you for such a lofty position. No, I had other things in mind. Serving lunch on Saturdays, for instance. Or helping kids with homework on

Wednesdays; our first hour is devoted to tutoring. And there's always cleaning up after they leave – dishes, sweeping, bathrooms. 60 teenagers can leave quite a trail.

"60 kids! I don't know how to tutor, or cook, or talk to teenagers! What was Judge Goodman thinking?"

Duke's amusement waned but his voice remained calm. "What did you think community service entailed? Promotional photo shoots? Nobody around here is above doing whatever it takes to get the job done. If my chef doesn't show up, I flip the burgers. If the janitor calls in sick, I mop the floors. That's how business works. It's the same with the Joy Chorus. These kids only get what we give them. You better decide now you are going to give them whatever they need. Or go back to the Judge and explain you're too sophisticated to mingle with the likes of us. See how that goes. He might find an opening on the crew cleaning up highway trash. Might be tricky in those shoes, though."

Clayton cleared his throat and put a warning hand on my shoulder. "Duke, point taken. You just tell Anastasia what she needs to do and she will do it with a good attitude. And forgive me, both of you, for not preparing Anastasia better regarding her assignment. That was a lack of good judgment on my part and I am truly sorry. She will be here tomorrow."

Clayton's grip tightened on my shoulder. "I'll be here. "

Duke nodded. Note to self – don't insult the guy who supervises your community service, you might end up on a chain gang. See Judge Goodman? Learning already.

# CHAPTER 4

Wednesday started off with a bang. Literally. Maria dropped my breakfast tray, spilling coffee, juice and a green smoothie all over my fluffy white hotel robe. Just as I mopped the sludge off my lap the phone rang. Maria pounced on it like a live grenade. She was awfully twitchy. I could hear Sterling from across the room even before she handed the phone to me. Clayton had filled him in after court, but I'd refused Sterling's call. Sympathy you pay for lacks the warm fuzzy.

"Hello Sterling. Don't bother trying to make me feel better. If a binge at the bar couldn't do it, there's no hope for you. I have a second breakfast tray on its way, so can we make this brief?" Maria scurried about collecting dishes from the floor. A sharp pain pierced my left temple, revenge for indulging in that final Long Island Iced Tea the previous night.

"Anastasia, we need to talk. (Nothing good ever followed that statement). It sounds like you will be in Texas these next few months; you need to make some adjustments." Pause. Long pause. My agent must have broadcast the news I was fired by Fame. Or Maria. It seems I had a long list of paid staff happy to spread the news of my humiliation.

I gave up waiting. "Adjustments, Sterling? I haven't had any time to think about my schedule! First I'm hit with community service – 100 hours, 4 hours at a time! - then I'm dumped again, this time by a bunch of narrow minded executives who won't admit I'm right about their stupid ad campaign. You should be busy suing them for breach of contract. I pay you to take care of me. Call me back when you have some GOOD news!"

"Anastasia, this can't wait. I'm sorry, but you are in a precarious financial situation and I AM taking care of you. Your expenses are escalating and you have no income. Rent here in LA, Clayton's fees, my fees, your Neiman Marcus bill, Maria – these all add up and you have been at a high burn rate since your arrest. Suing Fame is futile. You can't afford the attorney's fees, and they would probably win. Besides, you need to work; nobody will touch you if you are in litigation over a contract. I know this is a lot to process, but I recommend you sublease your apartment in LA, let Maria go, and quit shopping! Once you serve your time in Texas you can regroup. Travelling back and forth to LA racking up hotel bills will put you under. You have enough saved to get you through this hiccup if you scale back. Way back."

Grant Adams, my ticket to happiness, had become my passport to hell. Six months ago I was flush with cash, riding the wave in Prada. Now I was rag dolled, gasping for air. He sucked me into his Hollywood wave with charm and good looks; any girl would have fallen for it, and many did. My simple Midwestern upbringing made me vulnerable to career phonies like him. Grant took advantage of me, popped my lifeboat, then lounged on shore while I drowned.

I fell onto the bed, drained.

"Anastasia? Are you still breathing? Silence from you is scary." I grunted. Sterling wasn't too scared – he kept dropping bad news like it was my morning breakfast. "Maria can help you find an affordable place to live. You can't stay in that hotel for 4 months. Then she needs to return to LA. Once we unwind things here, she can look for a new job. I've given her a head's up."

That explained Maria's tizzy this morning. Everybody got the memo of impending disaster except me. My staff was jumping ship, leaving me alone at the wheel with no back-up.

\*\*\*

I arrived at The Watering Hole early for my 2:00 shift. It seemed like a good idea to smooth things over after Duke's scolding. I was dutifully dressed in jeans and sneakers, ready to mark off day 1 of

'My Texas Sentencing: Redemption through Community Service.' This had the makings of a good narrative for an interview one day. Celebrities always reminisce about their grueling start in the business, juggling loathsome jobs while living in a cold water flat (what is that?). Since my first job was a fat contract with Fame Cosmetics, this could fill in that chapter nicely. People like to believe that even super models must overcome obstacles. It makes us more relatable. I brought a journal to take notes; details make an anecdote real and I did not want to forget the local color. Selfies would document my story.

Duke was on stage, playing a complicated solo on the guitar. He was very attractive for a man his age (50? 60?). And very talented. I hung back in the doorway, unseen, until he set his guitar down. "Wow! You are an excellent musician, Duke. I didn't realize you played. I have seen lots of great performers and you could go head to head with many of them!"

Duke did not respond, packing his guitar away in its case. I tried again. "Have you ever considered being in a band? Touring? I could introduce you to some people in LA. You shouldn't hide that talent away in a barn. These days, lots of older musicians are successful. Most of the classic rock bands are practically ancient. Mick Jagger has made 70 the new 40!"

"I'll think about that Anastasia. Thank you for your vote of confidence. Now come with me and I'll show you the kitchen. We have a lot to set up before 3:00."

Behind the swinging doors was a beehive of activity. One cook was filling quesadillas at a furious pace. Another was mixing a huge bowl of fresh guacamole. Duke beckoned to a man in an apron. "Mo! Come over here a minute. You need to meet our latest addition. Mo Buckley, Anastasia DeMars. Anastasia will be helping us out for the next few months."

Mo approached with arms open wide. He was like a grizzly bear, tall, black, and imposing. I was buried in a hug before I could speak. "Welcome aboard, Anastasia DeMars. That is a mouthful! I tell you what – I'll call you Anna, you call me Mo. That work? We are too busy around here to get caught up in formalities. Do you cook?"

Mo's enthusiasm was almost contagious. "Not really, but I'm happy to do whatever else you need." Was Duke hearing my good attitude? Did he notice my sneakers?

Duke patted Mo on the back. "Anna is still in the dark about what goes on here. Maybe you can fill her in, show her around, prepare her for the onslaught. I'll be back for rehearsal. Put her to work!"

Mo pushed Duke out the door. "OK, Anna. Since you are new to the crew you can start by following Tish here. Tish, this is Anna. Can you get her a t-shirt? Anna, just do whatever Tish does. You'll catch on." Tish looked at me with disdain.

Everyone in the kitchen wore matching t-shirts that said JOY CHORUS on the front, THE WATERING HOLE on the back. Tish handed me an XXL. I am not even a medium, much less an XXL. She seemed unconcerned about the sizing problem. "Fashionable? No. But Duke insists we wear them so the kids know who the adults are in the room. Some of the volunteers are alumni and not much older than the Chorus members."

I slipped the shirt over my head. I'm tall, and in the right circles this could pass for a mini dress. I swam in it. An apron helped tie up the loose sail. If Fame Cosmetics could see me now...they would confiscate my remaining stash of Warrior Red lipstick and demand I change my name. Oh wait, Mo already did that. The carefully assembled Anastasia DeMars was shattered in one bear hug. I was back to Anna from Illinois, wearing a tacky t-shirt, in need of affordable housing.

Tish announced to the kitchen "This is Anna! She's new!" then hit the ground running, dragging me in her wake. We delivered dishes and food to the main hall, iced down buckets of bottled water, and hauled the tables to one side of the room to give the chorus rehearsal space. At least I think that's what Tish said. Music was blaring in the background, people in black t-shirts were scurrying, so I just followed her lead. I silently thanked Duke for the suggestion of tennis shoes. This was hard labor, and the kitchen floor was slippery. I did not need a repeat of humiliation by shoe drama.

At 2:45 Tish shouted, "Unlock the door!" and a tidal wave of kids came pouring into the barn. They descended on the food like vultures wearing backpacks. Girls, boys, all heights, all sizes. The unifying force seemed to be an unsatisfied appetite for chips and queso. Just as fast as they devoured the snacks, tables were cleared. Most of the staff bussed dirty dishes to the kitchen, then found a seat amidst the masses.

Tish stood on a table and immediately the room fell silent. Impressive. "Math over here with Mo. English with Rooney by the stage. I'll tackle science." Tish pulled me up on the table with her. "This is Anna. She's new, so she gets Jenga duty. If your homework is done you can join her in the back. We begin practice at 4:00 sharp so get to it!"

Jenga duty? I guess even an uneducated lipstick model can supervise Jenga. From my tabletop perch I observed what's known as fruit basket turnover. The kids grabbed their stuff and shifted locations to find a seat at their station of choice. Lots of talking, but everything was orderly. I remembered my high school cafeteria as anything but orderly – everyone jockeying for a spot at the right table, food fights, an angry Mrs. Wilson desperately trying to tame the natives. Mrs. Wilson was the nerdy computer science teacher and we got a kick out of pushing her buttons. But we were harmless suburban kids just looking for a break in our boredom. If I saw some of these kids on the street, I'd reach for my bodyguard (dang, I needed to fire him too).

I made my way through the chaos to the Jenga table. A crowd of boys were already setting up the game; there was a noticeable shortage of girls. Mo appeared behind me, arms crossed. "Really? None of you guys has math homework to do? Francisco, last week you were buried in algebra. Did you find a tow truck to haul you out?"

Francisco considered his reply. "Well, I was thinking a Jenga lesson might help me understand the x and the y better." All the guys laughed. Mo did not. Francisco, and 3 others, conceded. They picked up their backpacks with a backward glance. Mo leaned over to whisper in my ear. "You might be the motivation they need to keep up with their homework."

Four boys remained. I was a Jenga rookie, so the students became the teacher. I'm lousy at Jenga. I got too excited, acted too quickly, and the whole tower came tumbling down. The irony was not lost on me; the entire universe conspired to remind me that my life was in pieces. My competitors erupted in victory whoops and cheers. I was tasked with picking up the blocks while they laughed at my novice mistake. The whole room followed their lead. I surrendered, took a bow, and promised to win next time. My tussle with Officer Friendly over the Jimmy Choos taught me this: if you can't beat them, join them. Plus, I was outnumbered. Better to let them laugh with me than AT me. Simon, a very small freshman who needed no help with his advanced AP Calculus homework (he was very chatty during our game), offered to be my Jenga tutor. He revealed that all volunteers were subjected to this initiation. Newbies did not stand a chance against these Jenga pros; the real test was in how you handled the heckling. Simon gave me a thumbs up and I felt an unexpected flush of satisfaction. That skinny boy captured my heart. By the look on his face when we high fived, I may have captured his heart as well. Or it could have been abject terror. I wasn't practiced in reading teenage boys' body language.

Suddenly it was 4:00. Time flew when you were concentrating on keeping the tower intact. Mo took a seat at the piano and began to play. Kids milled about, taking their spots. Simon leaned over to whisper in my ear before he ran off. "I'm sorry your pretty shoes were ruined." So the cat was out of the bag. I wondered if anyone else had guessed my identity, then witnessed a wave of twittering pass through the ranks like wildfire. Maybe they recognized me as the face of Warrior Red? After all, the campaign rolled out a full year before that 8 second video. I shouldn't just assume the worst. But nope. The commotion was more mocking than reverent.

Duke tapped on a music stand to get everyone's attention. "Hey! Focus, gang! We have a lot of work to do before our Christmas concert. Ty, I know Shika is fun to look at but you don't belong in the soprano section. Join your fellow baritones. Anyone else in the wrong octave? If so, move it!" Duke noticed all eyes were on me.

"OK. Before we start rehearsing let's review a few things. One, most of you have a rap sheet of things you wish you had not done. Two, I know what most of those things are. Three, this is a place where we leave all that behind. In here we are all for one, one for all. That said, if I hear that ANYONE disparages a Joy Chorus member, volunteers included, you are OUT. No pictures, no gossip, no exceptions. Don't make me prove my point. Understood? Let's go Mo. "Frog Song" from the top." With that simple statement, Duke proved he already cared more about me than Grant ever had. Judge Goodman put me in good hands.

The kitchen sounded busy with clean up but Tish offered me a seat. I appreciated her lack of curiosity about my movie debut; she seemed to be in charge, so she probably knew why I was here. "Watch and learn, Anna. See that rag tag group? Duke is a magician. Even squeaky Simon will surprise you. Getting them going in the same direction is the hard part, but once they hit takeoff it's pretty remarkable."

Hard to imagine. Rag tag was an understatement. The boys were a mishmash of sloppy t-shirts, baggy jeans and sneakers. The girls were equally motley in crop tops and flip flops. This I could fix. I'm skilled at making someone look good for the camera. If these kids were preparing for a concert, they needed a make-over. Duke must not know much about branding. My huge volunteer t-shirt was evidence enough of that. The girls would be easy, the boys might be trickier. Maybe I could convince some of them to cut their hair. How do you steer a grungy group of guys into a blazer or a button down?

The chorus interrupted my thoughts. They were transformed from a jumble of awkward misfits into a swell of full volume harmony.

*Win or lose, sink or swim*
*One thing is certain we'll never give in*
*Side by side, hand in hand*
*We all stand together*

*Play the game, fight the fight*
*But what's the point on a beautiful night?*
*Arm in arm, hand in hand*
*We all stand together*

*Keeping us warm in the night*
*La la la la*
*Walk in the night*
*You'll get it right*

*Win or lose, sink or swim*
*One thing is certain we'll never give in*

*Side by side, hand in hand*
*We all stand together*

After some practice, Duke grabbed his guitar. Mo left the piano for an electric keyboard. The Frog Song (whatever that meant - there were no frogs mentioned at all) went from a sweet ballad to a rock anthem. Tish nudged me. "See? Pretty cool, right?"

"Tish, Duke and Mo are really good! They should try out for one of those TV talent shows. Do they ever perform here at The Watering Hole?"

Tish stared at me in shock. "Anna, have you been under a rock? Duke and Mo are the founding members of the Blue Valentines. They have won Grammys! They've played with everyone – George Strait, Pam Tillis, Merle Haggard." My face must have gone blank. Tish tried again. "Springsteen! You've heard of Springsteen?"

Now my face went red. There was my mom's voice in my head again; she suggested I do some research about this assignment, but I didn't think there was anything to learn about a kids' choir. Flying by the seat of my pants was landing me in the dirt. I grew up in Illinois! We did not listen to country music. I'd bet very few people in Chicago had heard of the Blue Valentines, or Merle what's his name.

I tried to recover; I've always been quick on my feet. "Of course! I don't know why I didn't put 2 and 2 together. But what are they doing at a barn? You'd think they'd be out on tour, not directing a bunch of squirrely high school kids in a choir."

Tish leaned back. Did I say something wrong? She didn't look mad, but she didn't answer me either. I hadn't fooled her – she knew I was clueless about Duke and Mo. Had I hurt her feelings? She did volunteer here; maybe she thought I was trashing the group. I seemed to step in it a little more each time I opened my mouth, but I am a slow learner and kept forging ahead.

"Not that there is anything wrong with the Joy Chorus, or working with kids...and the barn is very nice. But it must seem tame compared to touring with Springsteen! Are Duke and Mo under house arrest or something to keep them here?"

My joke landed like a lead balloon. Tish considered her reply carefully. "We are all here because we want to be. Fame has its upside, but it also has its downfalls. Maybe you've heard about those?"

With that she headed towards the kitchen while I nursed the sting of her jab. So yes, she knew who I was. And she had a point. But the upside was so incredible! I relished the perks my modeling income afforded, but fame opens doors closed even to the rich. The red carpets, mingling with other famous people, the flash bulbs! Fame made me popular. I was building a base of social media followers, and young women listened to me. The increase in Warrior Red lipstick sales was testament to that. Why did girls buy Fame Cosmetics? Because they wanted to be me, and their copycat lipstick was step one. My potential to influence an entire generation of girls was immense. Not to mention the free shoes, designer clothes, and tickets to the hottest shows. Everyone wanted the "It" girl to be seen in their stuff at events. Yes, fame was fickle, and my detour to The Watering Hole proved how she must be carefully managed. But I could cultivate fame again, even without Grant Adams.

At the swinging door, Tish looked back. "Come on. Lots to clean up." I followed her into the mess.

# CHAPTER 5

As soon as the kids cleared out of the barn, Duke and Mo dragged the tables back to their original position. I jumped in to help. Pretty girls are assumed to be helpless at physical labor, but men underestimate the prowess required to walk a runway wearing 6" heels. In flats, I can run a marathon and still keep my makeup fresh.

Wednesday nights featured an open mic inviting local talent to perform. Duke thanked me for my help. "You are off the clock, Anna, and can go any time. See? Teenagers aren't as scary as you thought. You survived day one with minor cuts and bruises. Of course today was just your introduction…Jenga is tame. Next time we'll put you in charge of crowd control."

My face must have registered panic because Duke laughed. "I'm just teasing you, Anna. Stick to Jenga for now. Although I expect a mob will have their homework completed by Saturday. Jenga with you has more appeal than math with Mo. Leverage that."

I was confused. Jenga duty seemed like babysitting, unless some girls joined the group. I could teach the girls a thing or two about putting a better face forward.

"Leverage Jenga for what? I told you, I am out of my league here. I don't speak teenager. But I do have some ideas to improve the overall appearance of the group. I am an expert in style! I could rework your image to be a little more edgy. No offense, but the Joy Chorus sounds like a geriatric church choir. The kids are good, and I might be able to get you some good exposure, but you've got to update your brand to get the media's attention."

Duke's face went blank. Granted, my huge t-shirt and disheveled hair were hardly alluring, but he had seen me photo shoot ready yesterday. If he was a famous rock star, he must know the importance of marketing.

"Just get to know the kids, Anna. Invest time in them. In return, you earn the right to be heard. You have more to say than you think. You might even learn a thing or two if you listen."

Why did everyone assume I wasn't listening? I am a gifted listener. True, I don't always listen to my mom, but most 20 somethings ignore their mother's advice. Parents don't understand the pressures my generation faces. But I listen to my friends. I listened to Clayton when I wore those awful shoes. On my first day at the Joy Chorus, which was very stressful, I listened to Simon; I knew all about his knack for calculus. I was a good listener! But nobody ever listened to me, so it wasn't worth going to battle on Day One. I hadn't forgotten Duke was the guy reporting back to my Probation Officer. I changed the subject.

"Duke, what's open mic night like? Can I stay and watch?" I couldn't face an evening with Maria detailing the affordable housing options available. On Friday she would abandon me for LA. Until then, I'd leave her alone to get me settled.

"Sure. Dinner service starts at 6:30, performers begin at 8:00. You can sit anywhere. We charge at the door on Wednesdays, no tickets. Most of the volunteer crew works the evening shift, so talk to Tish if you need anything."

That left an hour before the doors opened. I changed into civilian clothes and wandered around the barn. On closer inspection, the vintage decor covering the walls was memorabilia signed by performers. Photographs of Duke, Mo and their band drew a timeline of their career. I recognized Willie Nelson with a young Duke (sporting black hair!), and Mo embraced Springsteen in the 1980s. ZZ Top, Alabama, Lynyrd Skinner – those groups I'd heard of, even if I couldn't recite their playlists. By the looks of it, many others were country artists I didn't know. But clearly the Blue Valentines were famous. Famous! And stuck here in small town Texas instead of touring. It made no sense.

In the back of the barn a wall was dedicated to the Joy Chorus with photos of the kids practicing and performing. A framed poster titled "Our Story" featured a picture of a woman named Joy:

*Joy Valentine believed music can build a bridge between all people willing to cross it. As a high school music teacher, Joy saw many kids longing for a place to belong. So she created one. The Sing Gang offered snacks and tutoring to any high school student willing to sing in an after school choir. Joy's famous brownies coaxed them in, the friendships formed through music kept them coming back. The Sing Gang began performing at schools, nursing homes, and private parties. With its membership and reputation growing, the Sing Gang relocated to The Watering Hole music venue for rehearsals and regular concerts.*

*Joy's vision expanded to include teenagers from all area high schools. Graduates followed her example and volunteered their time to serve kids who came behind them. Upon Joy's untimely death, the Sing Gang members changed their name to The Joy Chorus in her honor. Joy's mission, to reach high school kids through friendship and music, thrives today under the leadership of her husband, Duke*

*Valentine, and their friend, Mo Buckley. The Joy Chorus is a non-profit, 501(c)(3) and is staffed entirely with volunteers. We appreciate your generous support.*

No mention of the Blue Valentines. No boasting about Grammys. No effort to capitalize on their fame for donations. Just a beautiful tribute to Duke's dead wife, and I told him the choir's name stunk. This was all Clayton's fault! He and Duke were obviously acquainted, he should have filled me in. And Maria? Her JOB was to keep me informed. I paid her to do that. I fought back tears. How was I supposed to avoid these land mines if my staff didn't do their job? Duke must think I was an idiot. Or an insensitive monster. Or both. The tabloids would love to get their hands on a faux pas like that. Duke didn't strike me as the type to entertain rag magazines, but he did send a report to my probation officer. Reports can get leaked. My reputation needed some time to recover!

Tish was setting up for the dinner crowd. I flagged her down; maybe she could help me mend fences with Duke. "Tish, I need your help. I stuck my foot in my mouth with Duke."

Tish continued to set the table without looking up. "I wouldn't worry about it. All those years in the music business made Duke pretty thick skinned. You don't know him well enough to offend him."

"Well, I'm not sure if you know why I am here, but Duke basically holds my future in his hands. I don't want to get off on the wrong foot.'"

"Sounds serious. Does Duke know he's responsible for your happiness? I can't even get him to plan for next month! An entire future seems like a lot to sign up for."

"OK, maybe it's not that dramatic. But I don't want him to hate me. How do I fix it?"

"What did you do?"

"I told him the Joy Chorus needed a makeover. And that the name sounded like a geriatric church choir. It's not my fault! I just now read the story on the wall. I had no idea the Chorus was named after his wife. I'm good at crafting an image for the media, and thought changing the name might help the group get some better press. You must admit, the name doesn't scream COOL to a high school kid!"

Tish moved on to the next table. "Anna, what we are doing here works. Are there things we can do better? Sure. But before you go moving the furniture, you need to learn how the house was built. After you've been here awhile it will make sense. In the meantime, understand the hole Joy left is still raw. Stay away from touching it."

"OK. Thanks. I'm not always good at keeping my mouth shut, but I'm working on it. You wouldn't know that by following me around today; I've left a trail of stupid remarks all over the place. But I don't try to hurt people's feelings. I'm just so out of my element here. I don't speak Texas! The rules are very different here. In LA – that's where I'm from – you work from a script designed to keep you out of PR trouble. I guess I should quit complaining about what I pay my agent and be glad she keeps me on course, in LA at least. Clearly I need some backstory here. Will you help me? Did you know Joy?"

Tish looked me in the eye. "Yes. She was my mom." Then she headed back to the kitchen.

That shut me up. Diane would have paid money to see me speechless. I felt like I was running over hot coals, hopping to relieve the burn only to land on another ember.

\*\*\*

Did that make Duke Tish's father? I hadn't heard her call him dad, but she referred to Joy by her first name so that wasn't a good test. I picked a seat in front of the stage, totaling the wreckage from my big mouth. I had offended Duke, Tish, and anyone they talked to about my comments. In Hollywood you could get deleted from the A list with insults far less damaging than my day's work. True, the only list here was Jenga vs. math, but I did not want to end up on the road crew. All things considered the Joy Chorus was a good assignment for community service. Judge Goodman might try to teach me a more severe lesson if I blew this on day one. I needed to figure out a way to get back in their good graces. I couldn't donate money – that would look sketchy. Maybe I could get them a gift, a thank you for taking me on. Nothing big, just something small and thoughtful. I loved spa services; maybe a facial for Tish? A massage for Duke?

Mo plunked down in the chair beside me. "So Anna, what do you think of our crazy gang here? This afternoon was only the beginning! Open mic night is always a crapshoot. One time we had a duo show up called Little Sammy and the Man. Little Sammy was a dummy and the Man was his puppet master. The Man sang without moving his lips while Little Sammy's jaw opened and closed to the beat. Weird. But we are an equal opportunity stage – anyone willing to make a fool of themselves is welcome to come on in."

Mo was either a great actor, or had not heard about my swath of destruction. I wanted to believe he knew all about it and was the forgiving type, but my better judgement warned me to tread carefully. No sense adding to the casualties. "Today was great. Open mic sounds fun. All good."

Mo handed me a flier listing the acts for the evening. "We have lots of regulars, so I can promise some great music tonight. But no guarantees on the outliers! Stay at your own risk. Our famous brownies will ease the pain if someone is terrible. Just make sure your order includes ice cream. Wait, do you eat brownies? Or ice cream? You look like more of a kale salad girl!"

I was ready with my MODELING IS A DEMANDING PROFESSION SO OF COURSE I DO NOT EAT BROWNIES tirade, but bit my tongue. Literally bit my tongue. Pain is the only deterrent that gets my attention when I am rant ready. Instead, I smiled. Paused. Mo's face displayed no disdain, just friendly teasing. "Mo, I would love a brownie. After a salad. I can't really be one of the gang without trying the famous brownie, right?"

Mo was pleased. "Nothing makes a cook happier than watching a skinny girl enjoy a brownie."

"Did you make the brownies, Mo?"

"I did indeed. We wear many hats around here, Anna. Keeps us nimble. You are off to a good start – passed the Jenga test. Who knows what other talents you may discover?"

Does sticking foot in mouth qualify? I was a master at that. But I sailed through our chat without further injury, so maybe there was hope. He ran off to wear the stage crew hat while I watched a hodge podge of performers come through the door. No sign of Sammy and the Man tonight; most of the musicians seemed familiar with the set up. A very tall cowboy sauntered in carrying a battered guitar case. His entrance sparked lots of waving and smiling from the girls on staff. He returned their attention with a shy nod of his head. I admit, I'm not one for the outdoorsy type. Grant was a Don Draper kind of handsome, always perfectly styled. This guy had mud clinging to his boots. His jeans were well worn Levis, his eyes already crinkly from squinting in the Texas sun. I guessed he was in his late 20s. He could have played Clint Eastwood's grandson in a biopic. Cute enough if you needed a date to a Western themed party, but hardly the type to walk a red carpet. I loved red carpets. Photographers calling your name, posing for the camera after a day of primping. I dreamed of finding my picture in *Celebrity* magazine on the Best Dressed List – and I had made it twice. Rachel, my stylist, liked to take the credit, but I made the final selections. I would have chosen those dresses even without her nod of approval. Stylists are very touchy, and I didn't want to poison the well with designers, so I gushed about her whenever possible. But I knew the truth.

Cowboy settled in at a table next to the stage. The tooled leather strap on his guitar read BEAU. He was the first act listed on the flier. I was surprised to see so many people show up for a crapshoot of a show on a Wednesday night, but The Blue Valentines were last in the set so maybe they were the magnet. At 7:45 Mo took the microphone to welcome the crowd. "It's open mic night at The Watering Hole! We are a family here, so fill in the spots closest to the stage and get to know your long lost cousins. The fun begins in about 15 minutes with Beau Laurel. After him, all bets are off since we have two acts debuting tonight. Applause is free, so be sure to bury our performers in it. Artists are notoriously fragile and we don't want any cracked egos at the end of the night."

Tish appeared with a brownie in hand. "Compliments of Mo. He takes his brownies very seriously. Next to music, food is his love language and he demands we all worship at the temple of chocolate. It's pointless to fight it; Mo is relentless. I recommend you surrender and enjoy." Her deadpan delivery was hard for me to read. Was she mad? Just following instructions, or extending an olive branch? In LA you always assumed someone was setting you up for a stab in the back, which actually simplified things; they expected you to do the same, so everyone looked out for Number 1. Here the tone was different. Tish didn't seem angry. Just cool. I couldn't afford any more missteps so I defaulted to my Midwestern upbringing and tried nice.

"Thanks Tish. Share it with me? I can't imagine downing that mountain of chocolate on my own, but I don't want to be in trouble with the baking gods. This way we can both tell Mo we paid our toll for the day without risking a sugar coma. Please?"

Tish sat down. I relaxed just a bit. "Tish, I'm sorry I was such an idiot earlier. I promise to follow your advice and quit trying to fix things. Not that there is anything wrong here to be fixed! I meant I will try to learn how the house was built before I start moving the furniture. Not that I will move the furniture! But before I even offer suggestions. See? I am listening."

I was rewarded with a slight smile. Tish offered me a fork and we dove into the brownie. I couldn't remember the last time I indulged in such a decadent treat without first calculating calories, or the exercise required to cancel them out. Heaven. I closed my eyes and savored the creamy chocolate. The hot brownie and cold ice cream combined to throw a party in my mouth.

"Been a while, has it?" Tish eyed me with amusement.

"Forever. I am a model, and brownies are a food DON'T."

"Sounds like being a model is overrated. Enjoy the show. Make sure you let Mo know you accepted the brownie challenge and loved it. He is a shameless baking diva and won't rest until we all throw ourselves at his feet."

I felt a huge sense of relief. Maybe it was the chocolate swirling around my confection starved brain, but for the first time in months I wasn't anxious. I sat back to enjoy the concert, even if country music was not my thing. Beau Laurel took the stage with no preamble and began to play. His voice was not what I expected; deep and warm, nothing twangy. There was nary a mention of booze, trucks, or girls in short shorts (this is what I thought country music was about). His music was soulful, the ballads were sweet. The audience showered him with applause and he left the stage without ever saying a word beyond "thank you".

His table had been commandeered by other singers unpacking their guitar cases. The only seat left open close to the stage was Tish's, and Beau Laurel maneuvered through the crowd to sit next to me. He folded himself into the chair, still nodding thanks for the enthusiastic response to his performance. "I'm sorry – this seat taken? I should have asked." His eyes were sharply blue. Lose the cowboy hat, hire a stylist, and he could pass for ruggedly handsome. Or keep the hat, hire a stylist, and he could run with the Nashville crowd. Surely Tim McGraw didn't buy his jeans at the feed store like this guy. With a little attention, Beau might break out of this barn and into the real music business. He was certainly talented. But it took a lot more than talent to launch a successful career. My advice? Work the silent type angle and keep them guessing! My career soared until I opened my mouth.

Beau waited patiently for my answer. "Oh yes, that's fine. Nobody is sitting there." What a dork. He probably thought I got lost gazing into his steely eyes. Our waitress fluttered by, asking him for his drink order. "Just water, Melissa. But don't worry, I'll leave you a tip." Melissa DID get lost gazing into his eyes until he turned towards the stage. She scurried off as the second act began. I wondered if Beau was meant to draw the crowd, and the Blue Valentines to keep them. Everyone in between was clearly an inexperienced amateur, but not a bad lineup for $10 at the door.

Finally, the Blue Valentines took the stage. Mo played the keyboards, Duke the guitar, and the band rocked the house with Tish singing backup. She'd ditched the kitchen worker uniform; her tight black jeans and sleeveless blouse made you think the girl serving brownies was her sloppy twin. That poker face disappeared under the lights. The music seemed to transport her to another realm, far from the duties of keeping this place running. They did wear a lot of hats, from selling tickets to bringing the house down all in one evening. I had underestimated Tish.

The crowd erupted in cheers at the end of their set. They were amazing! I couldn't believe they traded big stages for Wednesday nights in a barn. Their music was part rock, part country, but it brought everyone out of their seat. Beau hadn't said a word since he sat down, but he laughed as I jumped to my feet. "I think the Blue Valentines have a new fan. I haven't seen you here before." He had to shout to be heard over the applause. The band took a bow as the lights went up.

"I had never heard them play until tonight. To be honest, I'm not a country music fan, but they are good!"

"Really? You fooled me. But the Blue Valentines make everyone a fan – they can play anything. I'm Beau Laurel. And you are???"

"Anastasia. Actually, you can call me Anna."

Beau offered me his hand. "What brings a non-country music fan to The Watering Hole? Seems a bit out of the way for someone passing through."

This was tricky. If he'd figured out who I was, I didn't want to lie; that would only reinforce the tabloid image that I was shallow and petty. If he had no idea who I was, I didn't want to open with "Hi, only a community service sentence would ever get me in a country music barn like this." I settled for less is better.

"I'm working with the Joy Chorus for a while and stayed for the show. I heard the brownies were worth passing through. Oh, and you were very good too."

"I'm only pretty good. The barn's acoustics make everyone sound great. Kind of like singing in your shower. But thank you."

"What's so special about the barn's acoustics?"

Beau pointed to the walls. "See the wood slats? They absorb and reflect the sound without an echo. Most venues have a lot of flat painted surfaces that diffuse the sound – that makes the bass boom and high end notes ring. The high ceiling helps too. Duke and Mo found this barn in Tennessee and rebuilt it here. It has the best acoustics of any place I've played."

"Have you played many venues?"

"I've played my share. But I'm more of a songwriter than a performer. The Watering Hole lets me play new material while I'm still working on it."

"A songwriter? As a hobby, or are you a professional?"

Beau looked away. "I write for a few Nashville artists. Lucky for me, some of my songs have been well received. But my family ranching business puts food on the table. Everyone eats; not everyone likes my music. Cattle is a more reliable living."

"That's too bad! You have a great voice. Songwriters do all the hard creative work, and unless you are John Lennon, you get none of the credit. No glory in that."

"I can do without the glory. Songwriting just happens for me. I would do it even if nobody ever recorded my songs. But I love the cattle business too. I enjoy the best of both worlds and never leave home. What do you do when you aren't a Blue Valentine groupie?"

What do I do. Hmmm. I knew what I used to do. I knew what I hoped to do in the future. But at the moment?

"My mother insists I'm destined for great things, but for now I'm a model." I couldn't help but smile. I loved being a model.

This is when I usually get the wide-eyed look of recognition, the swooning over what a glamorous job it must be. Beau wasn't impressed. "There can't be much modeling work around here. That seems like a big city profession. Is it a hobby, or are you a professional?" He was teasing me.

"I live in LA. And I do it professionally. I'm just here for a short time."

"There must be a good story behind a big city model landing at The Watering Hole in Pleasant, Texas. Might be the makings of a good song. Why isn't modeling a great thing?"

"Oh there's nothing to love about actual modeling. You must obsessively watch your weight, and hope you don't get a zit on shoot day. There's a horde of other models gunning for your job, hoping you get a rash, or fat, or caught in some dumb PR nightmare so you lose your contract." I was getting louder; Beau unconsciously leaned back. Time to backpedal with a smile.

"But the perks of modeling are great. I love opening a magazine and seeing my picture there. Sometimes I get to keep the clothes, and during a shoot they pamper you like royalty. When you represent a brand, the company showers you with event tickets to increase exposure of their product. You meet lots of celebrities, plus everyone wants to date a model. That's the fun part. The perks, not necessarily the dating part. Sometimes that gets complicated."

Beau seemed confused. "So you hate the work, but you're willing to obsessively diet and fight off backstabbers just for some event tickets?"

Wow, he made it sound pathetic. Maybe I wasn't explaining myself clearly.

"No! I get paid very well too. My trainer makes the dieting not so bad, and my agent and assistant usually handle the ugly stuff. And my lawyers (I said this under my breath). So if I show up and do my job, I get to enjoy the fringe benefits."

Beau nodded. "Gotcha. You get paid lots of money to do a job you hate. Then you pay a trainer, agent and assistant lots of money to keep you in that job."

That sounded even worse. I tried again. "You don't understand! It's thrilling to be recognized for your work. Modeling is more than taking a pretty picture. The more famous you get, the more influence you have. I have thousands of girls who follow me on social media. They look up to me."

The crowd was thinning and Beau started packing up his guitar. "That's impressive. What life lessons do you share with these thousands of girls?"

"Mostly fashion and beauty tips. Those things give a young woman confidence. They are important!"

Beau nodded. "Yes, I'm sure they are. It was nice to meet you, Anna from LA. Maybe I'll see you here again." He tipped his hat, just like in an old Western movie, and rambled out the door.

I turned to see Tish follow him with her eyes. Her face was neutral, hard to read as usual. It seemed like she had been standing there for a while. She caught me watching her and walked my way. "So, country music still not your thing?" She gestured towards Beau leaving the building.

"I must admit there were a lot of surprises tonight!"

"Yeah, Beau will do that."

"I meant YOU. No offense, but the girl on stage was nothing like the Tish I met in the kitchen. Gives me hope I can reinvent myself when necessary. Why are you schlepping brownies instead of singing under the bright lights?"

"I don't know Anna – why are you playing Jenga with 9th graders instead of jet setting off to Paris for Fashion Week? Life can get complicated."

Ouch. I hit a nerve. I didn't mean to! Texans were more sensitive than models, and that's hard to do. I was trying to give her a compliment.

"Tish, what I meant to say was you were great up there. It's obvious you love performing. I get it! I love being in front of a crowd too. There is something about the energy! Those butterflies right before your big entrance, and the thrill that comes when they recognize you. It's addictive. Do you sing with other bands, or only The Blue Valentines?"

Mo interrupted before she could reply. "Anna, you still here? See, this place gets under your skin. What about our girl Tish? She is the straw that stirs the drink, behind the scenes AND on stage. And did I see you rubbing shoulders with the famous Beau Laurel? No better introduction to country music than hanging out with Beau!"

Tish ducked out from under Mo's arm. "Got to go. Receipts to tally." She seemed in a hurry to duck more than just a bear hug.

"Is Beau famous? I confess to being country music stupid."

Mo whistled. "Famous? Well, he's famous in our circles. And his songs are famous in all circles. Heard of "Chasing Home"?"

Of course I had. "Chasing Home" was the soundtrack to last year's hit movie of the same title. The story follows a refugee from a war torn region who returns to his native land in search of the family home. He finds his village destroyed, but learns that Home is found with the people you love, not in a physical place. It might have had some political message too, but I don't remember that part. I love a good tear jerking drama. An animal protection group adapted the song for their pet adoption campaign, showing 'before' shots of mangy mutts transformed into 'after' shots of lovable doggies. It was very effective. I almost caved and went to the shelter, but my schedule at the time didn't leave much room for a dog. Those commercials were tear jerkers too.

I was impressed. "Did Beau write that song?"

"Yes, he did. It was originally just a skeleton of a ballad, sitting in Beau's unfinished pile. Dylan Worth (the star playing the refugee) and Beau are friends, so Dylan convinced the producers to listen to Beau's demo. Beau changed the arrangement for the movie, and they changed the name of the movie to *Chasing Home*. The song was even nominated for an Oscar. Dylan came down to The Watering Hole when the single debuted; we had a drop party here. But Beau will never tell you that story. He's the silent type. Though he seemed pretty talkative with you here in the front row."

I couldn't believe Beau was friends with Dylan Worth! I met Dylan a few times at award shows with Grant. Dylan was the guy who took the gritty roles, the ones that made him lose weight, or shave his head, or forget to bathe. The opposite of Grant's 'super hero in a cool suit' roles. He was married to a nice girl from Texas – what was her name? His wife wasn't in the business. I remember commenting on her Texas accent at the *People's Choice Awards* after party.

Mo was baiting me. Did everyone notice my conversation with Beau? Tish seemed a bit annoyed. Maybe she had a thing for him – all the waitresses did. The last thing I needed was co-workers jealous over a romance that didn't even exist. Everyone assumes pretty girls want to collect guys like hunting trophies. I was no threat to their Beau Laurel pursuits.

"Beau was explaining to me why the barn has good acoustics. Nothing more. But I don't want to step on any toes. Is he dating anyone? Not that I'm interested! But today I've learned how easy it is to put my foot in my mouth, and how hard it is to extract it. I'd like to avoid ticking anyone else off, especially Tish."

Mo laughed. "No need to worry about Beau and Tish! She is NOT his type. Far too moody for his taste. But we are all entangled around here. The short story? Duke and I have been friends forever. We started playing music together as kids, taking any gig we could get. The Blue Valentines came later when we got the itch to tour. We started at rodeos, in bars – that's where Duke met Joy. Her daddy owned a honky tonk in East Texas. Back then we called ourselves the Bullfighters. We thought it made us sound tough. But Duke had written a sad ballad about being a lonely blue Valentine, and Joy's dad thought that was the name of our band. Once it went up on their marquis, the name stuck. Joy sang backup for us, like Tish does now. We had a big bus and all the band members' kids tagged along. Tish wasn't 5 years old when she started reaching for the mic."

"Sounds like a big happy family. What made you leave the road for The Watering Hole? I googled the Blue Valentines. You made it big! Not that the barn isn't great, I just can't imagine working that hard for a big break then throwing it away."

Mo nodded. "Well, the music was exciting, but life got tricky. Tish's younger brother Jordan was born with some disabilities and Joy needed to take care of him at home. The only way to keep their family from falling apart was to bring the music here. The barn was Duke's idea. Our reputation was a good draw. We booked quality acts for weekend shows, and during the week we fostered new talent. Kind of made the barn a destination for up and coming artists."

"When did the Joy Chorus start?"

"When Jordan was in high school. Joy taught music there; it gave her a reason to be at school if Jordan needed something. And Joy just loved teenagers! She started the chorus as an after school club to give kids a place to hang out. If a kid didn't want to sing, she put them to work on lighting, or designing posters for their concerts. Jordan manned the sound booth. He still does. He wasn't here today, but you'll meet him on Saturday. Turns out lots of kids were looking for a place to make friends, and the club grew like crazy."

"So what happened to Joy?"

"She was hit by a drunk driver going home from the barn one night."

"I'm so sorry! That's awful."

Mo teared up. Five years later and he still cried talking about it.

"You asked me about Beau, and I narrated the life and times of the Blue Valentines! Sorry, Anna. You are doing fine. And Beau is not dating anyone. I best go help Tish close up for the night."

I didn't know what to say.

"Thanks Mo. It's been a long day. I think I'll head back to my hotel. Oh, and I loved the Blue Valentines! Country music may grow on me yet."

"Yeah, Beau will do that to you. See you Saturday."

Who would cry for me five years later if I didn't make it home tonight? Besides Frank and my mom, I couldn't think of anyone.

*\*\*\**

It was 11:00 pm before I got back to the hotel. Maria was waiting for me with printed lists of hotels and short term apartment rentals. Evidence of room service littered the coffee table. I should have asked Maria to join me at the barn for the show. Texas had been all work and no play for her.

"I'm sorry, Maria! You didn't need to wait up. I'm exhausted. We can figure out my living arrangements tomorrow."

Maria was annoyed. "I was worried about you. I texted you several times and didn't hear back. Without a car, I had to order room service; hope that's OK. I packed up most of your things so we can clear out tomorrow. I fly back to LA on Friday if you think you can manage here on your own."

Sure enough, I had texts from Maria and my mother, all ignored. I shooed her out the door. "I'll be fine. We will catch up tomorrow over breakfast."

# CHAPTER 6

A hot bath restored my body but my mind was racing. I met a famous songwriter, he was friends with a famous actor, and all these people hung out in a music barn in Texas. Who could have guessed a community service project – OK sentence – would be so interesting! This morning, the next four months stretched out like purgatory, but now I could see some benefits; The Blue Valentines were well connected. And maybe, in time, I could help the kids with their image. A few months off the LA grid would also boost my financial situation; there was nothing to spend money on here. Cutting back on staff and living expenses should put Diane and Sterling at ease until I could land a job. All in all, it was a day well spent.

I relocated to a less expensive hotel closer to the barn and set out to explore my new home town. Pleasant was a jeans and t-shirt kind of place (when you weren't appearing in court), so I stocked up at Joey's Closet, a boutique staffed by Joey herself. I found the perfect skinny jeans for $38 dollars - $38 dollars! I was reluctant to try them on but Joey insisted, and since we were new friends I couldn't say no. In LA I paid more than $300 for a pair of jeans that didn't feel this good. I treated myself to 4 pairs, all in different colors. I usually dress in black – or white – but Joey sold me a floral blouse to go with my new pants. For $32! Dressing here, with no thought to a paparazzi ambush, was a breeze. I could wear flats. And nobody would recognize me in pale pink jeans and a floral blouse anyway.

In addition to the Courthouse and Theater, Town Center green was bordered by shops and local restaurants. Even hick towns harbor a Starbucks these days. I sat under a green umbrella with a protein box, but Starbucks clearly took a backseat to Jay's All Day Diner. Jay's had a lot more traffic. Today's lunch special, highlighted on the chalk board sign, was either chicken fried chicken (wasn't that redundant?) or a Cobb salad, both served with sweet tea and a slice of pie. Little kids ran on the grass, moms gathered nearby, and a steady stream of business people left their offices at noon. Small town Texas was hopping, at least outside of Houston. Suburban Chicago had parks, but the giant mall was our town square. Looking around I felt gypped of an all-American childhood. Downtown Pleasant was 2 miles off the interstate and light years away from the rat race. I didn't worry about anyone stealing my purse off the back of my chair.

I stashed my shopping bags in the car before walking the full Town Center loop. Clayton peered back at me from the *Greater Tuna* poster. Good thing I hired him before I scrutinized his community theater involvement. The Ace Hardware advertised Kendra Scott jewelry right beside a special on BBQ grills – this I had to see. I was shocked! Ace boasted one of the most eclectic gift shops I'd ever seen. Designer jewelry, elegant serve ware, a full line of Vera Bradley. From flip flops to Pandora charm bracelets, you could pick up a birthday gift while you got your paint mixed. And they gift wrapped everything for free! Genius.

Next to the hardware store, L'Etoile Hair Salon and Spa offered the best in European services (it said so right there on the sign). The Bistro featured California wines, Pet Palace groomed your doggie, and Miss Maggie's Dance studio had a recital coming up in December. Folks said "hi" as you passed them on the sidewalk, men held the door for any woman entering an establishment at the same time. People smiled. I sat down on a bench, soaking in the sun and the charm. I was tempted to stretch out and fall asleep, but imagined public napping crossed the line.

"Well look who's here. I know a woman who could be your doppelganger. Perhaps you've heard of the famous Anastasia DeMars? Though you are much more approachable. The real Anastasia wouldn't be caught snoozing in public, wearing sneakers and a t-shirt."

My eyes flew open to see Clayton grinning amiably. "Today I'm Anna Martin, community servant, enjoying the magic of small town America. But Anastasia DeMars is available for a modeling gig if it doesn't interfere with kitchen duty. Hey, I have a bone to pick with you! You sent me into battle with no armor. I shot myself in the foot several times on Day One at The Watering Hole. Would it have killed you to fill me in on who everyone was? Or that the Joy of the Joy Chorus was a woman, now dead? You put me in a terrible spot."

Clayton wagged his finger at me. "Objection, I did no such thing. You never asked. I've seen you google, find, and buy something in the time it takes me to dial the phone; you could have taken five minutes to look it up. I'm paid to get you out of trouble, remember? Isn't your staff in charge of due diligence?"

Hmmm. "My staff is on leave of absence. I've had to scale back a bit. My Texas attorney cost me an arm and a leg, so I'm currently without an assistant, a stylist, a driver or a trainer."

Clayton refused the bait. "Well, your arms and legs look just fine, and I'm pretty sure attorney fees were a drop in the bucket compared to your shoe budget. And your new wardrobe sure beats the orange jumpsuit you might be wearing without my help."

"I was never going to be locked up in an orange jumpsuit, Clayton. I accidently leaned on a police officer! Hardly a capital offense."

"Either way, it does my heart good to see you enjoying the rhythm of our little village. Maybe you'll find that life outside of LA isn't so terrible after all. Millions of people lead very happy lives without ever being featured in a magazine."

But I wasn't those people. My interlude in Pleasant was temporary. I should follow up with Diane to see if she'd gained any traction in securing some work for me. I'd consider my time here a vacation, some much needed rest after the break up with Grant. But once this stint was up I needed to get back to my people. Awards season would coincide with my jail break (figuratively of course), and LA was never more exciting than during awards season.

"Clayton, somebody has to be featured in all those magazines so it might as well be me. But I admit, today I'm happy to be Anna, chillin out in front of Jay's Diner. Can I buy you a coffee?"

"I appreciate the offer but I'm due in court. Maybe I'll catch up with you on a Wednesday night at the barn? I hear the local talent is pretty entertaining."

Had he heard about my conversation with Beau? News travels fast in a small town, but that didn't seem gossip worthy.

"Probably not as entertaining as the local theater. I hear a revival of *Greater Tuna,* starring a certain lawyer, is in the works. Don't want to miss that. See you soon."

Clayton raised one very bushy eyebrow at me.

"Goodbye, Anna. Enjoy your afternoon."

And I did.

***

Maria headed back to California the following morning, pretending to be concerned about leaving me behind.

"Are you sure you'll be alright? The next few months will be over before you know it. I am going on vacation with Leo so you won't be able to reach me. I hope you don't think I'm abandoning you! We've been planning this trip for a year, and he almost gave up on me ever getting away. I think he might propose – well, hoping anyway. I color coded folders with all your important information; they are in the file box in your room. Bills are paid through the month. Sterling's office will send your mail once a week. I forwarded it to a PO box for the time being. How will you get things paid next month?"

"Maria, I know how to write a check. Off you go." And off she went.

Before I could even feel a little bit lonely, my mom called. "Hi sweetie! Anything new in Texas?"

I told her all about my foot in mouth Day One at the barn. She laughed and told me about her first job – fired on Day Two for complaining to a fellow waitress that the food was over priced and the staff under paid. It was a family business and the coworker was family. Ooops. That's why she suggested I check out the players at The Watering Hole. Experience is a good teacher. Unfortunately, youth can be a poor learner. But no scolding from Ginger. She was happy to hear me considering a piece of lemon chess pie at Jay's. I didn't know what lemon chess was, but it sounded more diet friendly than double chocolate peanut butter mud pie.

"You sound good, Anna. Some time away from the Hollywood scene might be refreshing."

"Because I am destined for greater things than dating the likes of Grant Adams?"

"Let's remember you said that, not me. But it could be nice to regroup out of the spotlight. These past few years have been a whirlwind; I don't want you to get lost in it. Remember when you were a kid, putting on shows in the basement? You were always the Director, drafting your neighborhood friends to play a part. When Jenny Cox was too shy to go on stage you put her in charge of the cookie table. You gave her a title, Refreshments Boss, and told her the pink apron was a very special uniform. It was her idea to charge a dime a cookie to raise money for your next production. You know where Jenny is now? She got her Master's degree in Economics and is teaching at University of Illinois! You have a gift for getting everyone on board behind a great idea."

"Jenny Cox! She used to hide in the corner, afraid I was going to make her sing, but more afraid of being left out. You took us to Walmart with her bake sale money to buy costumes. Guessing you padded the profits?"

"The parents took a collection! You might not remember, but we made a deal - since costumes made you a professional troupe, you had to rehearse before selling tickets. That saved us from a few torturous performances! But I must say your turn as Mary Poppins showed great promise. If only you could have made that umbrella fly…"

"Well, my story lines were limited because you were the only mom on the block who wouldn't let me watch *The Little Mermaid*! The other girls were mad about that."

"I was not going to let my daughter watch a movie about a girl who gives up her VOICE just to catch a man! Who does Disney think he is?"

The irony was not lost on me. Good thing my mom hadn't seen Grant drag me onto the patio during the interview just to shut me up. It would have broken her heart. Mary Poppins would never let a man get the best of her; she knew how to exert influence without inciting a riot. Or trading her soul for a magazine cover.

"Thanks, mom. You're right, Mary Poppins is a better role model than Ariel. I'll do my best to live up to her here in Pleasant. But you must admit, Ariel's clothes were better."

"Much better. I was never a fan of hats."

"I love you mom."

"I love you too, Anna."

Laughing made me hungry. I discovered I loved lemon chess pie.

\*\*\*

Saturday's practice was less frantic than the Wednesday after school shift. Kids wandered in with bed head, dropping their backpacks on tables. We didn't feed them on Saturdays; the kitchen staff was busy preparing for the evening concert crowd. Mo greeted me like his best friend before getting right to work on algebra. Duke had a group learning to play guitar in the corner, and Tish put me in charge of updating every member's contact information on the computer. Until yesterday I paid an assistant to help ME do this kind of thing, but I caught on fast. Tish was everywhere at once – directing kitchen staff, giving the box office instructions about ticket sales, talking to a local radio station about promotions. She redirected kids when they lost focus on homework as she ran from the kitchen to the office. Anyone with a question looked to Tish.

At 10:45 her frenzy stopped. The front door opened and a young man in a wheelchair breezed in. All the kids yelled "JORDAN!" in unison and he waved back, heading towards Tish. Her face lit up in a smile, bossy checklist forgotten, and she leaned in to give him a kiss on the cheek. "Hello, handsome. You're late. I'll give you a pass just this once." So this was Jordan, Tish's younger brother. She obviously adored him. I hadn't seen her greet anyone else with that kind of enthusiasm. Or sweetness. Jordan had Tish wrapped around his little finger. Maybe that's why Tish, talented performer, wasn't on the road pursuing her dream. Jordan needed her. They all needed her.

I couldn't think of one person who needed me. My mom and Frank loved me, but they didn't need me. Fame Cosmetics had a new "My True Story" model; they replaced me in no time with an adventure girl whose lipstick stayed in place even while skydiving. Grant certainly didn't need me. Hey, he might not even remember me. Tish was scrambling to find things for me to do at the Joy Chorus, so they didn't need me. Maria had Leo, my agent had other clients. I had achieved the dream of all millennials, freedom from the burden of responsibility. My only concern was for myself.

Simon peeked into the office. "Hello Miss Anna. I was hoping to give you Jenga tips today but we are starting practice. I didn't want you to think I had forgotten. Maybe we can try on Wednesday?"

Simon. I could barely hear his voice over the clatter of chairs being moved, but his familiar face warmed my heart. "Of course, Simon! I wouldn't miss it." I was rewarded with a blush as he ducked out to rehearsal.

Music filled the barn. If you closed your eyes, all the voices blended together seamlessly; remarkable for such a weird mix of teenagers. Tish popped in to check on my progress. I had an idea.

"Tish, I heard Duke say something about a Christmas concert. What do the kids wear when they perform? Please tell me it's not this t-shirt!"

"Funny, Anna. They wear black pants and a white shirt. We let the girls add necklaces to dress it up a little."

Black pants and a white shirt? Dressing up is half the fun! In high school, prom was just an excuse to get a new dress. We spent more time getting dressed and taking pictures than going to the actual dance. Half the fun of modeling was getting made over and wearing great clothes (OK, maybe not half. I loved the paycheck, and seeing my picture in a magazine, but a big part of the fun was the clothes.)

"Wouldn't performing be more fun in a better outfit?"

"I'm sure it would, Anna, but many of our kids have limited resources. We don't want to make them pay for something they can only wear while performing. The Joy Chorus is a non-profit. We don't have the funds to buy all 50 kids new clothes. But all donations are greatly appreciated. If you want to take them shopping, just let me know. Maybe you could get them on the cover of *Celebrity* magazine while you're at it?" Her tone was sarcastic, but I couldn't tell if she was teasing or being mean.

"Thanks for the green light, Tish. I'll get right on that." I took a break from data entry and went outside to make a phone call. Rachel answered on my first ring.

"Anastasia! You disappeared! I hear you are in Texas? Good grief girl, get home. How long are you stuck there? I'm already busy with awards show season but I can pencil you in."

Rachel was my stylist. Hairdressers and stylists are like therapists – they know more about their clients than anyone else. We, the clients, never know anything about them. It occurred to me this might not be a good arrangement. She knew I was arrested, in Texas, and out of the Hollywood scene. I had no idea what she had been up to. I decided to let this go for the moment.

"Rachel, yes, I'm in Texas. It's a long story, and I won't bore you with the details, but I'm exploring a few professional opportunities here. I've met some amazing people along the way. Ever heard of the Blue Valentines? Beau Laurel? They are friends with Dylan Worth and all perform here at The Watering Hole venue outside of Houston."

My name dropping clearly caught Rachel off guard. "Of course I've heard of the Blue Valentines. And Dylan Worth is there? Are you working on something with him?" Her piqued curiosity set off alarm bells, but I decided to let that go too.

"It's too early to talk about anything concrete, but I have a favor to ask you. Would you like to be a hero? The Blue Valentines formed a non-profit that benefits high school kids. It's a choir called the Joy Chorus. Most of these kids don't have a lot of money, and they don't have any performance outfits. Could you help me find someone to donate dresses for the girls and suits for the boys? We're talking 50 kids of all shapes and sizes. It doesn't have to be anything over the top, just nice."

"That's not my thing Anastasia, you know that. I work with designers, not big retailers."

"What if I made it worth your time? Perhaps an introduction to Dylan Worth? He might need a new stylist. That would be a feather in your cap."

"Well, I do have a few contacts I could call. It sounds like a good cause, and it could be a great marketing opportunity for a company. They would get good exposure with the Blue Valentines connection. What's the non-profit called again?"

"Thanks Rachel. It's called the Joy Chorus, named after Duke Valentine's late wife. So don't make any snarky remark about the name!"

"Got it. I'll get back to you next week. And keep me in the loop if you develop a project with Dylan Worth. That sounds interesting!"

I hoped Rachel wasn't friends with any of Dylan Worth's contacts. I'd have to unwind that little white lie later.

***

After practice the staff kicked into high gear. Saturday concerts were the bread and butter income of The Watering Hole. Tish found me in the office, still doing data entry. "Anna! I forgot you were still here. No need to stay."

"Well, about that, Tish. I don't have anything pressing to do today. Can I help out here?"

"I think you are limited to Joy Chorus hours towards community service."

"I know. Can I volunteer for the fun of it? Otherwise it's a movie all alone. I don't know anyone in Pleasant except for Clayton, and I'm pretty sure a chick flick is not on his wish list."

Tish hesitated.

"I can answer phones, sell tickets at the door, do more data entry if you like. Please?" I made my most pathetic puppy face. It worked.

"OK. Once the concert starts you can just enjoy the show. In the meantime, grab some lunch in the kitchen, then answer phones. We get a lot of last minute ticket requests. I'll tell Shirley to put you to work."

Yes! I hate office work, but it was better than a Saturday afternoon all alone. Bubba James was tonight's headliner; that promised to be interesting. Who names their kid Bubba? Let's hope it's a nickname. On my way to the kitchen I stopped by the booth. Squawk, the sound engineer, taught at the local community college. He worked with some of the Chorus kids interested in a technical career. His tattooed sleeves declared he was an Alabama, ZZ Top, and Mom fan.

"Hey Squawk. I heard we had a celebrity in the house so I wanted to meet him. Are you Jordan? I'm Anna, new girl in town."

Jordan turned his chair to get a better look at me. His smile was captivating. "Who said I was a celebrity?"

"It was obvious by the shout out when you arrived today. You certainly know how to make an entrance. Does Hollywood know about you?"

Squawk laughed. "Don't tell Hollywood about Jordan! We need him here, plus we don't want him to get a big head. I think Anna's flirting with you, dude. Better tell her about your girlfriend."

Jordan blushed. "I've been to Hollywood – no thanks. I like my job. Squawk and I are a team. And

Daisy isn't worried about new girls in town. I gave her a promise ring."

"Well then, Daisy is a lucky girl. I look forward to meeting her. Nice to meet you, Jordan. Glad to know someone has their eye on Squawk. I have a feeling he could get into all kinds of trouble on his own. See you around, boys."

I got to work. The show was sold out, so I took advantage of today's calls to promote the future schedule. I grabbed a handful of M & Ms from the apothecary jar on the front desk; when I was a kid I used to keep a tally of completed homework assignments by moving candy from one bowl to another. Then I'd eat the treats when I was done. Without the promise of chocolate, I never would have gotten through algebra. Shirley was impressed with my ability to keep disappointed fans on the line, selling them tickets to an upcoming show. She underestimated the motivating power of candy. As a model, I had to earn permission to eat anything forbidden (in my mind anyway. There is probably a chapter in a psychology book somewhere explaining the complicated mechanism of food as a reward for weight obsessed models.) Old habits are hard to break.

Shirley was impressed. "Anna, I thought you were new to country music. Have you even heard of Colby Jensen? Or the Moonshine Guys?"

"No! But I looked at the flier for next month to see who was performing, then found them on iTunes. I can see which songs are most popular. I tell callers those are my favorite tracks, and they get chatty about theirs. If they aren't Colby Jensen fans I ask them about another act on the list. When I sell them tickets, I gather their contact information. We have email lists, right? Once we know who they like, we should email them when similar musicians are performing. It would be an easy way to promote new talent. We could even sell a bundle - pitch the headline act, but throw in a Wednesday night ticket at a discount, or even free. Better to fill the seats; we can at least sell them food and drinks. Besides, who wants to play to an empty house? It's a win win! And I make it a game. For every caller who unexpectedly buys a ticket, I give myself an M & M. It makes the time fly."

Shirley tried to keep up, but I think her experience was better suited to bookkeeping than marketing. "Wow, I never thought of that. I think I'll leave answering the phones to you and get busy working on payroll." Good idea, Shirley. I was on a roll. Bubba James was wildly popular, so the phones kept ringing and I kept selling. It was 5:00 before I knew it, and my cup was filled with M & Ms. I could never eat all that candy. But it was fun to see how many extra tickets I sold in full color.

Tish poked her head into the office. "How's it going? Any questions, Anna?"

Shirley practically popped out of her chair, which is impressive for a woman of a certain age and weight. "Tish, Anna is a machine! See all those M & Ms? That's how many future concert tickets she sold this afternoon. And she has some marketing ideas we should consider. Colby Jensen's show is almost sold out, and he's a new talent."

"How did you do that?"

I explained how I hooked Bubba James fans into giving Colby a try, and asked if I could throw in some free Wednesday night tickets to close the deal.

Tish looked skeptical. "Sounds like you are selling the tickets without the freebies, so why bother?"

"It will make them feel good about taking a risk on Colby, and we'll fill more seats on Wednesdays. It doesn't cost us anything since the seats are empty anyway. Add in the food and drink they buy, it's all profit. Maybe we turn them into regulars?"

Tish nodded slowly. "OK, if someone is hesitating go ahead and throw in some free Wednesday tickets. Let's see how that goes."

Shirley was almost giddy, funny for a quiet woman who enjoyed accounting. "Where did you learn to sell like that Anna? You make it look almost fun. I hate sales."

"I think of it as making new friends. Talking comes easily to me, and the alternative today was room service in my hotel room. Stick with what you do well, Shirley! Crunching numbers makes me want to me poke my eyes out. Just ask my assistant Maria – well, former assistant - she couldn't even get me to balance my checkbook, something I will now regret since I no longer have an assistant and still have a checkbook. Thank God He made people with your kind of brain. We'd all be swimming in a sea of overdrafts if I was in charge of the books. My M & M accounting might not pass bookkeeping standards, but I do love winning at a game. And by the looks of it, my cup runneth over today!"

Shirley seemed pleased. You probably don't get too many strokes for keeping a company from financial ruin. Bookkeeping only gets noticed when you DON'T keep them from disaster. With Maria gone I was beginning to appreciate how much she did behind the scenes. Just this morning I had to renew my rental car, pick up dry cleaning, and check my account balance to avoid afore mentioned overdraft. I should thank her for doing such a good job. Besides, I might need her to rescue me from any number of situations, color coded folders notwithstanding. I could surprise her with a nice dinner at that resort where she and Leo were headed, if only I could remember where it was. Maria usually tracked these things down for me. A gift card sent to her house might have to do. I have the best of intentions, I was just rusty on how to execute a plan.

"I'll help you balance your checkbook, Anna."

"Shirley, that is so nice! Thank you. And I'll talk on the phone so you don't have to."

Shirley hugged me. "God bless you!"

The pre-concert dinner crowd started to pour in around 6:00. First through the door was Beau. "Hello, Anna. Looks like they put you to work. Or are you just keeper of the M & M stash."

"No, I worked the box office today! The M & Ms are payment for my valiant efforts."

Beau laughed. "Sounds about right. Welcome to the music business. You get paid in personal satisfaction and the occasional M & M."

A Beau look alike piped in behind him. "Don't be so cynical, Beau! You'll crush the dreams of up and comers. Pay no attention to him. He's doing just fine."

"Anna, this is my brother Ben and his wife, Sarah. Ben can afford to be optimistic because he is NOT in the music business. Anna took a wrong turn out of LA and woke up in Pleasant."

A petite blonde woman said hi, and Beau's brother shook my hand. "Welcome to the Great State of Texas, Anna. Is your detour permanent?"

The crowd was arriving behind them so I didn't have much time to answer. "Just a few months. Long story." Beau pushed them into the barn with a backward wave. His guitar was slung over his shoulder.

"Shirley, is Beau playing tonight?"

"Yes, he's warming up for Bubba. Why don't you go on in and get a seat? I've got things covered here. You've more than earned it! Want your M & Ms?"

"No, but thanks for the fun, Shirley. I feel like I accomplished something today!"

The barn was filling up quickly. The show was sold out, so the only seat available was at a lone table in the back corner. Ben caught my eye and waved me towards the front. "Anna, are you stuck in the back 40? That's what we call the spillover tables. We have an extra seat tonight, why don't you join us? Sarah's friend couldn't make it at the last minute. We'd hate to see a guest stuck behind a post – that's not very hospitable!"

"I'm not really a guest, but I'll take it, thank you! The view is much better from here." I sat down next to Sarah. She had a welcoming smile. "So what brings you to Texas?"

What to say? Was I going to have this conversation in my head every time someone asked me why I was here? If I came clean now, these nice people might regret offering me a seat at their table. But if I wasn't honest, and they later found out I was here by court order (which they probably would), they might hate me. And how much to tell? Just the basics? The whole story of me and Grant? That was probably more than she bargained for. My hesitation must have been longer than I intended.

"I didn't mean to pry. We are just glad to have you!"

Sarah was simply being nice. I had to reach back to my pre-LA days to remember what that felt like. In LA, everyone is fishing for something; you keep your guard up to avoid being blindsided. I doubt Sarah could blind side a sleeping turtle. Kindness fairly oozed from her. So I came clean.

"Well Sarah, I got myself in a little trouble with the Pleasant County Sheriff and was sentenced to community service with the Joy Chorus. But I'm not a bad person! I just got a little excited over a pair of shoes...it wasn't the shoes, really, I was upset over my cheating boyfriend...well I thought he was my boyfriend. I found out he was more interested in a trashy blonde than me. In any case, I let my emotions get the better of me and I was rude to a police officer. That landed me in court. Want me to find another seat?"

I saw the look of recognition go off in Sarah's eyes. My t-shirt and sneakers were a good disguise; hard to recognize the hysterical model of the video in this get up. That's not such a bad thing. Before the incident – that sounds better than arrest – I craved being recognized. Now I was happy to give Anastasia DeMars a break and welcome Anna Martin back into my life. I watched the video play across Sarah's face like a ticker tape as she worked to connect my high fashion image with the girl in front of her. Then she patted my hand.

"Of course not! I'm sure there is a lot more to the story than a short video can tell. Miranda Lambert says behind every woman's scorn is a man who made her that way. Looks like you've landed on your feet, so good for you. How did you meet Beau?"

And just like that, Sarah made a friend for life. She asked all the right questions, curious about my modeling while avoiding the gossipy side of my personal life. I told her about my blunders on Day One at the Joy Chorus, and my success selling tickets. She was a sympathetic listener. By the time Beau took the stage we were laughing together about his "I write a few songs" introduction. Beau wore modesty like a superhero cape; under that cloak lurked a lot of talent, but not a lot of patience for the palm greasing side of the music business. He and Ben ran their family ranching business together, selling beef to area restaurants. Sarah taught third grade.

Beau's music was beautiful, pared down and acoustic. Nobody talked, nothing interrupted his resonant ballads. The crowd rewarded him with a standing ovation. Beau tipped his hat, then took a seat on the opposite side of Ben. He didn't seem to notice I had joined the table, or the thunderous applause from the audience. Ben clapped his brother on the back. "Not bad for a part time songwriter. Does Nashville know about you?"

Beau ignored him, ordering a steak and an iced tea. Didn't country music folks shoot whiskey? I had been listening to the radio since Wednesday and did not recall any songs about tea. Ben continued to tease Beau. "Sorry Anna, Beau thinks that by sticking his head in the sand we can't actually see him. Nothing personal. He'll emerge once someone else takes the stage."

Ben and Beau looked like brothers. Ben was a bit shorter, but they both had piercing blue eyes and a lanky build. That's where the resemblance ended. Beau ambled with a slow swagger whereas Ben was quicker on his feet. Ben said 1000 words for every one of Beau's, and he filled me in on the Laurel family between stage acts. Ben sold the meat from their ranching business, Beau managed the ranch on site. Sarah called them two halves of the moon, Beau the dark side, Ben the sunny. Together they had made the family business very successful, living in cottages on the ranch with their parents' house in the middle. Cult? Commune? Or just a happy family? I guess if your livelihood depended on a herd of cows, it's best not to commute.

Sarah was intrigued by my leap from college to model. The more I learned about how hard these musicians worked to get their big breaks, the less impressed I was by my own success. They had talent. I was lucky to be born tall with great skin. Ginger, my mother, is beautiful. Heads turn when she enters a room. In addition to being physically gorgeous, she radiates warmth and confidence. I'm what people call striking – over 6 feet tall, long legs, thick brown hair. Hard to lose me in a crowd, kind of like a giraffe. My face is plain, and without makeup I can pass for an average all American girl if I'm sitting. But a plain face is a model's ticket to work, because with makeup I'm transformed into all manner of facades. I make a good before and after story. The right makeup artist can even make me look like an ordinary, but dazzling, all American girl. That's what caught the eye of the Fame Cosmetics scout; typical girl becomes noteworthy when using their products. Make Warrior Red lipstick your signature and you can become famous too! Girls everywhere bought into that fantasy hook, line and sinker. But typical girls don't wear $1500 shoes. That's where the story falls apart, and I lose my contract. I overshot the narrative. Moderation has never been my strong suit.

"Modeling fell into my lap; it was never my goal. I majored in broadcast journalism. When I was a kid I'd pretend to be a reporter on the scene of breaking news and make my best friend Jane film me. I wasn't interested in world events, I just wanted to be on TV! Acting didn't appeal to me because you had to learn a script. I liked the rush of being caught in the middle of the action. It seemed very thrilling. Modeling is the opposite of exciting; everything is meticulously staged. But the money lured me away from school. I never finished."

"It's not too late to go back. How old are you, 23, 24? I hardly think you're washed up! Mo and Duke didn't even get their first record deal until they were in their 30s. You can't give up on a dream!"

"I don't know if journalism is my dream or not. The past 4 years have been a blur, and modeling is the least of it. The LA scene has a way of sucking you in. I loved the attention until it turned on me. But I don't want to end my modeling career with a failure. I was fired from Fame. That's so humiliating!"

Sarah had no idea how embarrassing it was to have your downfall played out on video, over and over again. I did not want to be forever known as the hysterical model pitching a fit about her shoes. Or the gullible ditz too slow to figure out the movie star was a playboy. I had to prove I was different from the bevy of bimbos swinging through Grant Adam's revolving door. Going back to school wouldn't set that record straight. I needed a new high profile modeling job. And fast. A model's expiration date was shorter than last week's milk. I had made a lot of money, but I had spent a lot of it too. How big was my nest egg? Not sure. My LA closet full of the latest trends, now headed to storage, suddenly seemed foolish. When could I wear that couture gown again? I had been photographed in it, so by Hollywood standards it was old news. Who knew beaded dresses had such a short shelf life? The designer promised me I'd have it forever, called it an investment. Hard to fund a 401k with that.

Poor Sarah. Here she was trying to encourage me, and my mind traveled the yellow brick road to the locked gate of Oz. When did I abandon the idea of a career in journalism? Must have been the day I saw the bottom line on my Fame contract. The money distracted me. I hadn't thought about what I'd given up until Sarah called it a dream. Her face wore a look of concern.

"Anna, people will forget about that video. We've all made dumb mistakes. Why not do something you love?"

"Do you love teaching?"

Sarah beamed. "I do! Kids are so impressionable and it's fun to see the lightbulb go off when they learn something new. My upbringing was very modest, and my parents dreamed of me becoming an attorney, but what I learned in one semester of law school was that I hated law school. Teaching brings me a lot more joy."

Joy. That was never part of my job criteria. Money, visibility, swag? Those things, yes. And those things made me happy, but that's not the same as having joy in what you do. Maybe I was trying to make up for losing my pink bedroom as a kid. When my parents split, my mom and I lost a lot of security. My father was a successful salesman and the money was flowing. We left a big house and yard for a beige apartment with brown carpeting. I remember throwing myself on the floor in a fit about leaving my canopy bed behind. My mom sat on the floor next to me, silent. When I was drained she pulled me into her lap, confessing that every day spent in that house made her sad. I did not understand infidelity, but I knew what a liar was. My dad lied to both of us all the time. We could never count on him to do anything he promised. I later learned she traded child support to gain full custody of me – and with that, he was gone. We made a pact that day, sealed with a pinkie swear, to pick people over stuff, love over regret, and home over a house. I couldn't have told you what regret was, but I trusted her. My 6 year old self was relieved in one way, sad in another. I didn't miss the arguments, but I missed my princess palace. And I missed the idea of a dad, if not my particular one. Now I know the princess palace was paid for with debt; his "success" was borrowed. The house of cards was going to collapse sooner or later, and my mom got out before the roof caved in.

My most vivid memory of my father was him applauding my kindergarten dance routine. He couldn't make it to the recital – business – so my mom urged me to give him a preview in our kitchen. I put on my costume and tap danced my way across the floor. He cheered, told me I was beautiful, and declared I'd be famous one day. Then he made me promise to save him a front row ticket when I made it big. Forget all the steps along the way, he was only interested in the prize at the end. We left in the summer before first grade, and I had not seen him since.

My mom was true to her word. She never disparaged my father or pined for what we left behind. Our little apartment was filled with friends and laughter. Frank Martin rode in on his white horse when I was 8 – literally. My mom read that little girls who rode horses gained confidence and positive self-esteem, so I rode horses. Frank read that horseback riding was good for physical rehab.

He was recovering from a motorcycle accident and his therapy brought him to Angel Ranch where my weekly lesson took place. Our lives were forever altered that day. He entered the arena on a white horse christened Gabriel (I am not making that up), hijacking my mom's heart. The three of us got married and he adopted me. Frank is my real dad.

Bubba James interrupted my thoughts by taking the stage. I expected a guy named Bubba to have a beer gut and poor grammar. Nope. Bubba was buff, like a gym rat. I also expected a Bubba to sing with a twang and a drawl. No again. Bubba was more of a rocker than a crooner. When he wasn't performing, he worked as a mechanic, and on Sunday mornings led worship at the Fellowship of Grace Community Church down the road. At least he used to. Bubba was on his way to stardom; his hit single "Why Make It Easy" got him a Country Music Awards nomination. He'd even scored a duet on the awards show with Eric Church (never heard of him, but guessed he was famous). Since then he'd been on tour, but always made time for The Watering Hole. Ben shared a wealth of information.

Our front row seats made further conversation difficult, so we sat back and enjoyed the show. Bubba scanned the crowd; he seemed to be looking for someone. His eyes landed on Tish, standing in the back of the barn, keeping watch over all the servers. He smiled. That was something Ben left out. Bubba had a thing for Tish. Tish caught his eye then looked away. Did she not see the spark in his eyes when he found her in the crowd? Or did she see it, and not return the favor? Bubba pretended not to notice. He just kept finding her, even as she moved around the floor. Tish pretended not to notice as well, eventually leaving the main room. Sarah caught me watching their covert dance. She leaned over to whisper between songs.

"Yes, Bubba has it for Tish. Bad. She's a hard nut to crack, that one. He wants her to go out on tour with him, but she won't leave Jordan or Duke. She was out on her first tour when Joy died, and she's been going 90 miles an hour ever since keeping the plates spinning here. I think she's afraid something terrible might happen if she leaves again. It's too bad, because she loves being on stage."

I didn't understand. My dream was snatched away from me over a PR stumble, and Tish refused to chase hers when the door was wide open. Some people just don't appreciate an opportunity! Bubba was on the rise and he wanted Tish to fly with him. I'd hitch my wagon to his if I was her. Making it in the music business was obviously hard, and he was offering her a fast track ticket.

"Why doesn't Duke tell her to go? Things here seem pretty manageable."

"Try telling Tish to do anything! She is stubborn. Her toughness helped them all regroup after Joy's accident, but now I think she's stuck. It's been 5 years and she deserves a chance at her own life. Bubba isn't giving up; he can be as stubborn as Tish, but it's been a tug of war for a while. Sorry, that was probably more information than you needed. Tish would kill me if she knew I was telling you this."

"You didn't tell me anything I didn't see for myself. Hard to miss it. If Tish thinks it's a secret, she's fooling herself. Bubba's face told the whole story."

When the concert was over, and the crowd began to wane, I grabbed my bag to head out. Ben wouldn't hear of it.

"Anna! Hey, hang around for a drink and meet Bubba. I promised Sarah a night out. The more the merrier."

Tish appeared with a tray of drinks. The sound and lighting guys pulled up chairs and I felt like an intruder crashing a frat council. Tish said nothing, making it even more awkward. But Ben insisted I stay, escorting me to a seat next to Beau.

"Anna, Sarah, what can I get you ladies to drink?" Ben played host while Bubba announced his arrival with a whoop. "Tish, what's a guy got to do to get some music in this place? There's a dance floor calling your name! I didn't come all this way to dance alone. Hey, who is this? Maybe you'll two-step with a hometown cowboy if Tish won't? I'm Bubba."

He reached out to shake my hand and pulled me to my feet. "Tish, start the music! We've got a live one here!"

"I don't know how to one step, much less two-step! But I'm game if you are. I'm Anna." Beau plugged in his phone, filling the barn with a song about the Boondocks.

"Hello, Anna. Two-stepping is easy – just follow my lead. That's where Tish and I run into some trouble." He yelled that over his shoulder to be certain Tish heard him. "Are you good at following?"

"Probably not! The last time I followed a man I got arrested. Maybe if you take it slow I can catch on without running a red light." I gave up on worrying what anybody might think about my run in with the sheriff.

Bubba ignored my stepping on his boots and kept moving me across the floor. "Arrested! Was he worth it?"

"No! He wasn't worth the gas it took me to GET arrested! But it landed me here, so let's call it even. I needed a break from myself and this barn is a great place to get lost."

"Ha! I come to the barn to FIND myself. I'm apt to get lost out THERE. What are you running from?"

Two-stepping puts you face to face with your partner and Bubba's gaze didn't give me space to ignore his question. We just kept dancing while he waited for my reply.

"I'm running from a woman named Anastasia DeMars. She's the one who made me act like an idiot, humiliate myself publicly, and lose my job. Because of her I ended up in court, was sentenced to community service far from home, and had to shut down my swanky life in LA. Now, instead of working to support said lifestyle, I'm playing Jenga for free with a bunch of teenagers."

"Sounds like she's out to get you. What did you do to tick her off?"

"I followed her around and did whatever she did."

"I thought copycatting was the best form of flattery. Guess she didn't see it that way?"

"She loved it. But I took the fall when the mess hit the fan."

"Has she tracked you down? Apologized? Thrown herself at your feet asking forgiveness?"

"Not exactly. Let's just say I'm learning who my real friends are."

Bubba smiled. "That's why I come back whenever I can. My real friends are here. People out there will eat you alive if they think they can make a buck off you. That woman – is she from around here? Her name sounds familiar."

"No, you've probably seen her name in the tabloids. She was a hot topic there for a while."

"That explains it. People looking for publicity are usually self-serving jerks. Be grateful you learned early. And thanks for the dance. Not bad for a beginner. Go get you some boots – makes two-steppin a lot more fun. Cavender's Boot City up the road can fix you up. In boots you'll be taller than most men, but I don't think that will stop you."

"Any man worth his salt won't be put off by a tall woman in boots. Thanks for the lesson! By the look on Tish's face I might pay for it, but in this case, it WAS worth it!"

Tish was watching us, her frown something less than neutral for once. Bubba grabbed her with both hands. "OK, let's show the new kid how it's really done!" They were good, in perfect synch. Tish relaxed, Sarah and Ben joined them, and the tension leaked out of the room. Squawk looked at me with admiration.

"You've got more guts than I do to poke that bear. It's been a long time since anyone has given Tish a run for her money. You might be just the thing to help her see Bubba's not gonna wait forever."

Tish cranky, what's new? It wasn't my fault. Bubba pulled me on to the dance floor, not the other way around. And what if I did? She didn't seem interested in him, at least not until he gave me a little attention. Some women make things harder than necessary. You like a guy? Go for it, or don't blame me if he'd rather dance with someone fun than someone grumpy playing hard to get.

The crew scattered to refresh their drinks. Ben two-stepped Sarah by our table. "C'mon Beau, it's not polite to leave a woman unattended when there's dancing. Anna, forgive him for his backward manners, we were raised better than that. Dance you two! Bubba gave her the basics, let her practice."

Beau asked with a raise of an eyebrow. I answered with a warning. "I'm in if you're not afraid of me stepping all over you. I was a two-stepping virgin until today, so no promises, but I'll do my best to follow."

Beau stood up and extended his hand. "I'm not afraid of much, and leading is what I do best. Let's go."

Dancing with Bubba was easy. We talked, and if I clomped on his feet he never let on. But after some initial instructions, Beau was silent. Every mistake landed me on his foot, or had him catching me mid fall. I got worse, not better. Eventually I had to stop. "Hey, aren't you supposed to make this easy? I seem to be doing all the work, and doing it badly! Where does the leading come in?"

"You're fighting me, so I thought I'd let you lead. Ready to try it my way?" I nodded.

"The two-step is just like walking – slow, slow, quick quick. Don't try so hard. Take it easy. We won't add other moves until you get the rhythm."

He whispered the beat as we moved, slow, slow, quick quick until I got the hang of it. I listened, and sure enough, right there in the music, was the tempo. After a few songs Beau added a simple spin, giving me time to work out the kinks. Just when I thought I was getting good he threw in a side by side maneuver that left us tangled up. Ben clapped and whooped.

"That's Beau in a nutshell! Just when you think you have it figured out he startles you with some tricky move. Don't let him fool you, Anna; under that quiet exterior lies a complicated mystery man. You're doing great. Let's get a beer."

Beau apologized for tripping me up. "I thought you were ready. You'll get it next time."

I laughed. "No harm, no foul. But I see there is more to two-stepping than just walking!"

He conceded. "Walking is a good place to start. The rest comes with practice."

We joined the group at the bar, and when it was time to go Sarah made sure to say goodbye. Texans were so much nicer than my LA circle. If one of those friends tracked me down at the end of an evening it was to catch up on the latest gossip, and if it didn't involve me I probably spilled it. Sarah just wanted to wish me well. I left the barn happy. For the first time in months, I didn't dread the coming week. There was a pair of cowboy boots in my future. Do they make red boots? I'd love red boots.

# CHAPTER 7

I spent the next few days settling in to the Pleasant life. If I ever wanted to model again I needed to work out. A 24-hour gym offered a treadmill, but the attendant looked at me like I was an alien when I asked for directions to the massage room and spa. True, the low monthly fee should have tipped me off that facials weren't part of the landscape, but no need to be rude. Brownies would quickly find their way to my hips without warfare, so the 24-hour gym it was. On the up side? Spin classes are universal, so I jumped right in. I always feel better after I sweat.

And after I eat. I was becoming a regular at Jay's All Day Diner. My little hotel suite had a tiny fridge, currently filled with a sideways bottle of white wine. The crowd at Jay's was eclectic. In the morning, retired folks gathered to chat over coffee. Lunchtime brought in moms with kids, business people, and round two of retired folks chatting over coffee. Jay's offered everything from all day breakfast, to burgers, to salads, to milkshakes. If it wasn't on the menu, Jay might even whip it up for you; all you had to do was ask. Just don't ask for anything "diet." Jay believed in real food with real flavor. No phony franchise meals here. When Jay took the day off to go fishing, his sign read CLOSED.

I was just finishing my turkey patty and grilled veggies (Jay frowned when I ordered, but he's given up on me eating a bun) when my phone rang. It was Wednesday and I knew today would be lucky. How? My hair. This morning my hair behaved, without frizz or funky cowlick. I had tested this theory over the years and my hypothesis stands: good hair opens the door to serendipity, bad hair forecasts trouble. When I landed in Houston on the day of my arrest I should have known I was headed for disaster; humidity blew my hair up like an inflatable helmet. If I had been paying attention I would have gotten right back on that plane. It wasn't until my mug shot made the entertainment news that the lightbulb went on. Thinking back to my life's high and low points, I was batting almost 1000. Dance marathon when I was discovered? Hair performed beautifully in a French knot, even after 24 hours on my feet. The exception that proved the rule was the day of my sentencing; perfect hair, yet sentenced to community service anyway. Today promised to be lucky. My hair was smooth and fly away free, pulled back into a sleek ponytail.

"Hello, Rachel! Tell me you have good news!"

"Anastasia, I always have good news."

My stylist was a master at walking the gossip tightrope. She hinted at the latest romance or scandal without mentioning names, never betraying a confidence while teasing her clients with just a whiff of whodunit. Elopements, splits, secret trysts? Rachel was the first to know. She dropped enough hints so that when the news broke, you realized she had known all along. Rachel was a good stylist, but LA was brimming with good stylists. Her secret weapon? Discretion, and her warm personality. Everyone wanted to be her friend. We confided in her, trusting her to keep her mouth shut while hoping for a morsel of chatter about someone else. I didn't even know where she lived.

"Anastasia, your mission of mercy is a good story, and good stories always sell. I made a few calls and connected with the Head of Marketing at Belle Bridal. You've heard their slogan, "Be the Belle of Your Ball"? Well, they design bridesmaid dresses for mass production. Tall, short, skinny, chubby, they've got a dress to fit. Grace Jackson, the woman I spoke to, sang in her high school choir and believes in the life changing power of music, or at least that's what we'll tell anyone who asks. She offered to donate the girls' dresses and guys' suits. Belle Bridal even threw in shoes. All you need to do is arrange a fitting; I have the number of the local store manager. Oh, and one more thing. Grace wants a print ad featuring all the kids in their new outfits. They are running a "Belle Heroes" campaign this Fall and will feature your group with an emotional pitch about how Belle Bridal rocked their world. Seemed like a fair exchange, and hey, what teenager doesn't want to see themselves in *Celebrity* magazine?"

"What celebrity doesn't want to see themselves in *Celebrity* magazine! Rachel, you hit it out of the park. Thank you! I'll be sure to connect you with Dylan Worth as soon as possible."

"Anastasia, if that works out, great, but don't worry about it. Being the hero has its own perks. Keep me posted on the progress, and send me an early copy of the ad when it's ready. Get the kids to sign it? I'd love to frame it and hang it in my office. It was fun to do a good work! Who knows, this may be the beginning of a whole new chapter for me. I can change the world, one fashion assist at a time."

"Rachel, I tell you what – feel free to tell everyone what I'm doing in Texas, and how you made some kids' dreams come true."

"I just might do that, Anastasia. Look for the email with the local Belle Bridal information. And stay in touch!"

See? Good hair day, good news.

\*\*\*

I burst through the door at The Watering Hole that afternoon and almost knocked Duke over.

"Hey, where's the fire!"

"I'm the fire! Duke, how would you like to see the Chorus kids decked out for the Christmas concert? Dresses for the girls, new clothes for the boys? All for free?"

"I'd like it."

I told him all about Belle Bridal's offer to outfit the kids from top to shoe clad toe. He was ecstatic.

"Anna, that's amazing! How did you pull that off? New in town and you're already shaking things up."

I basked in Duke's enthusiasm. This was fun, surprising people with good news. Put me in charge of image management and I'm a pro, just please don't make me do math.

"What's the catch?" I turned to see Tish standing behind me, her eyes narrowed. She must have heard my pitch to Duke.

"The catch? No catch really. We need to set aside a day ASAP to get the fittings done. Belle Bridal does want to do a print ad featuring the kids in their outfits, but I'd see that as a bonus, not a catch. The kids would love it!"

Tish's eyebrows went up. "Have you agreed to this deal, Anna?"

"No, I haven't agreed to anything yet. I need to contact the Director of Marketing at Belle to iron out the details. My stylist in LA helped me find a company willing to donate the clothes."

"I don't think your Hollywood stylist should be making deals for us. Are you sure the offer is free? Did it occur to you that the kids' parents might not want them used in an ad? And our practice time is limited. I don't think we can spare a day to arrange fittings for 50 kids. But I'll consider it. Send me the information you have so far, and I'll follow up after I discuss this with Duke and Mo."

What was her problem? This was all good for the Chorus. And Rachel was just trying to help! No secret agenda, no hook, just people offering to do a nice thing for a group of kids. She was getting on my nerves.

"Tish, what parent is going to turn down the free gift of a whole new outfit? I think they would love to see their kid, and the Joy Chorus, featured in a magazine. It will generate great exposure. And no, I will not send you the information. This was my idea, through my contacts, and if anyone follows up it will be me. Talk amongst yourselves – just let me know your decision, although I'm pretty sure the kids will be disappointed if you put the kibosh on it."

That put Tish back on her heels. "Did you tell some of the kids already?"

I ignored her and headed to the kitchen to begin set up, almost knocking Mo over as I flew through the swinging door.

"Whoa there! What's the hurry? Not much to run for in the kitchen unless it's a brownie you're after. Or a t-shirt. Why are you swimming in that thing? I can get you a smaller one, unless you like the muumuu."

Mo was always cheerful. How did he do that?

"You have smaller t-shirts?"

Mo pointed to the cabinet. "Sure. Here, a whole drawer full. Take what you want and throw that big one in the laundry pile."

A whole drawer full of small t-shirts and Tish had given me an XXL. I was fuming now.

"Thanks, Mo. Tish must have thought it would be funny to stick me in this tent. What did I ever do to her? I just showed up to help! Coerced I admit, but still, I jumped right in. Who does she think she is?"

Mo clucked his tongue. "True, your tall beautiful self just showed up on her turf and right off the bat the kids love you, Beau befriends you, and Bubba takes you dancing. Not sure what she is so fussy about."

Mo has a way of smacking you down without making you mad. That takes some skill. My mom could do that – compliment you on the way to a stinging observation. Ginger taught what she called the Pretty Girl Proverb: people will assume beautiful women are bitchy and self-centered, so you must go the extra mile to prove them wrong. Ginger was better at the nice part than I was. Not that Tish wasn't pretty, she was, but I am 6 feet tall and hard to miss in a room. Mo might have a point. I tend to enter by knocking the door down rather than ringing the bell. Tish didn't ask for me to be at the Chorus, and I didn't go the extra mile to prove I wasn't bitchy. But she wasn't without blame. Tish could learn a thing or two from the book of Ginger's proverbs. The truth is we were off to a bad start. It was her turf. I was here by court order.

I took a deep breath. Mo handed me a small t-shirt with a smile. Just being in his orbit made my blood pressure go down. I didn't mean to invade anyone's territory. But OK, I could probably back off. I just had so many good ideas! Thanks to me, we had sold all those concert tickets. Shirley would still be peddling Colby Jensen seats one at a time if I hadn't stepped in. But artists are notoriously temperamental, and I would have to learn to tiptoe around their fragile egos. Fine.

Mo left me alone with my thoughts while I got busy setting up for practice. I had graduated from Jenga. Duke asked me to work with the kids on the debate team. I was a master at debate. If you were persuasive in the strength of your delivery, the facts were secondary. Human nature compels us to look for information that supports our own position, so the key is to win an audience to your position early.

Tish was noticeably absent. After snacks I gathered my kids in a corner of the stage, dividing them into two groups on opposing sides of a table. The debate topic was up to me; the point of our practice was to develop confidence in delivery and formulating a strategy. I gave each team their position to argue, and 15 minutes to prepare. The topic? Pros and Cons of Speaking Your Mind to Your Boss. Discuss.

Duke came by to see the kids at work. His only comment was "how did you ever come up with that?"

*\*\*\**

Sarah called me on Thursday night. I was getting lonely on my days off from the Chorus and answered the phone on ring one.

"Anna, I hope I'm not disturbing you."

"Good one! No. Any interruption to my life in this small hotel suite is welcome. What's up?"

"Well, Ben and I had an idea – no pressure. We won't be offended if you say no. But we have a small guest cottage here on the ranch that nobody is using, and it seems silly for you to live in a hotel when it sits empty. No maid service, but you'd have more space and a full kitchen. It's not far from The Watering Hole."

A guest cottage on a ranch! Community service was giving me a full education into life on the range. I recommend hotel living if you are in the Four Seasons; extended stay mini suites, even with maid service, are depressing.

"Sarah, that sounds great. Can I rent it from you?"

"Oh no, that's not necessary. Do you want to see it before you commit? It's nothing fancy."

"Believe me, this hotel is less than nothing fancy. I accept!"

"You can come by tomorrow evening; I'll text you the address. Any time after 6:00."

"Sarah, you are an angel. Thank you!"

She might be the nicest person I have ever met.

My Texas story was getting better by the day. If I was going to live on a ranch, I needed some boots; might as well dress the part. On Friday, I headed to Cavender's. Jeans, jewelry, wall plaques – Western wasn't just for hoe downs, it was a lifestyle. A tall guy named Blake offered to help. He was a walking advertisement for the store in his boots, cowboy hat, and a silver belt buckle the size of a dinner plate. Blake took one look at my Tori Burch flats

146

and guessed I was new at this. There were so many pretty cowboy boots! And why go plain when a red pair with embroidered flowers called your name? Or turquoise with sparkly inlays?

Blake was a ranch hand when he wasn't selling boots, so he steered me towards something practical. I compromised; for every day, brown with some studded details. For dress up? Full on bling. The right boots make any pair of jeans something special. Add a blouse, or better yet, a dress, and you were good to go. I hauled my pile of clothes to the checkout. Blake politely carried my loot to the car. We parted with a handshake and I promised to come again. Let's hope Blake was paid on commission; if so, he was celebrating that night. At least I didn't get arrested in Iowa. No fun clothes there.

Back at the hotel I changed into my new boots and blouse before heading to Sarah and Ben's. Not far from the freeway the landscape changed dramatically. No strip malls! Just cross fenced land with pastures and cows. I passed a lot of trucks, but few sedans, on my way to the ranch. GPS started to beep as I approached a huge iron gate declaring this was HONOR RANCH. Green pastures bordered the drive, and over a small hill the main farmhouse came into view. A porch ran the length of the front, and large magnolia trees shaded the lawn. Honor

Ranch could have been the set for the homestead in *Forrest Gump*, all Southern and welcoming. Maybe they served sweet tea and lemonade to guests lounging in the rocking chairs. (I had learned all about sweet tea at Jay's All Day Diner – not the same as tea with sugar in it! Oh no, sweet tea combines carefully brewed tea with simple syrup... ignorance of the art immediately brands you a foreigner). Further down the road I could see another house, a bit smaller, and off to the side sat two small cottages. Sarah's SUV pulled up next to me.

"Hey! Follow me. Our house is out back."

As we parked, a swarm of waggy and barking dogs surrounded our cars to greet us. Sarah shooed them away, shouting over the noise.

"Sorry! Hope you aren't afraid of dogs. If so, your hotel might start to look good. They run the place! We are just staff."

Good thing I wasn't wearing stilettos here. Boots were perfect for navigating potential hazards hiding in the grass. My mom had a cuddly Cavapoo – Cavalier and poodle mix – with the brains of a Cavvie and the curly coat of a poodle. In Ginger's terms, the perfect mix of dumb, sweet and non-shedding. My doggie experience did not prepare me for the swirling mob of hair and tongues all vying for my attention.

"They don't bite, do they?"

Sarah laughed. "No! But they might try to lick you to death. Back up, all of you! If you ignore them they will eventually give up. But for now, they think you came just to visit them."

I waded through the pack onto Sarah's front porch. Her house was charming – simple wood floors, a surprising mix of traditional and contemporary art, lots of family photos. She grabbed some keys and we headed back into the yard to see the guest cottage. A sign by the front door said WELCOME TO SOJOUNER HOUSE. It was adorable! Two small bedrooms, a fresh gray and white palette, a cozy sitting area in front of a wood burning fireplace. An old fashioned cherry red range anchored the kitchen, giving it a retro, but farmhousy, feel. Rugs were scattered over the wood floors. My LA decorator could learn a few things here. Her design for my upscale condo wasn't half as interesting or comfortable as this little corner at Honor Ranch. One more person I could release from the payroll.

"Sarah, I love it. Are you sure Ben's parents are OK with me staying here? What if they have guests in the next few months?"

"Oh, they have plenty of room. This was the first house Boone and Kit built on the property. They lived here with the boys while the main house was under construction. Then Ben and I lived here when we were first married; we updated it while OUR house being built. Beau lives in the other cottage, and his is NOT updated. Through the years the Laurels have had all kinds of people stay here – missionaries on leave, ranch interns, an interim pastor from church. No maid service! But good water pressure and great neighbors. They were thrilled to hear someone could use it, especially someone who is serving the Joy Chorus."

"Serving is a stretch, Sarah. Do they know that what I am serving is court ordered?"

"Boone and Kit don't scare easily. In fact, YOU might need a warning! They are big personalities. Most family business is openly debated at the dinner table, guests or no guests. Don't mention anything you don't want discussed over pie!"

"Is that awkward since you live so close?"

"I've learned to manage it. The good news about Kit and Boone? You never have to guess where they stand on anything, and they can take it as well as they give it. When Ben and I got married he made it clear to them we needed our own life. Close proximity could not mean meddling! If they wanted to see us, they should call first. We lived in this cottage to test it before we built our house, and they've been great. Then Boone had a battle with cancer; it helped that we were settled on the ranch."

"Is that why Beau came back from Nashville? To help his dad?"

"Now that is a complicated answer! Yes, in part. Beau loves managing the ranch, and his dad couldn't keep up during treatment without help. But Nashville wasn't Beau's dream come true. He was ready to be back home."

I thought Nashville was every country musician's Mecca. All the big names lived there – hey, they even made a TV show about it. Why wouldn't a successful songwriter want to be in the thick of it? Most people run to, not from, opportunity.

"Must have been a girl?"

Sarah got busy turning off the lights.

"Sarah, come on. There are only two reasons a musician on the rise would leave Nashville - he was on the lam, or heartbroken. Besides, I'll probably hear all about it from Kit if I'm invited to dinner since no subject is off limits."

Sarah conceded. "Good point! Have you ever heard of Misty Hart?"

"Of course. She's a pop/country crossover singer, right? She's the girl?"

Sarah nodded. "She's the girl. Misty played at The Watering Hole, and Beau was instantly smitten. She convinced him to move to Nashville to work on an album together. He wrote most of the songs and played guitar on a few of the tracks. When he wasn't writing, he was playing any gig he could get. Then late one night he dropped by the studio with coffee. Misty was making final adjustments to the album before its release. He discovered why the record was taking so long to complete – Misty and the producer were busier working on each other than the album."

"That's awful! And so cliché! I should hook her up with Grant Adams; they are made for each other."

Sarah's tone was sad. "It got messy. Beau was naïve to the business side of the industry. He didn't have an agent, or a contract. He trusted her. Misty didn't share any songwriting credit on her album, never shared the proceeds with Beau, and threatened to counter sue him if he challenged her. He was outgunned. She had the label's attorneys backing her, and he had nothing in writing. Kit and Boone were prepared for a showdown – they never liked Misty - but Beau refused. He packed his bags and came back to Pleasant to work the ranch with one condition: his parents not discuss Misty, and they all move on. Beau can be stubborn and they knew he meant it. Beau still writes, and he has connections that get his music to the right people, but he doesn't have the stomach for the cut throat game in Nashville."

Poor Beau. Used! I knew exactly how it felt to be dumped and humiliated. Pleasant wasn't a bad place to lick your wounds, but Beau shouldn't let Misty Hart have the last word on his music career. I wasn't going to let one terminated contract derail my modeling future. Lots of people make comebacks. Geez, look at Cher. Or Tony Bennett. He hooked up with Lady Gaga to completely jump start his career, and he's old! We were young, with plenty of time to regroup and take another stab at it.

"Anna, please don't bring this up to Beau. It will just make him mad. Nothing makes Beau angry more than pity. But at least you know the short story; you will be neighbors, after all. When would you like to move in?"

"Is tomorrow too soon?"

# CHAPTER 8

I loved my new tiny house! Kit and Boone brought me a welcome plate of cookies soon after I arrived on Saturday afternoon. Sarah wasn't kidding. One of them could fill a room; together they were a lot to take in. Kit knocked once before throwing the front door open.

"YOO HOO! I hear there's a skinny model around here who needs some good Texas cooking. Anyone home?"

Kit found me unpacking my bag in the closet.

"Hello! You must be Anna? I'm Kit and this is Boone. Welcome to Honor Ranch. Cookie?"

I am tall – 6 feet without shoes – but I felt dwarfed by Kit. Her booming voice, oversized turquoise jewelry, and confident stride made her one imposing woman. This was magnified by all of us being crammed in my small walk in closet. Boone was 6'5" if he was an inch, quieter, but equally intense. His handshake could crush a coconut. I waited for them to back out into the bedroom. They were waiting for me to take a cookie. I was going to lose this standoff.

"Cookie? I'd love one!"

Once I was nibbling on a delicious treat, we moved the party to the kitchen. Kit and Boone each pulled up a barstool. Kit smiled, taking me all in. I was very disheveled. I hadn't expected visitors, and unpacking was best accomplished in sweat pants and a messy ponytail.

"Sarah tells us you are here for a few months. Glad you can keep the dust bunnies cleared out; we hate to see Sojourner House sit empty. It's happier when occupied."

I felt a slight advantage standing up, so refused the offer of the remaining barstool.

"I offered to rent it, but Sarah insisted I stay as a guest. Thank you. I confess, my hotel made me sad."

Kit handed me a second cookie. "Sad? We can't have that. And you aren't a guest – just part of the family. That's how it works here. We serve dinner most nights in the main house, and you come any time you like. If we are out, Millie will find something for you to eat. She's our housekeeper. But no ceremony; don't wait for an invitation. The door is always open. You might run into Sarah and Ben, or Beau, but we are just as happy to have you by yourself."

Boone spoke up at last. "Let's leave the girl to settle in, Kit. Don't want to overstay our welcome."

Sarah had trained them well, at least in the leaving part. I made a mental note to lock the door when I was home. Not sure that would stop them, but at least I'd get a moment's warning. But Sarah was right – they had good hearts. I could tolerate a little nosiness if the payoff was living in Sojourner House.

Two rockers graced my front porch, so I grabbed another cookie and surveyed the landscape. My only experience on a farm was a second grade field trip to Miss Warner's family homestead. She showed us how to milk a cow. I remember being confused. My beautiful teacher, who wore pink high heels, was the same person in work boots with her hands on a teat? It was my first lesson in understanding that people had lives outside their connection to me. I experienced a similar feeling when Ginger met Frank; she was more than just my mother, she was a woman with hopes all her own. In both cases, a flash of intense envy and fear surged through me. I was not the center of the universe after all.

Beau came around the corner in a muddy truck, parking outside his cottage. I waved and he headed my way.

"I heard we had a guest. It's not Hollywood, but where in LA can you find Texas longhorns grazing outside your front door?"

"True. Not even Neverland Ranch had longhorns. Can I offer you a cookie? There is a plateful in the kitchen that threatens my girlish figure."

"Ah, so you've met my parents. My mother believes all friendships begin with chocolate. She and Mo are soul mates. Yes to the cookie and a glass of milk. I'll get it."

"Sorry, no milk. I just moved in."

"Oh, there is milk. Have you opened your fridge?"

The refrigerator was stocked with milk, fruit, and yogurt. The pantry bulged with all manner of snacks. Beau grinned. "Southern hospitality. Kit would have to answer to Sugar if she didn't roll out the red carpet for guests. You'll find lavender soap and bath salts in the linen closet, fresh scones on your doorstep tomorrow. After that, just ask Millie for anything you need."

"Who is Sugar?"

"My grandmother. Kit was raised on a big ranch in West Texas. Sugar loves a crowd and kept the house full with parties, BBQs and relatives. Spoiling the guests at David Ranch kept them coming back, and that meant Sugar was never lonely. I spent summers there as a kid. Most of my education in ranch management came from my grandparents, not school."

"Is David your Grandfather?"

"No, David is the shepherd boy who defeated Goliath with a slingshot in the Bible. My Pop came from nothing. His family were dirt poor share croppers. He and Sugar scraped together some money for a farm in the middle of nowhere and grazed a few head of cattle on it. A little oil discovery helped them buy more land; lots of land. Thousands of acres. Pop always said that first oil well was the slingshot the Lord gave him to beat poverty. He named the ranch David to remind him where his help came from. Pop is the most humble man I've ever known."

"That sounds like a plot for a movie, Beau. Poor guy strikes it rich, has a great family, doesn't let the money corrupt him...never mind, nobody would believe that story! People love to hate a villain, and every family has a rebel. Is that why your mom ended up in Houston? Oh sorry, that wasn't very polite! It's none of my business. I didn't mean to suggest your family story has a villain – just referring to what sells in a movie."

Beau raised his eyebrows and waited. Yes, I wanted to hear the rest! You don't throw out a teaser like "struck it rich" and not finish the tale. Rags to riches, obscurity to fame, those were my favorite stories. Beau continued.

"My parents met at Texas Tech University. My dad was a chemical engineer, never the ranching type. When they got married his job brought them to Houston, and frankly I think Pop and Sugar were a lot to take in for a young guy who didn't know how to work cattle. But city life was not for my mother. She bought this land and built Sojourner House so we could stay here on the weekends. I was roping fence posts and goats as a 5 year old."

"Your dad was a good sport to trade in the city for a long commute to work from out here."

Beau grimaced. "That's one way of looking at it. My parents hit a rough patch; let's just say my dad began to wander in a season of family stress. My mother gave him a choice – relocate to the ranch with her, or stay in the city without her. He was a man of honor when she married him, and she expected him to stay that way. My mom sees things in black and white – not a lot of gray – so we all moved out here. She named it Honor Ranch as HIS reminder to keep his promise. Again, subtle is not her mother tongue. Sorry, that was probably too much information. I don't usually discuss family skeletons with newcomers."

"We all have family skeletons. Some people just dress them up better than others. Most of mine wear tutus and bowties. Your dad must have guts. I've only met your mother once, but I wouldn't want to test her!"

"She's mellowed through the years, believe it or not. But my dad knew she meant business. Eventually he jumped off the corporate hamster wheel and joined her in the ranching enterprise."

"What happened to David ranch?"

"My uncle Billy manages it. Sugar and Pop are still out there. They started a program called Bootstrap for troubled kids. High school boys live on the ranch, work on their GED, and learn ranching skills. After a year or so they are ready to get a job. It's part school, part hands on training. A lot of the benefit just comes from structure and hard work. My grandparents are in their 80s and spend most of their time now working with the Bootstrap staff. I come from hardy stock."

"I guess! Don't you people ever relax?"

Beau pondered that one. "Relax? I'm relaxing now."

"No, I mean take time off, enjoy the fruits of your labor, retire! You've heard of it?"

"Retire is another word for dead in my family."

"Retire is another word for FINALLY if you ask me! You work hard your whole life, you deserve some fun! I hope to make a lot of money so my mom and Frank can kick back, play golf, and go on a long cruise."

"I thought you already made a lot of money. Sent them on any cruises lately?"

"I offered, but they only want to go with me and I've been too busy."

"Maybe they want to see you more than they want the cruise."

This man could be exasperating. "Not all of us have the luxury of living next door to our parents."

Beau shrugged. "Most of us live where we choose."

He did not understand the modeling business, and I was not interested in educating him. Better to steer him back to familiar waters. "When do you see your grandparents now?"

"I fly out about once a month for the weekend. Time is short, and a visit means a lot to them."

It had been more than a year since I was back in Chicago. Ginger and Frank came to LA a few months ago, but at the last minute I was invited to an important premier; many industry movers and shakers were also invited, so I couldn't miss it. My parents spent much of the weekend exploring on their own. Maybe they would come visit in Texas since I was handcuffed to Pleasant. Being an only child was a lot of pressure.

"Once my community service obligation is over I should take my parents on a trip. Europe maybe."

"Do they want to go to Europe?"

"Doesn't everybody want to go to Europe?"

"I don't think the destination is as important as the time you spend together."

"OK Beau, does your family vacation together?"

"Again, vacation isn't part of my family's vocabulary. But we did take a trip to Israel a few years ago with our church. Very cool to walk in Jesus' footsteps, very little down time. Perfect Laurel family "vacation" – we took in all the sights and had one afternoon to float in the Dead Sea. Good busy/relaxation ratio for the likes of us."

I would NOT be asking the Laurels for travel advice. The best part of a vacation for me was lounging while a pool boy served drinks. "I don't like swimming in the ocean. It freaks me out. I'm afraid something will bite me. But the Dead Sea is dead, right? No fish?"

"No fish. You know why?"

"Hmmm. Too many bath salts?"

"Pretty much. It's so salty you can easily float with no inner tube. You just lay back – it's weird. And no danger of a shark bite; nothing can live in the Dead Sea because it has no outlet. All the water that flows into it stays there. The minerals have no place to go so they collect at the bottom. After about 30 minutes your skin starts to burn from the salt. Our guide reminded us that people aren't much different; if all you do is take, and nothing ever flows out, nothing good can live there."

Good visual. Did he think all I did was take? He didn't even know me! I gave him the benefit of the doubt; maybe he was just reminiscing. I played along.

"So the moral is, don't be a Dead Sea?"

"You said it, not me. I'm headed to the big house for dinner; you are welcome anytime. It's a perk of living in Sojourner House."

"What's your cottage called?"

"My mother calls it the Stag Shack. She hopes I'll move on to a wife someday. I just call it home."

And with that he wandered off. It felt awkward to show up for dinner when they stocked my house with food. I didn't want to give the impression I was a freeloader, so I boiled some pasta and made spaghetti with the home canned red sauce nestled in the pantry. Dang, it was good.

***

The following Wednesday I showed up at The Watering Hole with Grace Jackson's email in hand. Belle Bridal needed an answer about the ad so we could schedule a fitting. Duke was in his office, thankfully alone. Waging war with Tish wasn't going to make my time here any easier, but I wasn't ready to fall on my sword for her.

"Hey Duke. I didn't mean to step on anyone's toes last week about the clothes and the ad. I was just excited about the opportunity for the kids. Here is the contract with Belle Bridal; you do what you want with it."

"Anna, no need to apologize. We didn't have a sponsor for the kids' clothes and you found us one. That's a win. I'll have our attorney review the contract, and if she gives it a thumb's up you can run with it. I think it's a great idea."

"Really? Thank you! Is Tish OK with this?"

"Tish is fine. This is a family operation, and like most family businesses the dynamics can be tricky to navigate. We worked it out. But it wouldn't hurt to lay low for a while." Duke gave me a wink.

"Gotcha. I will go to work with my head down and my mouth shut."

"Now THAT I'd like to see. Cancel the headliners! Anna is going to fall in line silently!"

"Funny, Duke. I can be a roadie. Just watch."

"I don't think roadie is your calling; you'll land center stage one way or another. Just give Tish a little room in the spotlight. The Chorus is her connection with her mom and she's worked hard to make it a success. She is fiercely protective of it."

"I get it. But she seems happier performing than managing the barn. Her talent is remarkable. She lights up like a Christmas tree on stage! The Chorus is in good hands with you and Mo; why doesn't she go on tour with Bubba? At least give it a try? I'd jump at the chance if I was her."

"Sometimes it's easier to see the obvious from the outside. Tish will figure it out."

"Maybe she needs a push."

"Maybe. Tish is stubborn. She has to think she jumped, not got pushed."

"So get her some qualified help at the barn. Make it easier for her to walk away. There must be a music teacher who would help with practice and administration for a little extra income. Tell Tish you are doing this new person a favor by giving them a job. Hey, tell her whatever will work! I'm here for a few months and can fill in some gaps. Once the Christmas concert is over the Chorus can reboot, and Tish could go on the road."

"Food for thought. Thanks, Anna. But let's keep this between us?"

"Absolutely. Head down, mouth shut, at least about this. Trust me!"

Men can be so thick. Women are skilled at getting what they want by coming in through the window. Men always want to bust the door down. Tish just needed someone to make it easy for her to say YES to Bubba, but not TELL her to say yes to Bubba. And Bubba should start looking for a different opening act. I saw how jealous she got when we danced. Nothing makes a girl want something more than the possibility of losing it. Just watch two women reach for the same hanger in a store! That garment is suddenly the only thing each of them wants. Smart retailers carry limited stock; scarcity produces demand like nothing else.

I have in my closet – well, now in storage – a very expensive purple leather swing jacket. Sounds cool, but it's not. The sleeves are too long, the jacket is too short, and the leather is so soft any scratch puts a hole in it. But a beautiful blond woman saw me take it to the dressing room and asked me to pass it along if I didn't buy it because it was the last one. So what if it didn't fit, so what if I don't like purple, so what if it cost a fortune, I had to have it because she wanted it. The salesgirl probably paid her to ask for it. Hey, the beautiful blonde might have worked there too. I have never worn that jacket. And now I'm paying to store it, along with a bunch of other things I'll probably never need. Ah, the seductive power of almost losing something.

*** 

Lacey Morrison was tickled pink (her words) that Belle Bridal would be outfitting the Joy Chorus kids. As manager of the local store she hoped to receive kudos from corporate by making this ad look good. After practice on Saturday she descended on the barn with racks of sample outfits, 4 additional fitters, and pop up dressing cubicles. A portfolio of photos helped us decide which styles to choose.

The kids thought I was joking when I told them about their *Celebrity* magazine debut. Lacey's arrival, with her scores of beautiful dresses, put the girls into a tizzy of chatter. Good thing Lacey was practiced in managing large groups of tipsy bridesmaids.

"Kids, listen up!" She had a surprisingly loud voice for a petite brunette in high heels. "Boys will try on pants and jackets outside in the parking lot! We have pop up dressing rooms, and it won't take long for the guys to be sized. Girls will stay here in the main area! You can look at all the samples, but please follow directions for your fitting!"

We kicked the boys out and went to work with the girls. Lacey got their attention by holding up a gorgeous ensemble.

"Let's think long term. These costumes should be versatile and last for a few seasons of concerts. You also have a wide variety of sizes in the group. If we start with a soft black skirt, we can switch up the tops in different seasons. For the Christmas concert, and the ad, this pleated black skirt paired with an embellished top would be fabulous. This one is flattering to all body types."

The gold matte sequined top had cap sleeves, and the fabric was stretchy for easy fit. It caught the light without being too flashy.

"In summer, you girls could wear this breezy sleeveless blouse with the skirt. Add a funky necklace and you have a whole new outfit! Who wants to model?"

Lacey selected 3 girls of different sizes to model a variety of tops with the skirt. She was a genius. Her original choices won hands down and each girl was measured.

"It will take about 4 weeks to get everything in; I'll put a rush on the order. In the meantime, Grace from corporate will contact you with details about the photo shoot. And one more thing! Don't let the kids take their outfits home. Keep them stored in their garment bags and hand them out at the last possible moment before a concert. Trust me! I've gotten countless emergency phone calls from panicked brides whose maids tore, stained, or lost their dresses. Best to keep them under wraps. This was so much fun! I loved seeing the girls light up when they put those clothes on. You are doing a great thing here, Anna. Thank you for including us. I hope you will consider Belle Bridal on your big day!"

She was thanking me? I should be thanking Rachel for setting this up. I texted her a photo of the girls modeling our new concert ensemble. Hopefully Lacey would be present for the photo shoot – I liked her. She was genuinely nice, thankful to be working in the field she loved, and happy to make some high school kids smile. Hanging out with the Joy Chorus seemed to bring out the best in people.

The girls were already chattering about how to do hair and make-up for the photo shoot. One spin in a pretty dress and they were primed for publicity. Amazing what the right outfit can do for a girl's confidence.

The boys were no different. The following week Duke had to break up a tie debate – plain black or patterned?- in order to get practice underway.

# CHAPTER 9

Several weeks into my stay at Sojourner House I ventured to the Main House for dinner. It was time to offer my help at the Ranch. OK, OK, I was hungry. My cooking expertise rivaled my ability to keep my mouth shut, meaning both skill sets were deficient. I had plowed through the pantry goods, and on the nights Jay took off I was stuck with drive through. My jeans were protesting. Fritz, my trainer, had checked in. Was I being diligent with my cardio? I was too embarrassed to answer. I had rediscovered my love of sleeping, but didn't think Fritz would consider that acceptable cross training. Beyond time spent at The Watering Hole I wasn't sure how the days passed so quickly, but pass they did. I learned all about country music (thank you, internet), and even practiced housekeeping by cleaning my little cottage. But cooking mystified me. I caved and hit the path towards the house.

I knocked on the side door. Nobody answered, so I let myself in. Music spilled out of the living room and I could hear Ben and Sarah laughing. Sounded like a full house. Millie caught me peeking into the kitchen. "Come in, Anna! I was beginning to think you didn't like Southern cooking! What took you so long to join us for dinner?"

"Millie, nothing would make me happier than enjoying your Southern cooking! I didn't want to over step my welcome. But you've got me now and I'm hungry. What's on the menu?'

Millie beamed. If I were to cast a loving grandma in a movie, I'd pick Mille. She was pleasantly plump and her hands were strong. The fragrance of cinnamon and basil lingered in her wake as she hurried to prepare a sample plate of the night's fare for me – pulled pork, roasted potatoes and fresh green beans. Simple. Delicious. I was ravenous.

"Off you go into the living room. We will sit down in ten minutes. Your place is already set; we've been hoping you would show up."

The whole family erupted into shouts and applause when I appeared. I took a bow, which is the appropriate response to a standing ovation. They meant it when they extended an invitation to dinner.

Ben greeted me with a hug. "Anna, your timing is perfect! We had a little wager going about how long it would take for you to show up, and I think I just won the pool. Pay up, people. You too Rocky. I believe you said Anna would be too busy accepting dinner dates to find her way to our table? Looks like you were wrong."

Rocky worked with Beau managing the ranch. I had met him in passing on a few occasions. He was a man of few words, and he blushed at Ben's revelation as he passed him a $10 bill. Dinner dates – funny! My only dinner companion had been Jay. He plopped down in my booth one night, wanting my opinion of his latest menu addition; chicken fried steak salad. I told him to stick to fried, or salad, and keep the two apart. He rewarded me by leaving the seasoning, and dressing, off my grilled chicken Caesar. Feedback isn't always appreciated.

You learn a lot about families when you share their table. Dinner with my parents was always relaxed. Frank did the cooking, my mom sparked conversation with some interesting story, and friends were always welcome. Kate, my high school bestie, usually joined us. It took one dinner at her house to understood why. Her father was crabby, her brother was rude, and her mom ran around trying to make her dad and her brother happy – an impossible task. Talkative Kate was uncharacteristically sullen. I remained uncharacteristically tongue tied. We escaped before dessert. Kate and I never discussed that evening, but she never invited me to her house for dinner again. Kate turned down a scholarship at

Northwestern University to attend some obscure college in the Pacific Northwest, far, far from home.

Dinner with the Laurels was festive. Millie and Rocky took their places at the table, and after a prayer we all dug into Millie's feast. Boone whipped out a newspaper and Sarah leaned over to whisper "the quiz!".

Kit explained. "Boone harbors a secret fantasy of being a game show host. The best we can do is let him be quizmaster at the dinner table – a pathetic substitute for game show fame, but don't tell him that. We take our Isaac Asimov super quiz very seriously around here. Just shout the answer if you know it."

Boone announced the quiz category: American History. He started with a practice question. "Who was first in war, first in peace, first in the hearts of his countrymen?" Everyone at the table yelled GEORGE WASHINGTON. Well, everyone but me. Boone was patient. "See how the quiz works? Just jump right in. Now we advance to the Freshman level, indicated by the ONE POINT QUESTION (in unison!)." Clearly this was a regular tradition; even Rocky and Millie joined in the fun. The quiz got a lot harder after the practice question, but one of the answers HAD to be Abraham Lincoln. I waited until my best guess was Honest Abe, and sure enough, I got one right. Everyone else got it right too, but they gave me the credit. I went to a decent high school, I passed American History with flying colors, but my understanding of the Federalist Papers was obviously insufficient. Boone threw me a bone; the second quiz subject was Pop Culture. Ah, my milieu. I was the only one who knew that Nadya Suleman (aka Octo mom) had octuplets, and I narrowly won the Pop Culture quiz (Millie almost beat me with her knowledge of *People* magazine's list of World's Sexiest Men!). It's not rocket science, I get it, but a win is a win and I'll take it. Boone rewarded me a high five, and suddenly I felt part of the gang.

Dinner and the Quiz were followed by homemade cherry pie. Again, my jeans protested. If I ever intended to work again, I needed to lay off the comfort food. But it was so nice not worrying about every bite I ate! And just try saying no to Kit. What's a few pounds anyway? I could knock that off in a heartbeat if the right job came along. Millie began clearing the table and Sarah and Ben jumped in to help. I bussed my dishes to the kitchen before saying good night.

"Thank you for a great dinner and memorable evening. I must go back to Sojourner House and begin studying trivia immediately. Boone, any idea where I should start? Give me a lead on which quiz will come next time?"

Boone laughed. "Maybe consider a review of quantum physics and world economic policies? Or better yet, stick to what you know. You saved us on Pop Culture and were a delightful dinner companion; that trumps a history nerd any day. Don't be a stranger! The door is always open."

After a round of hugs, Beau followed me out the door. "Well, you survived dinner with the Laurels unscathed. That's quite an accomplishment. Not everybody embraces the Quiz with enthusiasm, and debby downers aren't invited back. Well done. See you around."

I had always enjoyed being an only child, the center of all attention. Dinner with the Laurels made me long for siblings.

***

Millie insisted I join the Laurel clan for dinner when I wasn't at The Watering Hole, and I took her up on that invitation once or twice a week. When it was just the two of us we ate at the kitchen counter while she entertained me with stories about Ben and Beau as kids. Ben played football and was Homecoming King. Beau tinkered with his guitar up in the tree house, or spent countless hours roping fence posts and the family dog. Paul was the prankster, the one who played video games instead of roaming the ranch.

"Paul? Who is Paul?"

Millie glanced at a photo of three boys perched on the kitchen desk. "Paul is the middle Laurel boy. He's a computer whiz who loves to tease. While the other two were out wrangling cattle, Paul would sit there at the counter while I baked, stealing cookies out of the oven. I never could say no to that boy. My own son, Eduardo, is the caboose in the group. He trailed those boys like a loyal soldier! Eduardo is away at college studying agriculture and hopes to manage his own ranch one day." A handsome guy in a cowboy hat smiled at me from another photo. Millie was obviously proud of all four. Funny I'd never heard anyone mention Paul before, but the subject seemed to be closed.

Dinner with the Laurels was loud and raucous. They argued good naturedly over who was the best new voice in Nashville, or debated the latest ranching methods. A few months ago my dinner conversations began and ended with Hollywood gossip; now I could extol the benefits of rotational grazing. I was rewarded with applause when I praised Honor Ranch for refusing to use chemicals, fertilizer, or drugs in raising their livestock. Boone and Ben both tried to take the credit, but Kit chimed in with the truth – Beau had been the first to insist on sustainable ranch practices. Beau insisted it was a team effort, and peace was restored with Millie's peach cobbler. She didn't allow fighting over peach cobbler.

The only cracks in the happy Laurel family façade seemed to be around Beau's refusal to discuss – well, anything. Ben hounded him to connect with Nashville artists, Kit lamented over Beau's lack of dates, and Beau ignored them all. Then there was the mystery of Paul. Was he dead? Missing? A gamer in Las Vegas? Curiosity almost got the best of me, but it seemed rude to ask. Hey, what happened to your son and why have I never heard a word about him? Curiosity made me antsy, but nobody took my bait. I first tried a comment about missing out as an only child. Ben's reply? "Siblings can be overrated." I asked Kit if she expected a big crowd for Thanksgiving. "I hope so – join us, Anna!" Now she thought I was fishing for an invitation. This was getting me nowhere. Maybe Sarah would fill me in. I jumped up after coffee. "Millie, you are off duty. I'll do the dishes tonight. You don't want me cooking, but I can load a dishwasher with the best of them." Millie conceded, and as I hoped, Sarah offered to help. We headed to the kitchen laden with plates. Subtle had failed at dinner, so I got right to the point over pots and pans.

"Hey Sarah, Millie told me Ben and Beau have a brother? She wasn't speaking out of turn. I saw the photo of the three of them and asked. Sorry, it's none of my business, but Beau has never mentioned him."

Sarah continued drying. "Yes. Paul. Paul is a sore subject. He is super smart, equally handsome, and kind of a computer geek. Whereas Ben and Beau love the ranching business, Paul is talented with technology. He's had a hard time finding his footing. Expectations in the Laurel gang aren't exactly low."

Neither Sarah or I heard Ben behind us with the last load of dessert plates.

"You failed to mention he is a selfish jack ass, a free loader, and an alcoholic. Sarah always gives everyone the benefit of the doubt, Anna, but Paul has blown through his 9 lives around here." And with that, Ben slammed the door and headed across the yard.

Yikes. Touchy subject indeed. Sarah continued drying.

"I think I'll let him cool off before I go home! Paul brings out the worst in Ben. Paul likes to play the victim, and Ben can't stand that. Paul never went to college, which was fine with their parents if he was working. But Paul started drinking heavily in high school and never quit partying. Kit and Boone offered to invest in a start-up so he could build a computer services business - with one condition. Paul had check in to rehab. He went, but didn't buy into the argument he needed help. After treatment, he lost the seed money gambling and wouldn't commit to being sober. You can imagine the hard feelings all around after that."

Sarah paused for a moment. This was obviously a painful subject for their family, and none of my business, but I was intrigued with how the Laurels navigated such a difficult situation. I couldn't manage a simple break-up from a loser without getting myself arrested. Sadness filled Sarah's voice.

"Ben and Kit play by the rules without a lot of patience for poor judgement. Paul majors in poor judgement. His record has multiple DUIs and tickets for possession. The final straw snapped when Boone was diagnosed with colon cancer. Paul has a mean streak. Instead of offering his dad support, he showed up here drunk right after Boone started chemo and accused him of all kinds of things. Blamed him for favoring the other boys, told him he hated him. Ben threw him out and we haven't seen much of him since. I think he works fixing computers, but I have no idea where he lives."

Skeletons indeed. Sad ones. You'd never know it to sit at the Laurel table playing the Quiz.

"What does Boone say about it? And Beau?"

Sarah sighed. "Boone is a softy. Paul broke his heart, but I think he feels sorry for him. They have tried to help him time and time again, and it always backfires. Paul's issues have put a lot of stress on their marriage and Kit won't tolerate it. She is more practical – Kit understands that Paul must want to get better before treatment will be effective, so she's cut him loose for the moment. Beau gives Paul a wide berth, but he isn't angry like Ben is. Paul really gets under his skin, as you just witnessed."

Beau joined us in the kitchen. "Where's Ben? He picked up a new account today and dad wants to break open the Macallan to celebrate."

Sarah pointed out the window towards her house. "He's home for the night. I'd leave it alone if I were you."

Beau looked first at Sarah, then at me. "OK. I'll take your word for it. Macallan, ladies?"

I felt terrible. I stuck my big nose in their family business and ruined a celebration. Siblings certainly make a family more complicated. I never had to compete for any attention from Frank or Ginger; they hung on my every word, even when I ignored theirs. I couldn't imagine spewing hate at them, and believe me, I had logged my share of hissy fits over curfews and dress codes (Ginger did not tolerate hoochiness. If I wore a short skirt, she insisted my top be modest. Tank top? Pants! My poor mother must have cringed when the tabloids came out with that photo of me in a strapless mini romper, stripper shoes making me 6'5". I should send her a photo of me in my jeans and loose blouse as an apology). Sarah declined the whiskey invitation, and I followed her lead. Beau shrugged and wished us a good night.

I ended the evening in my favorite porch rocker, pondering the Laurel family drama. It was like a car wreck you couldn't stop rubber necking – everything seemed so all American happy until Ben exploded in the kitchen. Why didn't Beau tell me about Paul? In our evenings on the porch I thought we were becoming good friends. I filled him in about my absentee father, shared how angry I was when Fame Cosmetics dumped me. For the first time since high school, I confided in a guy. Beau was my new Dwayne Chapin; an actual friend, with no dating potential muddying the water.

Dwayne was a math geek who tutored me in 10th grade algebra. In addition to being saddled with a nerdy name, Dwayne wore glasses, spoke with precise grammar, and was as muscular as a wet chicken. Add a weird hat and Dwayne could play the hero in a John Hughes' film (surely you have seen *Pretty in Pink.* If not, you must now go binge on all the Hughes classics such as *Breakfast Club* and *Ferris Bueller's Day Off.*) When I first met Dwayne, I was taller than any boy in our class. My size 10 feet earned me the nickname "Skies", short for water skies....I spent a lot of time in math class pining for Allison Draper's petite size six shoe. That might be why I was failing algebra. The future Anastasia DeMars was buried deep within an awkward Anna Martin.

Dwayne got extra credit for tutoring me in the library every Tuesday and Thursday after school. Looking back, I think my math teacher Mrs. Richards was encouraging us to combine forces against the warfare that defines high school (clearly Dwayne did not need extra credit.) It worked. We liked the same movies, hated the same posers, and spent many afternoons baking chocolate chip cookies in my kitchen. Dwayne's devotion to my math grade paid off in ways he couldn't have originally imagined. By my junior year, I had come out of the dork cocoon and Dwayne prospered in my wake. It was hip to be square when he sat with the pretty "new" girl at lunch (once I ditched the glasses and stood up straight, nobody recognized me. Anastasia DeMars was almost here). I needed Dwayne - he helped me pass all my math and science classes – and he needed me. By our senior year we drifted. He was elected President of the Robotics team, and let's face it, I had become a poser. But at graduation he hugged me and said thanks for being his friend. Dwayne was never anything but nice to me. I hope I was as nice back.

Dwayne got the last laugh in the end. After graduating from MIT, he developed an app that made a boat load of money. My mom sent me a copy of the *Chicago Tribune* story featuring his company. The photo, with a caption that read NERDS RULE, pictured him with his beautiful fiancé who was at least 6 inches taller than Dwayne. I'd like to think I had a hand in that. Sure, being a millionaire at age 23 might have boosted his confidence, but he practiced hanging out with an amazon in high school.

Hanging out with Beau, like Dwayne, was easy. By some unspoken agreement we never broached the subject of our exes. Kit was the only one who ever mentioned Misty, usually in the context of Beau "dodging a bullet with that one. Or a grenade. Or a nuke..." I don't think she liked her. Grant Adams was a closed chapter in my book. Our evenings on the porch lacked any romantic tension, so we were free to laugh at the staff's attempts to make love connections at the barn. At first I was slightly offended that Beau didn't seem interested. Guys were always interested, at least up front. True, I was a bit off my game. My flirting instincts seemed to flee once we settled into our rockers. But I was a little miffed. Then I realized he probably sought a low key cowgirl, not a sarcastic model who craved center stage.

Did that make me a diva? In Pleasant, maybe. By Hollywood standards I was practically an introvert. I had never posted nude selfies or released a sex tape. But norms were different here. Not that it mattered, because Beau wasn't my type. Too quiet. I couldn't figure out if he was heartbroken, or just naturally serious. I had no aptitude in reading someone who kept things close to the vest; that required a lot of quiet observation. No, information about Paul wasn't going to come from Beau. I would have to be patient. Since that's not my strong suit I opted for distraction and loaded up Netflix for the night. Show me a shiny object and sometimes I can quit obsessing.

***

One night after dinner at the main house, Beau followed me home. "My parents like you."

"I'm sure your parents like most everybody. They are very friendly. And Millie is an amazing cook. If I'm not careful I'll blow up like a bouncy house. How do you stay so slim?"

"I work. Managing the ranch keeps me in shape. And what do you have against bouncy houses? They can be fun."

"Fun, yes. Employable? Not so much. Eventually I need to get back to fighting weight so I can land some work when my community service is over."

Beau walked beside me silently until we reached my cottage. The night was clear and I offered him a seat on the porch.

"So, Anna, you're headed back to LA once your Joy Chorus assignment is done?"

The frogs were singing, serenading us as we rocked in tandem. "I'm not sure. I subleased my apartment, and I don't have friends there who would take me in. LA is a weird place – 4 months out of the spotlight and you are practically erased. But by spring my falling out with Fame Cosmetics will be old news; I should be able to get some work. Or I can always go back to Chicago while my agent gets things lined up. My mom would like that."

Beau shuddered. "Nashville was like that – everyone clawing their way up the ladder, desperate to get noticed. The only way to get ahead was to step on someone else. I'm not cut out for it."

"Do you ever miss the excitement?"

"No. Watching my back was stressful. I get excited about cows delivering healthy calves, or singing new material at The Watering Hole. I have family and friends here who would take a bullet for me, and vice versa. In Nashville I felt alone, always dodging bullets. No thanks."

"But Beau, isn't it frustrating to write a song and have it go nowhere? You are very talented. What if the only people who hear your music are the crowd at The Watering Hole?"

"Why is that nowhere? If the crowd at The Watering Hole appreciates a song, and I enjoy performing it, mission accomplished. Record sales are not my goal. The music business is just that, a business, and it is cut throat. Writing music is like breathing for me; it just happens. I'm not willing to do what it takes to be on the charts. Why should I? I make a good living doing what I love, managing this ranch. I have time to pursue my music, I'm with my family, life is peaceful. I already have what people spend their whole lives looking for. I am not trading that in for money or fame. The price is too high."

"C'mon Beau, it had to be pretty exciting when "Chasing Home" hit it big!"

Beau grinned. "True. People identified with the story in that song, and I made some money from it too. But I don't want one song to define me. I've written much better music since then, but guess what everyone wants to hear? I'd be just fine to never play it again."

"OK, well you're lucky; you can afford to dabble in your passion because you have a fall back with this ranch. If I don't work, I have no income."

Beau shook his head. "Why does work have to be modeling? You said yourself you only do it for the money. And you need the money to support the lifestyle – the trainer, the agent, the lawyers. Ditch the lifestyle and you can work doing all kinds of things. I've seen you sell concert tickets like they were sno cones on a hot day. No lawyers required, and you get to enjoy the cherry pie."

I did enjoy that cherry pie. But Beau didn't understand!

"I dropped out of college to model. I don't know how to do anything else, and I don't have a degree. Last time I checked, my commission on all those sno cone sales was a big fat zero! My options are limited."

Beau scoffed. "No they aren't. You have lots of skills. Figure out what you want to do and do it. Don't cave to easy just because the pay is good. What do you want your LIFE to look like? Start there. A job should fit into that, not the other way around."

"Is that what you learned in Nashville?"

"No, I knew all that before I went to Nashville. But I let a distraction drag me down a rabbit hole, chasing things I didn't want. Nashville taught me to go back to what makes me happy. I'm happy here."

I had been successful in LA, if making and spending a lot of money qualified as success. But I had not been happy. LA was a lonely place. The constant spin of events kept me busy, but not happy. And Grant Adams? What had I seen in such a self-absorbed jerk? I was willing to humiliate myself just to keep his attention, and he was willing to let me do it. What an idiot. Me, not him. Him too, but I was only responsible for my own idiocy. Geez, getting arrested may have been a gift. No telling what the headlines would have reported if I'd gotten my hands on him and that tart.

"Anna, what do you think about? When you lay awake at night, what do you think about?"

That was a good question. I used to think about how I could score a ticket to the newest premier, or which shoes looked best with my latest designer purchase. Hollywood gossip kept me entertained on sleepless nights. Those topics all seemed light years away from my life in Texas. But one topic did seem to dog me. I was reluctant to confess it.

"Tish."

Beau let out a snort. "Tish? Why! You barely talk to her. I'd keep that one to yourself. Nothing would make her happier than knowing she disturbed your sleep!"

"I'm trying to figure out why she won't just go on the road. She's obviously very talented. Tish comes alive on stage, but the moment the spotlight dims, she's back to Miss Grumpy Pants. It's hard to manage a business well when you hate being there. The Watering Hole is special! It has huge potential, and she treats it like just another B list concert venue. Shirley is drowning, trying to sell tickets to artists nobody has ever heard of. It's great to feature new talent, but you can't attract big names if that's all you do. The only nights that sell out are when you or the Blue Valentines play. The Watering Hole could be an act unto itself. Artists should be clamoring to play there. You told me yourself the acoustics are perfect."

Beau pondered this. "OK, so how do you get big names to forego a huge pay check at the Toyota Center for a gig in Pleasant? And even if you could convince an act to play at The Watering Hole, their agents would never go for it. Their cut would suffer."

I was hoping he would ask that. "First, you have to make The Watering Hole a destination for artists, not fans. Why did you leave Nashville? You dreaded the promotion side of the business, hated the press junkets and focus on sales. Most artists first went on the road because they loved the MUSIC, especially country musicians. Do you think Chris Stapleton spent years performing because he thought he might get a big break on the CMAs some day? No! He's an artist. He feels compelled to write and sing. And what is country music all about? Storytelling! So tell a story about The Watering Hole that makes those artists want to return to their roots, fall in love with the music all over again. Focus on the intimate atmosphere and exceptional sound quality. Then make it hard for them to book a performance. Everybody wants something they can't get! Charge a lot of money for a ticket; true fans will gladly pay up for the chance to see their favorite artist in a small setting, and posers will pay to say they could. Nothing sells better than authenticity. The Watering Hole could be a warm up for counting the big bucks at the Toyota Center the following day. Some might even give up the masses for the chance to enjoy the music again. You did."

"Back up a second. How do you make it hard for an artist to book the venue if the only other events are open mic night and Beau Laurel? And when did you discover Chris Stapleton?"

"I know things! You don't hang around The Watering Hole and not pick up a thing or two about good music. And Chris Stapleton is just the kind of artist we need to get the big ball rolling – someone who is true to his music, but has become a trivia question on the Isaac Asimov Quiz. If we play our cards right, artists will be begging us to book them in our limited Saturday slots."

"And how do you propose we book someone as hot as Chris Stapleton?"

"Pay him, of course. Or better yet, pay him and promise to donate the ticket sales to a charity of his choice. Good press follows philanthropy! Zac Brown has built an entire brand based on giving back; his Southern Ground mission is huge! Don't you have some favors you can call in? You must know some people in Nashville who want to be a part of a revolution, to return to the love of the MUSIC."

"Sounds expensive. Duke is working hard to make a go of it there; not sure there is room in the budget to pay artists with no profit to the barn."

He didn't shut me down - he thought this might work! I jumped up and started pacing. I think best when I'm on the move. "It's an investment! Get people talking, create a buzz, and agents will be banging the doors down to get a piece of the action. Promote non-promotion! Make it a semi-secret club, so exclusive that only those in the inner circle can access it. Agents LOVE that, especially if they can take the credit for discovering it. C 'mon, there must be someone you can ask to come perform! I know a marketing genius in LA who could get a press kit together. "

Beau nodded his head, deep in thought. "So when you said you were thinking about Tish, you were really thinking about The Watering Hole. That's a lot of strategizing for a place you plan to leave in a few months. What, nothing juicy in the tabloids to think about this week?"

That was mean. True, I showed up in Texas star struck by my own fame, but I hadn't mentioned LA or a celebrity in weeks. And I HAD given The Watering Hole a lot of thought. They were wasting a huge opportunity! My little game in the ticket office had already bumped up their profitability, and what did I get for it? A jar of M & Ms and the muted (as opposed to openly hostile) acknowledgement from Tish that I was "good on the phone." Why wouldn't anyone take me seriously? I am more than just a pretty face. I learned a lot from my rise, and subsequent fall, from the public eye. I knew how to get peoples' attention, and The Watering Hole would never get on the map with Little Sammy and the Man. Besides, I hate being bored. Fixing the bottom line at the barn was a lot easier than trying to fix myself; there were no regrets to factor in. Beau must have seen the anger on my face. I've been told I have a habit of narrowing my eyes and scowling when I'm mad.

Beau was repentant. "Sorry. That wasn't fair. You have good ideas. But your biggest hurdle may not be the artists, or the money. Tish will never go for an expensive idea that came from you. Hey, she didn't even like the free idea that came from you, and the Chorus will get a lot of good exposure from that one. Not to mention dresses and sport coats."

He felt bad about underestimating me – perfect. I looked him in the eye, and for once kept my mouth shut. He stared back. It was his turn for narrowed eyes and a frown. "No way, Anna. I am not getting in the middle. The Watering Hole is not mine, and Tish will know none of this came from me. I'm the guy who hates the marketing side of the business, remember? Besides, the last thing I want is a problem with Tish or Duke. They let me play my stuff, I fill their seats. All good and uncomplicated."

What a weanie! No wonder he frustrated Ben. How could you get anything done if you never took a risk? Uncomplicated is how Beau ended up living alone in the Stag Shack. I couldn't sit still, and the porch was too small for dramatic gestures, so I ran down the steps into the yard. "Beau! Don't think of it as a favor for me, think of it as taking a stand for the MUSIC. You love the music! So does Duke. Save the artists from the greedy grasp of agents and record labels! Help them see the light, help them return to their first love! Be the hero!"

Sarah and Ben waved to us as they crossed the lawn to their place. Ben laughed; no idea how much of my one woman act he'd overheard. I tend to get loud when I'm on a soapbox. "Beau, take it man! You don't get to be a super hero for a beautiful model every day of the week!"

Beau stood up, nodded goodbye, and sauntered off without a word. Cicadas joined the chorus as darkness fell. Music spilled from the kitchen while Millie finished the dishes. The dogs ran out for their bedtime trot around the house, chasing after an imagined rabbit or intruder before Boone called them in for the night. I watched Beau enter his little house from my soapbox in the yard, wondering what it felt like to be that confident in your place in the world. So confident you didn't need to be a hero to a traveler passing through.

# CHAPTER 10

Time flew. Lacey called to announce the clothes had arrived, and our photo shoot was scheduled for the first week in November. Belle Bridal wanted to shoot the ad at The Watering Hole; the kids could barely focus at rehearsal for thinking about their appearance in *Celebrity* magazine. A professional hair and makeup team started the day right, transforming our rag tag bunch of teenagers into camera ready models. It's amazing what some attention and a new dress can do for a girl. Photographers played with the lighting while Lacey surprised me with my own dress. She insisted I take a photo with the kids for Rachel.

You know that niggling in your gut that says hey, this might be a bad idea? That same little voice that told me not to chase after Grant, the whisper that warned me not to tick Tish off? It tried to get my attention, tell me I might regret this photo, but I ignored it. It felt great to be in front of the camera again! The kids followed my lead as we went from posed to silly, and after a few minutes everyone was relaxed and laughing. It was gratifying to see the kids having so much fun. The photographer declared I was a natural – had I ever considered a career in modeling?

November was pedal to the metal with concert preparation. Posters went up around town, Duke promised a mystery guest at the big event, and we were sold out. The Friday after Thanksgiving was typically a profitable night for a venue, but Duke always reserved it for the Joy Chorus Christmas concert. I worked my way through the calendar, selling tickets for artists through the end of the year, but noticed the Saturday after Thanksgiving was blacked out.

"Shirley, what's the deal? Did someone reserve the barn? That should be a big night for us. Are The Blue Valentines playing? We need to get some ticket information if we want to sell out."

Shirley shrugged her shoulders. "No idea. Duke just told me to rebook our original act and leave it open. Ask him."

Shirley, while smart, lacks a healthy dose of curiosity. I am full of curiosity, so I bee lined it to Duke's office. He and Tish were deep in conversation, and since I enjoy poking the bear, I hung in the doorway. Duke glanced up and beckoned me in.

"Anna, just the person I need to see. Listen, we are planning a special event on short notice and could use your help. Up for a challenge?"

Tish was surprisingly silent, pretending to be busy reading some sort of contract.

"Always! Let me guess – the Saturday after Thanksgiving? I saw it was blacked out on Shirley's calendar. Why the mystery?"

"We wanted to get the details nailed down before announcing it. Misty Hart plans to release a live album, and asked to record it here. She's played at the barn before and loves the acoustics. Ticket prices are high for this. She wants it to be exclusive, a way to reward her hard core fans. Live audiences can be tricky, so she needs a group who will cooperate during recording. Her team has promised to deliver about half of the ticket sales, and we are on the hook for the other half. The good news is we have access to her fan club data base. Can you help us fill the seats? Pour on some of that phone magic I've heard so much about from Shirley? It's $500 a ticket. We have never done anything like this before. Maybe we get Mo to throw in some brownies!"

Wow, what a great idea! I wish I had thought of it – oh wait, I did! My head was spinning with questions, but for once I listened to that little voice yelling at me to PLAY IT COOL.

"Duke, that's amazing! How did you pull it off? I thought Misty Hart's head was too big to fit through the barn door, not to mention this is Beau territory. How is he going to feel about his cheating ex headlining the marquis?"

Tish and Duke exchanged glances. Tish piped in. "First, we didn't court her; she called us. Her offer was too good to refuse. This could be a game changer for the barn. She also promised to help us book a few more exclusive events if we said yes. She's gotten so big, even her warm-up acts are headliners. On top of all that, she agreed to be our special guest at the Joy Chorus concert the night before. Once the press catches wind of it we expect a lot of good publicity."

"And Beau?"

Duke was clearly uncomfortable. "Maybe you could help us with that too. I don't want to burn any bridges with Beau. He's a reasonable guy, so I think he'll understand, but it might be easier to swallow if he hears it from you. Misty chewed him up and spit him out, but this is just a business decision. We are all on team Beau."

I should ditch modeling for acting; I was about to pull off an academy award winning performance. "I'll tell him. I'm sure he will be shocked to hear

Misty is coming back to The Watering Hole – he doesn't like to talk about her, so I think it's still pretty raw - but I'll smooth things over, point out how good this will be for the barn. He'll be OK."

Where was the applause? I guess the best reward a performer can receive is for the audience to believe the act; by the relief that ran across their faces, Tish and Duke bought it. Acting was kind of fun. But really, did Duke think Misty Hart woke up one morning and had an 'aha' moment to record at The Watering Hole? Come on. She was the hottest act in Nashville, and there were PLENTY of venues where she could record a live album there. It's true, we believe what we want to believe...or maybe my acting was just that good. Either way, Beau was going to be OK because he obviously engineered the event. That must have been some kind of string he pulled for Misty to make that call. I couldn't wait to hear all about it.

"Duke, I'll get to work on that list tomorrow. My phone charm will get those seats sold by the end of the week. After all, who doesn't want to see their favorite artist in an intimate setting? Just imagine the scramble for front row seats – prime real estate to catch Misty in your selfie. That Misty Hart is a genius!"

I was pouring it on, but they didn't seem to notice. Duke was busy tallying the take for the barn, and Tish was busy avoiding any more conversation with me. Humble pie must have been her appetizer before asking for my help. Duke was sweet to worry about Beau getting his feelings hurt. Things were looking up. Duke and Tish needed me to bridge the (imaginary) gap with Beau (making me the hero), and once Misty arrived I might be able to figure out what he ever saw in her (besides beauty, talent, and fame). I hoped whatever leverage he used to inspire Misty's 'aha' moment made him feel vindicated for how she treated him.

Beau did not share my urgency to chat about this latest development. He was nowhere to be found when I returned to the ranch, and my texts went unanswered. I made myself an early dinner of Cheerios so I could wait on the porch until his truck appeared at the cottage. My patience was tested. It was after 10:00 when he arrived, and I had to practically do cartwheels to get his attention. He waved but made no move to join me on the porch. I jogged across the yard to catch him before he disappeared inside.

"Beau! Hold on! Want to come have a drink? I'd offer you dinner but the menu is limited to cereal. I do have bourbon."

He hesitated. I could see the tug of war going on in his head. If he was avoiding me, I was going to make it hard. I don't appreciate being avoided.

I persisted. "Come on. I have some news to share. You might even be interested! But no pressure. I have been patiently – yes, patiently – waiting for you to come home, but I wouldn't want to interrupt your lonely bachelor routine if you have other plans." I had backed him into a corner and was standing my ground. He had to be borderline rude to get rid of me, and rude was not Beau's style.

"OK, one quick drink."

I grabbed two glasses and the bottle of Maker's Mark before joining him on the porch.

Beau reached for his glass without looking me in the eye. "I am not lonely," he muttered.

"Whatever. Guess what? We have a special event coming to the barn!"

Beau swirled his bourbon. "Is that so?"

Clearly he was not going to make this easy. "Yes, Beau. A famous artist – Misty Hart I believe – had a sudden notion to record a live album at The Watering Hole! You've heard of her? She's the one your mother calls The Weapon of Mass Destruction?"

Beau merely raised an eyebrow at me.

"Here's the funny thing. Misty told Duke she wants to make this event exclusive, an intimate evening with her closest fans. Sounds a lot like the plan I floated to you! Any idea how Misty Hart got wind of that plan?"

Beau shrugged. "Maybe great minds think alike."

"Beau! Don't be so modest! You obviously talked her into recording at the barn. When I asked you to call in some favors I didn't think you'd start with her. She's a big fish! I hope you didn't sell your soul to close the deal."

Beau shrugged again. "What does it matter? The barn and Chorus get some good publicity. Misty gets a live album out of the deal. And Tish has no idea the idea was yours. Win/win."

"For the barn it's a win. What about for you? I thought Misty was persona non grata."

"Don't worry about me. Misty and I brokered an armed truce. Our history is old news, and this might be the trick that puts The Watering Hole on the map. Since Duke and Tish don't know to thank you, I will say it for them – thank you for the idea."

"You are welcome. It's fun to be in on a secret. Oh, and head's up. Duke is worried about hurting your feelings by booking Misty. He has no idea you are behind this, and doesn't want you to think he is on Misty's side. So for the record, I made you feel a lot better about it, OK? I can't take credit for the promotion idea, but I will bask in the glow of gratitude for making hometown hero Beau Laurel comfortable with the return of his evil ex since it benefits the community at large."

Beau almost smiled. "So dramatic, Anna. But I'll play along."

"How did you get Misty to make that call to Duke? Compromising photos? Did you threaten to spill her inner most secrets? Promise to kiss and make up? Do tell!"

"Southern gentlemen never tell, Anna. And I do not blackmail people! Drop it. Duke needs to think Misty just wants to record a live album at the barn. End of story. Do NOT tell anyone about this. Understand? I know keeping things under wraps is not your first go to."

That wasn't fair! OK, maybe it was. I tend to vent my frustrations out loud more often than I look silently inward (and in my opinion, that kind of repressed emotion is what causes cancer and heart disease, so no thank you.) Fine. I nodded. All that waiting and no inside scoop, so nothing to tell anyway. Beau handed me his glass. "Thanks for the drink."

*\*\*\**

The next few weeks were a blur. I was very proud of myself for keeping our little secret, even when Shirley began to wonder why a big name like Misty chose the barn for her album, especially after her nasty split with Beau. Maybe, Shirley mused, Misty wanted to get back together with Beau. Maybe this was her way of making nice since Beau refused to go back to Nashville. I hadn't thought of that. No, that couldn't be true. Beau had no plans to leave the ranch, and Misty had no plans to leave her tour, right? Pleasant was far too small for the likes of Misty Hart. That couldn't be the hook. Beau must have threatened to expose something she wanted kept private. I hadn't seen a sneaky side to Beau, but maybe he played a card from his back pocket. In any case, the subject was closed between us. He meant it when he said he wasn't talking.

We all worked overtime getting ready for the Joy Chorus concert and Misty's big event. Decorations for the Chorus concert had to be mobile to accommodate Misty's set the following evening, so by the Wednesday before Thanksgiving I was exhausted. I hoped Judge Goodman had tickets to attend. Per his instruction I had embraced my assignment, and learned a few things indeed; how to wield a hammer, herd dozens of teenagers, and bake a brownie or two. No doubt my record would be expunged at the end of community service. Free at last, free at last!

Back in October I'd invited my mom and Frank for a Thanksgiving visit. Kit was relentless in her insistence they come, and I finally surrendered. Now I wondered if I could drag myself to the table to enjoy the day. Weeks of late night preparations had caught up with me. I breathed a sigh of relief when I learned a snow dump in Chicago delayed my parent's early morning flight. A few more hours of sleep were required before I could manage introductions between Martins and Laurels. It seemed very important that everyone be friends. I didn't want my mom to worry about me here. I had given her enough cause for concern with tabloid and video appearances of late. She deserved a break.

Lucky for me, Texas was showing off. Thanksgiving morning dawned clear and balmy. My parents exited the airport in down coats and boots, quickly shedding their layers before getting in my car. Frank couldn't stop talking about how nice Texas was (it's so green and lush! No tumbleweeds? Are those cows grazing right off the highway?). I filled them in on our cast of characters, from Millie to Rocky to Kit; my mom just listened on the way to the ranch. Ginger is nothing if not wise. She sensed there was a lot more happening in Pleasant than choir practice. I know this by what she DIDN'T ask. The most reliable intelligence is gathered by observing, not prying, and her radar was up and running. My mom isn't the only one who can read signals.

Our late arrival meant festivities were well under way when we made it to the big house. Kit greeted us at the door with hugs before taking Ginger by the arm. They disappeared into the kitchen while Boone offered Frank a drink. A fire roared in the fireplace and several tables were beautifully set for a celebration. My childhood holidays were low key, usually just the three of us. Midwesterners are committed to an unwritten code that requires holidays be spent with family. Even if you don't like them, even if you rarely see them, by golly you dress up on Thanksgiving and Christmas and gut out a meal together.

Our extended family was small and scattered, so the three of us created our own traditions. Fondue and church on Christmas Eve, lots of gifts on Christmas morning, and a rowdy game of Monopoly in the afternoon before cuddling on the couch for *It's A Wonderful Life*. My parents hosted a casual open house the day after Christmas where friends gathered to swap horror stories of their family holiday get togethers. Those parties made me thankful our zone was free from crazy relatives. Now, walking into the big house, I had a revelation – holidays can be a happy gathering of all the people you love, regardless of biology or connection.

Millie's son Eduardo was home from college. Rocky's entire family – wife, mother-in-law, and three kids – were working on a large puzzle on the coffee table. I think their dogs had joined the pack in the yard. Mr. Downly, a widower who lived up the road, was tucked into a corner of the sofa reading a book entitled *Thanksgiving: The Evolution of American Traditions.* I offered to help get things on the buffet, but Millie shooed me back into the living room with instructions to make sure Beau had his guitar for an after dinner sing along. The house buzzed with conversation and laughter. Aromas of the feast drew us all into a circle where we held hands and Boone prayed. Peace settled on us like a light rain.

Between turkey and pie Boone pulled out the holiday version of The Quiz. Mr. Downly had been a Thanksgiving guest before. His pre-dinner reading prepared him well for the graduate round of questions. And who knew Frank was a presidential historian? Even my mom scored a point with some obscure knowledge of which turkeys gobble (only males!). It dawned on me I had spent very little time with my parents since becoming an adult. We'd shared busy weekends here and there, or brief holidays between 'important' LA events, but I hadn't taken time to know them as people.

I sat back while my childhood filter lifted. My parents were funny and smart, thankful to be included at this lively table. Frank entertained the guests with tales of me as a little girl. I had stolen the show as a 4th grader in our Thanksgiving school play. Maddie Swanson won the lead role (much to my dismay), so I decided to go off script a bit...OK, a lot. My role was in the ensemble, one of several Native Americans invited to the first feast. It didn't make sense to me that Indians would speak English – they had just met the Pilgrims, after all – so I made up my own language and greeted Maddie in my 'native' tongue. She was befuddled, and just repeated her lines louder. I matched her volume for volume, and the audience roared with laughter. Mrs. Johnston never should have cast Maddie in the lead; she couldn't think on her feet. Eventually our teacher sent in Bill Kaufman to act as 'translator' so the play could move on. Mrs. Johnston's later scolding was lost on me. All I could hear was the audience laughing at my joke. I LOVED being center stage.

We left the table on the verge of a turkey and pie coma. Eduardo and Beau promised to wake us up with a round of Christmas carols by the fire. Ben joined the fun with a makeshift drum while Sarah played the tambourine. Millie handed out jingle bells for the finale and we belted out the tune at the top of our lungs. The evening had turned brisk, and Rocky appeared with a huge box of twinkle lights. No better way to work off dinner than to bedazzle the ranch with lights. By the end of the night the big house glowed with the holiday spirit. Brandy was our reward before Mr. Downly pronounced the evening a success. His departure was our cue to clean up. Everybody pitched in, and the party moved into the kitchen. Millie was given the night off dish duty, and Sarah insisted the parents all relax while the 'kids' finished the job. Ben washed, I dried, Sarah and Beau put things away. I noticed a small card propped up against the picture of Paul. It read:

'Children are a gift from the Lord; they are a reward from Him.'
Psalm 127:3-5

Sarah saw me reading it. "Kit and Boone were hoping he would call, at least. No word. Not a surprise, but heartbreaking anyway."

Heartbreaking indeed. He must be very angry, or lost, to miss this special day at the ranch. It was one of the most memorable of my entire life. If Thanksgiving was this much fun, what would Christmas be like?

# CHAPTER 11

I slept like a baby that night. Kit promised to keep my parents occupied as I headed to the barn for concert prep. I'd hired a hair and makeup team for the girls (my little treat – they LOVED their photo shoot makeovers) and rolled into the barn a few minutes after noon to check on the beauty squad set up. Maybe I could talk Tish into getting her makeup done too. Extending an olive branch seemed like a good idea, show her we played for the same team. She did have some egg on her face; fighting the ad with Belle Bridal had backfired. She may not know it, but the whole *BACK TO THE MUSIC* concert series was my idea too. Without me, the Joy Chorus Christmas concert would be a nice community fundraiser, not the national headline it promised to be once Misty showed up. I could afford to be gracious.

The kitchen was bustling with preparation for the night's crowd, but Tish and Duke were missing in action. Squawk pointed to the office. The door was closed, but he seemed to think they were in there. As I approached the door, I could hear Tish yelling. I cracked it open and got an earful.

"Dad (that was a first.) She is an attention WHORE! Having her here was a TERRIBLE idea! Why is everything all about her? Doesn't anybody realize she is just using us, and the barn, for her own career? She doesn't care about any of us!"

What ever happened, Duke wasn't as upset as Tish. "Patricia. (Patricia? Well, she was certainly NOT a Patty, so Tish made some sense. Amazing what you learn when nobody knows you are listening). I get it – you're mad. She's upstaged you. But we've worked too hard for a full year to let this get under your skin! Tonight is about the KIDS, not you, or her. I'm warning you – let it go for the weekend. We can talk about it next week."

Tish was fuming. Much as I craved the scandal details, I carefully closed the door. No need to get caught in that crossfire. Misty Hart must have done something wicked to set Tish off like that. The barn was raking in a hefty profit, plus publicity, by having her record here; that should cover a multitude of sins. Whatever it was, best to let Tish blow off some steam. Nothing stayed secret for long at the barn, so I'd hear about it sooner or later. I didn't want my happy Thanksgiving vibe to be dashed by Tish's sensitive ego. What did she expect from a celebrity who had treated Beau, the nicest guy on the planet, like scum? Yes, Misty was obviously here to further her career. Or she owed Beau a BIG favor, but they wouldn't know about that negotiation (I didn't either. That man was like a steel trap.)

I turned to see cute Emmie Jenkins motioning for me to come away from the office. She could hear the heated discussion, even if the words were muted through the door. Emmie had a look of panic on her face, and I'd never seen Emmie flustered before.

"Miss Anna, Jessica needs your help. We were waiting for the makeovers to start and she turned green. I think she's sick."

"Where is she?"

"She ran to the bathroom. I'm not sure she made it in time."

Let's just say she didn't. Lacey from Belle Bridal knew her stuff. That's why she encouraged us to hand out dresses at the last possible moment. I'm glad we listened. The bathroom was a mess (I will spare you the gory details), and Jessica was curled up on the floor next to the toilet. Her forehead was hot, she had broken out in a clammy sweat, and her sweatshirt was trashed. Good thing I was still in my grubbies. Duncan, our custodian, had ducked out for a late lunch when the glam squad moved in. I was on my own. First order of business was to get Jessica home. I didn't know what was wrong with her, but we could not afford to have a barf bug sweep through the troops.

"Emmie, can you grab Jessica's phone and call her mom? She needs to go home."

Poor Jessica groaned. She didn't want to miss the festivities, but was in no shape to argue. The bathroom was enough to make anyone sick, so I got her out in the hall with a cool towel on her forehead. Thankfully her mom wasn't far; we got her loaded into the car before most of the girls arrived. I put one of the seniors in charge of organizing the makeup queue while I went in search of a bucket and mop. Community service suddenly took on a whole new meaning. I didn't even clean up after my dog when she was sick, much less someone else's kid. But I was not about to go in search of Duke, or Tish, and have them ridicule me for being a wimp. My gag reflex would not win. Judge Goodman would be proud I think, and I discovered a new found respect for the highway clean-up crew (and Duncan!). Working with Tish, while challenging at times, was easier than picking up roadkill. Perspective is good, it makes room for some gratitude. I, however, had gained enough perspective for one day. Next step? Make sure nobody else had a fever and a queasy stomach.

I dumped the nasty bucket into the street out back. Cleaning up was hard work and I was sweaty, but there was no time to run back to the ranch for a shower. I dragged the mop and bucket back through the door, almost running down a woman in the hallway. It took a moment for my eyes to adjust to the barn after being in the sun, so I couldn't see who got in my way.

"Sorry, sorry. Might want to give me a wide berth. We had a disaster in the bathroom. Are you with the glam squad?"

A very petite woman with the prettiest sparkly boots stepped out of my way. "No, I'm headed for the dressing room, and looking for Tish. You might want to trade that t-shirt in for another one. I think the disaster in the bathroom is following you." She said this over her shoulder as she walked away. I must smell to high heaven.

Jessica's virus had found its way to my clothes. I had a flashback to when I was 8 and got my tonsils out. I kicked Frank out of their bed so I could sleep with my mom. The pain meds made me sick, and several nights in a row I lost my liquid dinner all over her and the sheets. Ginger settled me into the bathtub while she performed damage control. By the time I was bundled back into pajamas, the bed was fresh, the sheets cool. She kissed my forehead and rubbed my back until I fell asleep. Dang, motherhood is filled with thankless jobs. How many times had I made a mess, assuming the magic mom fairy would wiggle her nose to make things right? How many times had I made a wreck of things and expected Maria, or Clayton, or Diane to wiggle theirs? Being an only child meant I was always outnumbered by responsible adults; being a highly paid model meant I'd surrounded myself with staff. I was poorly prepared to handle the dirty stuff, but today I had mastered a mop and bucket. I felt strangely satisfied with my accomplishment. I should give Duncan a gift card. He more than earned it.

Sometimes I get lost on rabbit trails. While I was reliving my childhood medical drama, the woman disappeared. She seemed to know her way around, but criminals posed as all kinds of characters these days to rip people off. The chaos of the girls milling about made for a perfect cover if someone wanted to take something from the barn.

"Wait! Are you here for tonight's concert? Or part of the crew for tomorrow?" I rounded the corner to the dressing room. Right there on the name plate it read MISTY HART. This was Misty? The famous Misty Hart had big, flowing auburn hair and huge brown eyes. This fresh faced girl, perched in the makeup chair with a pony tail, did not look as tall as the Misty I'd seen on TV. I never would have recognized her in the grocery store. But Anna Martin looks nothing like Anastasia DeMars – that transformation takes a crew of trained professionals, which I had not yet encountered today. Misty clearly did not recognize me either.

Her assistant turned around. "May I help you? Miss Hart is not available for fans at the moment."

She thought I was a fan. Hilarious! I am the ANTI fan, and it took all my self-control not to berate her for how she treated Beau. Tish was mad, and that was a MUCH better way to deal with her. I had nothing to gain by harassing the very artist who was fulfilling my plans for The Watering Hole, and if Beau heard I'd broken my promise he would be very disappointed with me. Let Tish be the bad guy. Duke had warned her to wait until the weekend was over, but Tish could hold a grudge. Misty would get her due in time. So I took a deep breath, smiled, and pulled out the inner actor in me. She was getting some good rehearsal time in; I should alert my agent.

"Oh, I'm not a fan (couldn't resist that). I work here at The Watering Hole with the kids in the Joy Chorus. I'm Anna, their stylist."

I let that sink in, me with my sweaty hair in a clip, my shirt a smelly ruin. The assistant's eyebrows shot up into her hairline. Misty eyed me in the mirror.

"Their stylist? Not the maintenance crew?"

I maintained my cheery expression. "Around here we do whatever it takes – nobody is above a little bathroom clean up. I'll be sure to tell Tish you are here and hoping to see her. I'll close the door so the kids don't wander in. We wouldn't want them to interrupt your complicated hair and makeup routine. Keep the image alive and all that. Some of them might be fans."

I closed the door and spun headlong into Beau. "What are you doing here?"

Beau took a step back. "What happened to you." He waved his hand in front of his nose.

"I got caught in the crossfire between Jessica's stomach virus and the toilet. Never let it be said I shirk my duties. Misty Hart is in there."

He pointed to the nameplate on the door. "So I see."

We stood there for an awkward moment. Ah. He was looking for her. Maybe Shirley was right and they were working on a love connection. I stepped out of his way. "Guess I better get out of these clothes."

Beau's response was terse. "Good idea."

The general dressing room was right next door; I had stashed my bag there earlier. All the girls' dresses hung on rolling racks, leaving a small corner in the back where I could change. It happened to be next to the vent, and I could hear Beau and Misty if I listened very quietly. Misty did most of the talking.

"Why don't you play guitar on the record tomorrow, Beau? I'll name you in the credits. Nobody knows the music better than you. It might give the album a PR bump – local songwriting wonder plays backup for his ex, the difficult Misty Hart. Fuel some gossip. How long would it take for the tabloids to have us back together, expecting twins?"

"Not long, so I'll pass, thank you."

Misty let that go. "So who is Anna?"

Beau took his time answering. What was he doing in there? "She helps with the Chorus. And occasionally with clean-up." I could hear the grin in his voice as he said that. I'm glad my heroic custodial efforts gave everyone cause to laugh. I might need to seal this shirt in a bag and throw it in the dumpster. Yuck.

Misty sent her assistant on a hunt for sparkling water (good luck with that. Beer? Yes. Perrier? I don't think so).

"Is this Anna the wizard behind the curtain?"

Beau seemed to be a bit tongue tied. Misty persisted.

"Wow, the brooding Beau Laurel smiles. You and I both know this *BACK TO THE MUSIC* series was not your idea, and Tish seems to think it was mine. So let me guess – the gawky choir volunteer? How did she come up with a promotion plan like that? I thought you were trying to help Duke's bottom line at the barn. What's her cut?"

"Nothing. Sometimes people do things for the greater good."

Misty whooped. She had a hearty laugh for such a small person. "Not many, Beau. If you bought that line, you are a slow learner. Our breakup should have taught you the greater good usually translates to what's best for Number One. What do you get out of this deal, anyway? You were adamant about me not releasing those songs. Why the sudden generosity of spirit?"

Beau's tone now sounded irritated. "Look Misty, you got what you wanted and more. I gave up the music, you get a great live album, and the barn gets some press. Nothing else to talk about."

"Right. All for the greater good. Or maybe a girl? Seems like a long way around the mountain when a simple love song could do the trick; worked like a charm on me. By the way, I would have agreed to this gig even without the 2 bonus tracks. It's not too late to take those back. I probably owe you that."

"You probably do. But I've moved on. Knock yourself out. Just keep this agreement between us."

Beau closed the door a bit harder than necessary. She could still get under his skin. But breaking news – he surrendered the portfolio of music they'd been fighting over to get her here. And she poached 2 extra songs in the deal. Why would he do that? First Tish, now Misty; my eavesdropping left me with lots of questions and nobody to ask. That's the trouble with snooping, you only get half of the story. I went to work transforming Anna, smelly choir volunteer, into Anastasia DeMars. I came armed with a sassy dress, curling iron and makeup worthy of a super model. Misty's heels had nothing on me in mine. She would regret looking down her nose at me.

\*\*\*

Once I got the girls through hair and makeup it was show time, so no chance to drop in on any other private conversations. I handed out programs at the door before joining my parents at a table in the back row. This was Tish and Duke's night. Their tribute to Joy was a tear jerker. Lacey from Belle Bridal got a shout-out while the press politely took photos of the Chorus. Everybody knew they were waiting for Misty to make her 'mystery' guest appearance (which had been strategically leaked to the Houston paper and TV stations.) I was waiting to greet her nicely after the show. Nothing puts a stuck up girl in her place like being gracious to her, especially when you look your best. I'll give you gawky, shorty.

Before the concert began I entertained my parents by retelling some of the afternoon's events. I left the eavesdropping part out – that happened by accident – but had Frank in stiches over my encounter with the Diva of Country in my post-Jessica garb. Kit had indulged in an anti- Misty rant over lunch, so by the time Misty made it to the stage Frank and Ginger were prepared for the Wicked Witch of the West. Instead, Misty floated in like Glenda. Her blush pink blouse and embellished jeans hit just the right note of sweet. A humble wave to the crowd encouraged them to sit, and she pulled up a plain stool in front of the microphone.

"Friends, this is such an honor for me to be here. Aren't these kids amazing? I do not want to steal their thunder tonight, so let me end the evening with a simple ballad dedicated to the Joy Chorus called "True Joy." It will appear on the album I am recording here at The Watering Hole tomorrow night, and this is the first time I have played it in public. All proceeds from this single will benefit the Joy Chorus to fund the great work it is doing with teenagers in Pleasant County, so be sure to download the studio version once it is released."

Was she for real? The song was beautiful, pointing us all to the things that matter. Her simple delivery, just a girl with her guitar, brought it all home. Brilliant. If I hadn't met her earlier, I just might buy it. The rest of the crowd was on its feet, some wiping tears, others whistling. No wonder Beau had fallen for her, and no wonder he felt battered once he got past the floor show. "True Joy" must be one of the songs he had written. I had to admit she was talented, in music and promotion. Donating proceeds to the Chorus would make a great story in *Celebrity* magazine when the album dropped. I should be thankful; the *BACK TO THE MUSIC* series was launched the way I'd hoped. I just never thought Misty Hart would be the artist who kicked it off. My mom thought she was lovely, nothing like the "toxic bomb" of Kit's description. Yes, Misty had game.

Duke invited The Watering Hole inner circle to a cocktail meet and greet with Misty after the show. That was Kit and Boone's cue to exit. Before Kit dragged her back to the ranch, my mom gave me a hug. I swear that woman can read my mind.

"Last night you were all about jeans and sneakers. No ponytail today?" Ginger looked over at Misty, all flirty with Duke and Mo. Her raised eyebrows asked the real question – was I trying to impress a boy, or intimidate a girl?– but I played dumb.

"It was a special night for the Chorus. Can't a girl get dressed up just for fun?"

"Absolutely. Especially a girl who has nothing to prove. Enjoy the party! See you in the morning." Guess what? I can read her mind too. Translation: be nice, no need to get in another girl's face when said girl will be leaving in two days. Good advice, really, but I've been known to ignore good advice. We'd just have to see how things progressed.

I waited until most of the crowd around Misty thinned; even groupies eventually step away for an open bar. Sarah appeared at my elbow just as I was about to approach Misty. Maybe Ginger tipped her off, maybe Sarah read the look on my face, but either way she wasn't going to let me make a fool of myself with Beau's ex. I challenge anyone to be surly in Sarah's presence, her aura is so pleasant. Clever barbs dissolved in my mouth. Dang. Now I had to be cordial.

Sarah reached out to hug Misty, and introduced me as the Joy Chorus' newest family member. Talk about spinning things to the positive. Misty had to retract her claws now that Sarah was in the middle.

"Yes, we've met, although Anna was playing janitor at the time. Glad to see you are back to stylist tonight. I imagine the perks are a bit better. I understand you are responsible for getting the kids outfitted for tonight. Well done. They looked great."

OK, I did not expect her to be friendly. Sarah grabbed the ball and ran with it. "Anna got Belle Bridal to donate all the clothes for free. The Chorus will be featured in an ad for *Celebrity* magazine and the kids are over the moon about it!"

Sarah looped her arm through mine. I was fortunate to have such a grace filled friend. If birds of a feather flock together, I would need to abandon my snippy side. I guess there was no downside to being agreeable. After all, I might learn something.

"I loved your song, Misty. Very touching."

Misty hesitated before answering. "Thank you. That means a lot from someone who is not a fan." She smiled. I saw truce in her eyes. "I did not write it, though. Beau Laurel did. Perhaps you are a fan of his?"

Hmmm. She seemed to be teasing me. What had Beau told her? I opted for keeping things light. "I have yet to meet a person who is NOT a Beau Laurel fan!"

"True. He is annoyingly likeable. Would you two like to come back to the dressing room for a drink? I need to get out of these heels, and frankly, if I talk to you standing up much longer Anna, I may need chiropractic help for my neck."

Ben was waving Sarah down from across the room. I couldn't imagine Ben was a Misty fan; he and Kit seemed to be on the same page in most things. Sarah appeared torn, not wanting to leave me in an awkward situation. I sent her on her way and followed Misty to her dressing room. Beau had disappeared as soon as the concert wrapped, and the rest of the staff was enjoying free booze. Nobody saw us leave the party. I settled into a chair while Misty poured us a bourbon. I had never even tasted bourbon before landing in Texas, but here I was becoming a connoisseur. I'd never heard of Devil's River, but it was good. Misty tossed her shoes aside and tucked her feet up on the sofa. She cut right to the chase.

"So Anna, do I have you to thank for the *BACK TO THE MUSIC* series idea? When Beau asked me to kick it off, he was characteristically vague about whose brainstorm it was. You are the only new player in town."

"My idea, yes, but Beau must have been awfully persuasive to get the famous Misty Hart to sign on."

Misty swirled her drink, avoiding eye contact. "My agent loved the idea. And Beau is a hard man to say no to, right?"

Ah, there is was. One pour and Misty was already setting a trap. Kit might be right about this woman.

"We aren't dating, if that's what you're thinking. I'm only here in Texas for a short while, and I live at Honor Ranch in their guest house. Beau and I are friends."

Misty's gaze took stock of me.

"Beau keeps his circle small. He gave up a lot to see your idea take off. I don't know what you've heard about our history, but it wasn't easy for him to make that phone call. Beau went out on a limb for you, and he doesn't do that for just anyone. You must be very good friends. Treasure that. Beau is the real deal."

I sensed a shift in Misty. Her swagger had mellowed a bit, and regret seemed to color her remarks. The bourbon worked its spell and my guard dropped as well. If Beau wouldn't tell me what happened with Misty, maybe she would.

"Sounds like the rumors of a nasty split between you two were exaggerated."

Misty laughed. "No, probably not! He can bring out the best in me – you saw that tonight on stage. But it was a lot of pressure dating Beau, and eventually the situation brought out the worst in me. Throw his family in the mix and it was a recipe for disaster. It didn't take a rocket scientist to figure out we were a bad match. He wants to write music in a back room after a day of wrangling cattle. Me? I love being on stage! I always wanted to be famous. I grew up in a suburban duplex with my mom and three siblings. The closest thing I got to livestock was the neighbor's cat. I could not wait to get out of there. I love country music, but I do not like cows, or church, or his mother! Have you met his mother? She hates me! Kit accused me of scheming to get Beau to Nashville to pick his songwriting brain, then abandon him once my album charted. Turns out she saw right through me."

At least she was honest about her part of the break up. I felt myself warm just a little towards her. Or maybe it was the booze. The bourbon made it easy to push for details.

"If Beau loves the ranch so much, why did he go to Nashville? And why did you let him?"

Misty refilled our glasses. She was on a roll.

"Right before we met, my debut album had enjoyed lukewarm success. That's a nice way of saying nobody paid any attention to it. Beau had just hit it out of the park with "Chasing Home", and I needed songwriting help. I performed at The Watering Hole and sparks flew between us. As they say, timing is everything. Things at home were stressful for Beau. He'd wasted most of the previous year trying to help his brother Paul get sober. Have you met Paul?"

"No. Sarah told me he's an alcoholic. She mentioned he lost a lot of family money that was meant for a business venture."

"Sarah is sweet. Paul is a hateful son of a bitch. A charming one, but mean. When Beau and I met, his family was mad at Paul for losing that money. Paul was mad at Beau for trying to get him back into rehab, Ben was mad at everyone for not kicking Paul to the curb, Kit was mad at me for just showing up. It was a perfect storm for Beau to want out. So I convinced him to come to Nashville. We wrote a whole catalog of great music, and used some of the songs for my sophomore album *Glass Half Full*. It was a hit. Great, right? For me, yes. I was on tour promoting it, having a blast. Beau was sitting in Nashville waiting for me to come home. He wanted a life together and I was chasing a number 1 album. It was only a matter of time before it unwound."

That sounded like a predictable outcome. We've all seen the tabloid parade documenting the downfall of famous couples. Did anyone think Brad and Angelina would make it? Or Miranda and Blake?

"So where did the nasty come in?"

"Oh, the nasty came in thanks to Paul."

"Paul? I thought he went AWOL after the whole gambling thing."

Misty poured some nuts in a bowl and offered me a napkin. "Not without some parting shots. Paul was the puppet master in the Laurel family for a long time. It was easy for an outsider like me to see it, but they were all snowed by his pathetic "I don't fit in" game. Paul is just lazy. He's jealous of his brothers and played them all against the other to get what he wanted. He is a master manipulator. After he lost the investment money, Paul demanded a partnership stake in the ranch. Ben drew a line in the sand; it was him or Paul. Beau had to side with Ben. Paul never wanted to work on the ranch, and he couldn't be trusted even if he did. This all exploded at a Laurel family dinner where I put my two cents in – unsolicited, true, but nobody else would tell Paul to hit the road until he was sober. Paul did not appreciate my input. He sarcastically thanked me for the advice, then proceeded to get even."

Finally, the inside scoop! "What did he do?"

"He hired a sleazy photographer to stalk me. The headlines announced I was cheating on Beau with my producer."

"Were you? Cheating?" The bourbon had hijacked my manners.

Misty jumped up from the couch. "No! But the pictures ended up in the tabloids, and it was obvious I was cozier with him than I should have been. I didn't find out until much later that Paul set the photographer on my trail. But Paul got his revenge. Country music fans are NOT like pop fans. They have little tolerance for slutty. I got a bad rap in the press and had to do damage control. Beau has no stomach for all that drama. He refused to play the happy couple game for the cameras. Boone had just been diagnosed with colon cancer, so Beau came back to Texas. Looking back, I should have just let him go. But I picked a fight and told him I would release the remaining songs from our catalog if he didn't help me put the cheating story to rest. He was hurt. Those songs were about our life together, and it was falling apart. Beau didn't appreciate being blackmailed. He got a judge to impose an injunction, requiring written permission from the other to release that music. That's why those songs have been in purgatory until now."

Poor Beau. A fish out of water in Nashville, girlfriend wandering, his brother a train wreck. That impenetrable Laurel façade hid a lot of torment. And Paul? What a rat! I could not imagine Beau scheming to hurt someone the way Paul did. Misty refilled our glasses again. The bourbon was fueling her confessional.

"When Beau called me with the *BACK TO THE MUSIC* idea, I thought he might be interested in rekindling us."

Surely not – Misty was clearly not the girl for him. But maybe Beau was still smitten?

"And does he want to rekindle your romance?"

Misty laughed. "Oh Anna, I wish you could have seen your face when I said that! I think you might have a bad case of Beau Laurel! No, coming here has been good for me. We could never be together. I want the big stage! You understand that. I looked up Anna Martin, and imagine what I found; a model named Anastasia DeMars, most famous for walking the red carpet with Grant Adams and smacking a police officer with her designer bag!" Misty reenacted the viral video scene with an imaginary Officer Friendly.

The bourbon had worked its magic on me too. My defensive spiel dissolved into uncontrollable giggles. Misty did a pretty good impression of me. "Anastasia, ditch modeling and come to work for me! I got better press from this gig than all my interviews combined. And why stay so behind the scenes? Anastasia DeMars seems highly invested in grabbing the spotlight. I could put that to use!"

I almost caught her enthusiasm, then reality brought me back to earth. "Well, Anna Martin is trying to finish community service and reports to Duke. Tish hates me, but I am in the home stretch. I can't afford to rock the boat. Besides, I want to help the Chorus."

Misty eyed me up and down. "Tish Valentine hates you because you are a glamazon who threatens to steal the show around here. She is insecure and petty. Ignore her. This Series is the best thing that ever happened to The Watering Hole, and Tish never would have thought of it. She should go on the road and let someone else run the business. I'd hate to see the momentum from this Series lost because Tish is in over her head. Duke is a good guy, he deserves a break."

No love lost between Tish and Misty. The country music scene was a small, small world. Might be smart to watch my step.

"And Anna, where did you come up with the name Anastasia DeMars? Please don't tell me it was the Disney movie!"

"Ok, I confess, the Disney movie inspired me. What little girl doesn't want to be an undiscovered princess who eventually avenges her family? And Anastasia sounds much more glamorous than plain

Anna. DeMars is my mom's maiden name, so I'm not a total phony. Where did you come up with Misty Hart? A Hallmark movie?"

That hit Misty's funny bone. "That is my real name! I'm not kidding! My sister's name is Stormy!"

"And I suppose your brothers are Brave and Broken?"

Misty pretended to be shocked. "How did you guess?"

This was too much. "What? Really?"

Misty doubled over laughing. "OK, no. I do have 2 brothers, Ed and Joe. But don't think weird names started in Hollywood. My mother and her siblings were all named after Southern states – Georgia, Virginia, Carolina and Tennessee. You know why? Because my grandmother was born at home and the old doctor forgot her name when he filled out the birth certificate. He wrote down "Baby Girl." Her parents were simple country folks and didn't know how to change it, so Baby it stayed. Baby figured the clerk recording her own children's births would remember Southern states, so it seemed a safe bet."

Dang, I was not prepared to like Misty, but here we were drunk in her dressing room, laughing hysterically about nothing very funny. We must have been loud because neither of us heard the knock on the door until it escalated into a bang. "Misty, are you OK in there?"

That set us both off laughing again. Misty made her way to the door, not an easy journey after our cocktail hour. She fumbled with the lock and flung the door open. Duke stood there shaking his head.

"OK ladies, hand over the keys. You two are having WAY too much fun to be safe on the road. I'll get you home – let's go."

# CHAPTER 12

Sunlight drilled through my window too early on Saturday morning. In my fog the night before I had failed to pull the blinds, and was paying for it now. I vacillated between wanting to secure darkness (which required moving) and burying my head under a hot pillow. Eventually an overwhelming need for water and an aspirin settled the debate – moving it was. My feet cooperated reluctantly. The pounding in my head screamed DUMB DUMB DUMB to the rhythm of my heartbeat. Bourbon had seduced me, then ditched me like a prom date, leaving nothing but regret in its wake. It felt like roadkill had settled in my mouth overnight. The toothpaste was hiding, so mouthwash scraped the top layer of fur off my tongue while I searched for pain relievers. I hoped Misty handled her booze better than I did. She had a huge performance ahead of her. Me, I just needed to remember how to walk, swallow a pill, and sleep it off until later.

The pounding in my head synched with the beat of someone banging on the front door. I ignored it. Response time when wrestling a hangover is exceedingly slow, so they would probably give up before I could get there anyway. Nope. In addition to the banging, someone started yelling. "Anna? Are you OK?" A pack of the Laurel dogs joined the chorus, barking in tempo to this persistent drumming. I tried to match their enthusiasm, but my feeble "go away" was lost in the cacophony. The door opened just as I downed a handful of Excedrin – I'd forgotten to lock up in my drunken stupor. Didn't anyone respect the quiet that last night's booze demanded?

I had never heard Beau yell, so I was surprised to see his face come around the door. In all honesty, he may not have been yelling. Every whisper was currently amplified in my post- party state. But he had certainly been banging. Beau let out a slow whistle which escalated to a shrill screeching in my head. I covered my ears and eyes, trying to escape his scrutiny and the blazing sun he invited in behind him. He did not take the hint.

"Look what the cat dragged in. I saw Duke drop you off late last night so I thought you might need a ride to your car. Looks like you need medical intervention first."

This was humiliating. I was too queasy to care. The couch looked like a soft spot to land, so I collapsed face first. My mouth worked hard to formulate a reply. "You should see the other guy."

Beau seemed to be enjoying this. "By the looks of you, the other guy must be in the morgue. What's his name? By the smell of it in here I'm going to guess Jim Beam."

The label flashed before my eyes. "Devil's River," I mumbled.

"Ah, well you sold your soul with your eyes wide open then. The only remedy for that Devil is biscuits and gravy. With lots of greasy bacon and a Bloody Mary on the side. Or chicken fried steak and grits with cheese. Lots of cheese, all melty and hot. Or a big stack of blueberry pancakes…."

And with that I ran to the bathroom and emptied myself of what remained of the Devil.

Beau gave me a minute to regroup on the bathroom floor before handing me a tall glass of water. "That's step one. Sorry, it had to be done. Water is step two, followed by a hot shower and more water. Then food."

"You did that to me on purpose?" I groaned. The cool tile felt good on my cheek. Maybe if I just laid here all day - or week - I could recover my ability to string two sentences together.

Beau turned on the shower. "Drink the water. Get dressed and I'll take you to Mable's."

"Who is she."

"Mable is a guy named Gus who makes a great Southern breakfast. Been going there since I was a kid."

"I'm not hungry."

Beau laughed. "No, but I am. Trust me. The only way to fight last night's devil is to get moving today. I'll be back in 15 minutes."

I dragged myself into the hot shower after chugging the water. Hair scraped into a ponytail, face bare, I made it to the front porch in yesterday's sweats. Anastasia DeMars would have been horrified. The sun seemed determined to teach me a lesson by piercing through the armor of my sunglasses. Staying upright had its challenges, so I settled for the floor. Beau whistled his way across the lawn, unencumbered by sensitivity to noise and light. I begged him to be quiet and refused his offer of a hand, so he scooped me up and deposited me into the passenger seat of his truck. I leaned against the window and yearned for bed. The motion of the truck almost put me to sleep; the nausea receded, and the jackhammer in my head mellowed into a dull ache. There was a glimmer of light at the end of the hangover tunnel.

We pulled into a small dirt lot filled with all kinds of trucks, motorcycles, and a tractor. A faded pink shack greeted us with a WELCOME TO MABLE'S sign over the swinging screen door. The house was packed. Pungent coffee and frying bacon perfumed the air. A waitress nodded us towards a table by a big box fan, and after a moment of recurring queasiness I took a seat. This was clearly the local crowd. Beau greeted some ranching types while I did my best to disappear. There wasn't a menu in sight. The waitress brought me a big glass of tomato juice before I even ordered.

"I've seen this ailment before. Keep drinking. I'll bring you a biscuit, no gravy, to get things started. The fan will keep the smell of bacon on that side of the room. You're welcome. Beau? The usual?"

Beau nodded. "Thanks Fanny. Keep the coffee coming. The resurrection of my friend here may take a while."

I attempted a smile, but Fanny was already on her way. Beau worked hard to keep his smile to a smirk.

"Must have been quite a party at the barn last night. Yankees should be careful in the company of Southerners. You are not schooled in the seductive powers of a smooth bourbon."

I think I groaned, loudly enough to attract the attention of the table next to us judging by their amused glances. Let them think my misery was limited to a hangover. I did NOT want to get into a discussion with Beau about how I ended up interrogating Misty about him and his family. Changing the subject seemed in order.

"Well, if the booze didn't kill me I guess the grease here won't kill me either. Have they cleaned that grill since you were a kid?" A big guy, probably Gus, had the grill spitting with chicken fried steak, eggs and hash. The overhead hood labored under the accumulated exhaust of decades. Experts say kids have asthma these days because their environments are too clean; one trip to Mable's could fix that. Maybe that's the secret to Beau's superhero immune system. I had never heard him mention even a sniffle.

Beau refilled my water glass. "Breakfast at Mable's is legendary. Don't let appearances fool you. These are some of the wealthiest ranchers in south Texas. Huge land deals are made right here over grits and black coffee. No lattes, no granola, no strangers. You got a warm reception because you came with me. Show up in a slick suit or loafers, and you might not get a table."

What stranger could find this place, or want to. The peeling pink paint would deter most foreigners before they got in the front door. The biscuit, however, was life changing, even in my altered state. So light, so flaky, so buttery. Beau's platter of eggs, bacon, and pancakes filled up half the table. Portion control was not high on the list at Mable's. The aggregate cholesterol readings in this room could finance a new vacation home for a cardiac surgeon – if any of these people even went to the doctor. They radiated well being.

Beau dug in. "My dad brought us here on Saturdays when we were kids. My brothers and I had a running contest to see who could eat the most pancakes in a single sitting. I was happy to let Paul win, but Ben would eat until he had a stomach ache. Those two competed over everything – who got to ride shotgun, who got the prettier girl."

"And who usually won?"

"Ben always won. He never threw down a challenge he couldn't win. Paul flies by the seat of his pants, and Ben out maneuvered him every time. I think that's part of Paul's problem. Instead of just doing his own thing, he always tried to out do Ben. Paul couldn't beat him, and he didn't want to join him, so he settled for just ticking him off."

"How did he do that?"

"Paul called Ben Captain Rule Police and taunted him every chance he got. Ben got As? Paul flunked out. Ben was voted Homecoming King? Paul got suspended for smoking pot on campus during the game. The more Ben crowed about living up to the Laurel name, the harder Paul worked to tarnish it. But as kids, Paul was my hero. He was the master of pranks. Ben got the bad end of that stick."

"Only children miss out on all the fun."

"Yeah, well, the fun ended when Paul's partying turned into straight up self-destruction. He's spent the last ten years trying to rewrite family history to paint himself the outsider. Paul chose that role for himself. Sometimes I come here to remember what it was like when we were kids."

And to eat a HUGE breakfast. Beau was working his way through Gus' masterpiece pretty well.

"Do you ever see Paul?"

"No. My parents tried to get him help, and finally asked me to intervene. They thought he might listen to me, but nope. He went on the attack instead. Our family is not perfect, but we have always had each other's backs. Paul burned some bridges, especially with Ben. All Paul wants is money. And money is the last thing we are willing to give him."

Fanny gauged my recovery as progressing and delivered a scrambled egg with a steaming mug of coffee. I nodded a thank you.

"Are you mad at him? Sounds like he's pretty toxic."

"Mad? No. He needs help. But I don't trust him. Paul lies to everyone about our family, but trying to correct the record is a waste of time. I don't much care what other people think."

"So who is your hero now?"

Beau's face broke into a smile, chasing away the frown that seemed to accompany any conversation about Paul. "My grandpa. Pop is amazing. He has this gift – he sees the best in people, but never gives them a free pass. That's why Bootstrap works. Pop finds a good quality in every boy, and gives them a vision for who they can be. Then he expects them to live up to it."

"And do they?"

Beau pondered that for a moment. "Sometimes. Pop has a temper! Bootstrap gives these kids an opportunity, and he expects them to appreciate it. If they don't work hard, or they break the rules, they're out. But it's life changing for the kids who make it through the program."

I choked down the egg while the coffee went to work clearing my head. Or maybe it was the aspirin. Either way, that dark veil smothering my brain was lifting. I had never heard Beau be so chatty, but he had probably never heard me be so quiet. A crippling hangover seemed to be the key for keeping my mouth shut. I didn't spill the news that Misty had been my partner in crime, or that she filled me in on the Laurel family saga. He still thought I got drunk with The Watering Hole staff. No sense confessing now. I was learning a lot about Beau Laurel over biscuits.

"Who is your hero, Anna?"

Hmmm. Right now, I'd knight anyone who could restore me to pre-bourbon form, so Fanny was in the running. But seriously?

"Simon Eiler."

Beau leaned back in surprise. "The scrawny kid from the Chorus? Why!"

"Simon is 14 and a math genius, in school with 17 year olds who are half as smart. He is a math geek and owns it! I've never seen a kid so comfortable in his own skin. He has a teasing target on his back but he gives it right back with a smile. Need a tutor? Simon is the first to volunteer. He never talks down to anyone, just shows kids the other side of the math elephant so they can understand better. I've never heard him say a nasty thing about anyone. Guess who he asked to the Fall dance? Bethany Owens! She is a foot taller and 2 years older, but she said yes. And if she hadn't, he would have considered it her loss and moved on to the next girl. That kind of chutzpa will land him on the cover of *Forbes* magazine one day. He will then give the credit to someone else, because that's how humble he is. Nobody has ever accused me of being humble."

Beau laughed. "You surprise me, Anna."

"What, did you think I would pick a Kardashian?"

"Anastasia might, but not Anna Martin. Simon is a worthy hero. And let me be the first to accuse you of being humble. You have taken no credit for the *BACK TO THE MUSIC* series. I'm sure it's tempting to rub Tish's nose in something."

So tempting. I filed Beau's praise away to replay when Tish pushed my buttons. At this point it wasn't worth letting her get to me. She would be humiliated to learn I was the force behind the series, and humiliated people often strike. My own tangle with the police taught me that.

Beau paid the bill. I thanked Fanny and she invited me to "come see us again." That was probably directed at Beau, but I might come back without benefit of escort or hangover. The model in me was repelled by the display of butter and gravy; the human in me wanted a stab at Gus' blueberry short stack.

I was more steady on my feet that when I arrived, but Beau still guided me by my elbow through the maze of tables. "Do you need your car? I can run you by the barn, or you can leave it there and go with me tonight for Misty's concert."

Go with him? He didn't say ride with him. Was this a round about way of asking me on a date? No, of course not. Not that I wanted to go on a date.

"Anna?"

"Right – no, let's just go back to the ranch. The only thing happening between now and tonight is a nap.

Thanks for rescuing me today. Not sure I would have found upright without a push."

\*\*\*

The barn was a mob scene. Paparazzi were camped out in the parking lot waiting for Misty to arrive. The Joy Chorus kids charmed everyone as they collected tickets. Simon beamed when he saw me, and Beau promised to tell him a story later about a pretty girl and her hero. We made our way through the crowd to front row seats. A familiar face sat down next to Beau.

"Anastasia! Imagine seeing you here, in cowboy boots no less! Hello Beau, I don't think we've met. I'm Kelly Rogers from *Celebrity* magazine. I learned a lot about you in my research for this story. Sounds like you are the heart behind the music for Misty's new album. She has only nice things to say about you. What convinced you to release the songs to her after your breakup? Misty wouldn't tell."

Kelly should have dug a little deeper in her research of Beau Laurel. She would get nowhere probing him for information. He flashed her a brilliant smile.

"Miss Rogers, far be it for me to tell a lady's secrets." And with that he turned his back to her.

Kelly was unaccustomed to being ignored; most celebrities would sell their mother to get face time with her. She was speechless. Beau offered to get me a drink from the bar, and I offered to go with him. Kelly was left sitting there, nobody to talk to. Kelly had turned on me before. I had nothing to gain by walking into another one of her snares.

I tugged on Beau's sleeve. "Beau, did you catch that? Kelly interviewed Misty. This story might make the cover. What do you think she said?"

"I don't care what Misty said. I do not live and die by *Celebrity* magazine."

"No, but good press could launch the *BACK TO THE MUSIC* series into the stratosphere!"

Beau sighed. "Anna, for all your savvy, you are pretty naïve. That Kelly woman does not care about the music – she cares about gossip. Anything she prints will pander to that."

Did he think I fell off a turnip truck? Yes, she was digging for gossip! Gossip makes the world go round, especially in show business. Gossip was the hook! But success for the Series could ride piggy back. Our little venue could become the hottest ticket in country music. Beau was right, he was wise to stay in the background. Getting too close to the spotlight can get you burned, and he had no equipment to fight the fire. Misty, on the other hand, loved the spotlight. My guess was she handled Kelly just fine.

I patted Beau on the back. "You have to break a few eggs to make a cake, Beau."

"Let's just hope the cake is worth it." He maneuvered through the crowd towards the back of the room, away from Kelly and her snooping. The couple who took our front row seats were delighted. Misty put on a fabulous show, with a "Thank You" to Beau for contributing to her new album. Then she brought the crowd to tears with her soulful tribute to Joy. Simon and Jordan waved to me from their seats in the booth with Squawk. Melissa surprised us with Mo's famous brownies, which I devoured before the encore. My parents laughed with Boone and Kit at their table. All was well in my world, and I was thankful Judge Goodman had sentenced me to community service with these great people.

# CHAPTER 13

Have you ever been caught in a flash flood? The key word is flash. It sneaks up on you after an intense rainfall, turning lawns into lakes and roadways into rivers. Foolish people underestimate the depth of the water and regularly drive right in. You've seen the pictures on the news; guys, typically in big trucks, waving an SOS from their open window begging for a rescue. We had a flash flood in Los Angeles, and I mocked the macho men who were too stubborn to heed the warning signs of high water. From my couch, watching events unfold on TV, it was obvious they should have stayed home.

I should have paid more attention. As I floated about in my post-concert bliss, waters were rising around me and I missed the danger signs. Like those dopes on TV, I plowed into a hazard rather than take a detour to avoid it.

The morning after Misty's performance began with a farewell brunch for my parents. They had become fast friends with the Laurels in their short stay, planning to visit even after my stint in Texas was over. Not that I had a clue where I was headed. But I could not live in Sojourner House forever, and in a few short weeks my service commitment at the Chorus would end. Kit refused to discuss my departure, assuring me I had not overstayed my welcome. My mom encouraged me to stay in Texas, accepting Kit's invitation to celebrate Christmas at Honor Ranch if I was still there. She liked it that I now "ate brownies, wore sneakers, and had friends I didn't pay to hang out with me." I think she was referring to Maria, but I didn't ask.

My mom had a point; I was happy in Pleasant. Did I just think that? Happy in small town USA, herding teenagers and selling concert tickets at an obscure honky tonk barn? I'd read about Stockholm Syndrome, when hostages form attachments to their captors (OK, it was King Kong the movie, not a book, but the principle is the same.) Maybe I qualified. If someone had told me just a few months ago that I might want to stay here, I would have checked myself in for a psych evaluation. The absence of a nearby Neiman Marcus was enough to set me running. Yet here I was, planning Christmas with my parents at Honor Ranch.

The barn was closed on Monday, giving us all a break after the frenzied preparations for the Chorus concert and *BACK TO THE MUSIC* launch. I was enjoying a late morning coffee when Rachel texted me: "LOVE the Belle Bridal ad! Grace Jackson sent me an early copy. Being a fairy godmother is fun! Let me know when you leverage that choir gig for a job in LA. And get out of there before you start wearing boots and saying y'all!"

Red flag number one. Hard to imagine I could leverage court ordered community service into a windfall (and it is a Chorus, not a choir!). Besides, I had to address a few issues before heading back to LA. Mable's biscuits and Millie's pie had thrown a wrench into my modeling form. I asked Rachel to send me a photo of the ad, but she refused, didn't want to spoil the fun of me seeing it in print. I wondered if Tish got an advance copy as well, but my message to her went unanswered. Ah, red flag number two. It is all so clear now, but at the time I assumed everyone was recovering from our crazy schedule.

I did hear from Misty. She was headed back to Nashville on Cloud 9, excited to release her new single after such a successful concert.

"Anastasia, don't rot there in Pleasant! Your talents are underappreciated. I meant it when I offered you a job. You have a sixth sense about promotion and I want to maximize my momentum. Come to Nashville. You'd love it."

It's nice to be wanted. I told her I'd think about it. I didn't plan to think about it, but it seemed rude to refuse her outright. And what could I say, I planned to hang out here with no job or income, but that was better than riding the exciting wave of her success? I'd look like an idiot. Because it was idiotic.

Duke texted me on Tuesday morning: "No need to come in today." That's all – no explanation. Tuesdays is when I usually help Shirley map out which concerts need a promotion push and formulate our plan to sell out. She had replaced the M & Ms with marbles in a jar so my hands didn't get dirty. We had a wager going, betting on how long it would take me to sell the remaining tickets for a concert. Shirley had a hidden competitive side. I hoped she never entered a casino, it could prove disastrous. Shirley did not like to lose.

When I arrived at the barn on Wednesday afternoon all was quiet. The Chorus took a hiatus until after Christmas. I'd planned to help the staff pack up the kids' outfits until their next concert in the Spring. One thing I learned in modeling was how to pack with minimum wrinkling (FYI, rolling is sometimes the best way to ensure things stay fresh, but in the case of formal dresses, padded hangers and good garment bags are required). Duke intercepted me on my way in.

"Anna, come on in to my office. I have good news! Your extra work for the Chorus in concert prep means you've fulfilled your community service commitment. Judge Goodman signed off and you are free to go." Red flag, red flag.

I was stunned. Something was off – the barn was usually buzzing with activity, but Tish was nowhere to be found. Upon sentencing I started marking off days in my planner, counting the moments until I was free. Now I couldn't remember the last time I had drawn a red X, or even consulted my calendar for that matter. I fought back a rush of tears.

"Duke, I don't know what to say. I thought I had a few more weeks to figure out what's next. For the time being, I'd like to continue volunteering with the kids. Who will Simon dazzle with his latest Calculus discovery if I am not there?"

My humor fell flat. Duke was uncharacteristically quiet. And uncomfortable. He kept smoothing his hair while avoiding eye contact with me. An invoice on his desk captured his attention. I waited, finally stooping down to get in his line of vision.

"Duke?"

"Anna, I'm not sure that's a good idea. I appreciate all you've done for us here. Ticket sales have never been stronger, and the kids love you. But please understand I am in a tough spot."

"What kind of tough spot? Last time I checked you welcomed all the help you could get with the Chorus!"

Duke took a deep breath. "Yes. And I'm sure you think Tish is overreacting, but I'm walking a tightrope here. On one hand Tish and I are business partners, on the other I am her dad. In this case, the dad side had to win. Give it some time."

I was confused. "Duke, is Tish mad at me? More than usual? I know I rub her the wrong way, but what are you talking about?"

Duke looked like I had delivered a left hook, all off balance. "You haven't seen it? The Belle Bridal ad?"

"No……" A snake of anxiety slithered up from my gut to my throat. Duke handed me the advance copy. There I was, front and center in the 'extra' shot the photographer took as a souvenir. The layout was designed to mimic a story, not an ad, and if you missed the miniature ADVERTISEMENT buried at the top of the page you would never know it was a promotion. The headline read "Be the Belle of your Ball." Under the photo, the copy read:

*"Anastasia DeMars knows that beauty shines brightest when helping others. She volunteers her time at the Joy Chorus, a non-profit choir that gives teenagers in Pleasant, Texas a place to belong. Anastasia sets an example we should all follow this holiday season! She inspired Belle Bridal to make every Joy Chorus member the star of their show by donating dresses, suits, shoes and accessories for this year's Christmas concert.*

*Be the Belle of YOUR Ball! When you choose Belle Bridal to dress your wedding party you help us bring beauty to deserving organizations like the Joy Chorus."*

Alrighty then. Tish's rant last week made more sense. She wasn't calling Misty an attention whore, she was referring to me. That's why Duke had asked her to wait until the concert was over to deal with it. Tish obviously thought I had engineered the donation from Belle Bridal to promote myself. Rachel's comment about me leveraging this ad took on a new light.

"Duke, I had no idea this was the plan for the ad. Lacey at Belle Bridal surprised me with that dress. I did not order it. In fact, I think my agent will be ticked that I am featured in an ad without a contract! I did not give them permission to use my image, or call me a volunteer! Surely you can see it's not what it looks like!"

Duke swallowed hard. "Actually, the contract we signed with Belle spelled it out that anyone associated with the Joy Chorus could be featured in the campaign. The agreement was they give us clothes, we give them a photo op. No compensation for anyone, so you were under contract through the side door."

Great. My effort to do a good deed backfired, and I was the one with egg all over my face.

"So Tish thinks I arranged the Belle donation for my own career purposes? Really? Duke, c'mon."

"Anna, you insisted on running with the ball and Tish had no control. Ever since her mom died she has survived by carefully controlling everything here. The Watering Hole, and the Chorus, are her lifeline. You swooped in and invaded her territory. She doesn't know how to handle it."

Frustration traveled from my toes to my mouth. "No kidding! She is in over her head, Duke! The Watering Hole could be very profitable if you'd hire someone who knows what they're doing. Tish is an artist, not a business person. And she is miserable to boot! Snappy at everyone, barking at the staff. Everyone tip toes around her like she is a ticking bomb. The only time she appears to be happy is on stage, but she is too chicken to put herself out there. That's not my fault. And who do you think was behind the *BACK TO THE MUSIC* series? Tish? Misty? No! It was me! Did I do that for my career? NO! I did it for YOURS. You're welcome!"

With that I grabbed my bag and stormed out of the barn. You can make a quick exit when wearing sneakers. I fled to my car and flew onto the freeway at top speed. They didn't want my help? FINE! Let them limp along with Little Miss Crabby Pants at the helm, but hey, nobody would challenge her or hurt her feelings! Talk about small town drama. Queen Bee Tish had to be puppet master for her subjects, logic be damned. Let them all be miserable together, I didn't care. Simon might miss me, but nobody else would even notice I was gone. Thanks for the lessons, Judge Goodman – people in Pleasant were no different from the sharks in LA, they just wore boots and had less expensive haircuts. When it comes down to it, everyone expects the worst from each other and nobody disappoints. No good deed goes unpunished and all that. Somehow I found myself parked in front of Sojourner House, no idea how I got there. The tirade in my head (or out loud – I think I was shouting in the car) consumed my attention.

I should have known something was up when Lacey gave me that dress. Southern hospitality sucked me in to thinking it was just a gift. I felt like a fool, and she was not getting away with it unscathed. Lacey answered the phone with a chirpy hello.

"Anna! Have you seen the ad? So cute of all those kids! Belle's management is very happy with the outcome!"

Did this girl always speak in exclamation points?

"Yes Lacey, I saw the ad. Not what we talked about. The shot with me in it was supposed to be a souvenir, not the feature, remember? How did it happen that I am part of the story?"

Lacey paused. "You sound upset, Anna. I hope you aren't upset! That was the plan, but once *Celebrity* magazine put their cover story together, Grace thought it made more sense to tie the ad to the article. She thought the ad might get more attention if you were in the photo. At least that's what Grace told me when she sent the advance copy. I assumed you knew. You look great in the picture by the way!"

OK, maybe I was wrong about Lacey; she really was trying to do something nice when she gave me that dress. This girl did not have a deceptive bone in her body. Grace Jackson must be to blame. She used me to boost her ad's visibility without my permission. Or at least without me knowing she HAD my permission. Right. She was operating within the parameters of the contract. Any marketing professional would seek to maximize the impact of the ad, especially since Misty made the cover story. Misty. What had she said about me in her interview to tie me to the ad?

I sat in my car, unsure who to call next. Diane. I needed to give my agent a head's up before she opened a magazine to my smiling face. Her response? How can we use this to our advantage in securing more good press! Hmmm, let's wait until Misty's interview is published. Experience with Kelly Rogers made me gun shy. For all I knew she mocked my 'volunteer' work at the barn since it was court ordered. That detail neutralizes the hero factor. Nothing to do but wait until it hit the stands on Friday. It was too late to change anything, and I was NOT giving Kelly the satisfaction of thinking she got to me again.

I hugged the steering wheel and succumbed to the emotion of the day. I pounded the dashboard. Tish's words from last week, assumed to be about Misty, flung back at me like a boomerang. She called me an attention whore, accused me of using the Chorus for my own purposes. I'd gone WAY beyond the call of duty to help the kids, the barn's profits, and Tish. Let's ask Colby Jensen if anybody had heard of him before I started working in the box office! Talk to the kids about how much they loved wearing their new concert clothes. I did that! Tish sulked around playing the victim for Duke, slamming me for trying to make a difference. She was pathetic.

I heard a tapping. Kit's face was peering through my window. I wasn't sure how much of my tantrum she'd witnessed, but my face was blotchy and covered in streaky mascara. I told you I am not a pretty crier. I waved, hoping she would go away. She didn't. Tap tap tap. Kit is persistent, I'll give her that. I rolled the window down; no point trying to erase the damage on my face. Kit leaned into my car.

"Hello there, Anna! How's your day? I noticed your car screaming SOS and came out here to rescue it from you."

She had witnessed my meltdown. Great. Maybe Beau would show up and my humiliation would be complete.

Kit opened the car door. "Come inside. I'm sure we can solve your problem without incurring property damage. And if not, you can throw things. That sometimes helps."

Most people would offer hugs and sympathy, but Kit understood me better. What I wanted to throw was Tish. Or Belle Bridal. Or Kelly Rogers, depending on what she printed about me. I took a deep breath and tried pulling myself together.

"Thanks Kit, but I think I just need some time alone. I'll be fine."

Kit smiled. "That's what they all say. Come inside. Everyone is gone this afternoon, so it's just us. This is not an invitation. More of an order. You live in my cottage, so you really can't say no."

I followed her into the kitchen, dropping my head into my hands at the counter. Kit pushed a tissue box in my direction then busied herself making a cup of coffee. For a woman with a big mouth she knew when to keep it shut and wait. Silence was more effective than peppering me with questions. The events of the past few days spun in my head, gathering speed to form an ice pick drilling into my left temple. Crying always gives me a headache.

"I don't even know where to start."

Kit nodded. "Let's assume you are mad. Who ticked you off?"

"Tish. And a whole score of other people. I think. Not sure yet, won't know until this week's *Celebrity* magazine comes out."

"Let's start with Tish then."

"She hates me! All I've tried to do since I showed up at the barn is help. And what have I gotten for it? Blame and pushback. She called me an attention whore!"

"To your face?"

"No, I overheard her whining to Duke. No matter what I do, she is jealous. The kids at the Chorus love me, which should be a good thing, but she makes it all about me invading her turf. Profits have gone through the roof at the barn because I took over ticket sales, but she fights me on every promotion idea. I even engineered the *BACK TO THE MUSIC* series! Everyone pussyfoots around her because her mom died, and in the meantime, the barn is headed for disaster. Tish is the problem, not me! But she can't stand losing any control, so Duke told me my time at the barn was finished and not to come back. I got fired from a volunteer job!"

Tears erupted again. Kit ignored them. "So let me get this straight. You have helped the barn in all kinds of ways, but Tish is jealous so Duke kicked you out. Is that the short story? Sounds like I'm missing something. Duke is her dad, yes, but he also loves that barn and is a reasonable guy. Does he know the Music series was your idea? You'd think he would want to promote you, not fire you."

"He knows it now! I told him when I left. Did he think Tish came up with that brainstorm? Tish couldn't sell out a show if she GAVE the tickets away!"

Kit handed me a glass of water. "Anna, I'm confused. Back up. You're mad at Duke because he didn't guess the Series was your idea? Why didn't you just tell him in the first place?"

She made it sound like it was my fault! OK, OK, back up was good advice. I started over.

"Kit, when I was sentenced to community service at the Chorus I was humiliated. That video made me look like a spoiled Hollywood brat. The people at the barn – especially the kids – were nice to me. I wanted to help, so I arranged for Belle Bridal to donate their concert clothes. In return, the Chorus was to appear in an ad. Well, that ad ended up featuring me, and Tish came unglued. I didn't know they were going to use me in the campaign! But Tish assumes the worst about me every time. It's a stupid ad! I'm not trying to overthrow her! She's threatened because I know more about promoting the artists than she does. Tish is miserable at the barn, but she won't admit it. So Duke fired me to keep her incompetence under the radar. I could run that place a thousand times better than she does." I was getting wound up again.

I saw the dawning of understanding in Kit's eyes just as I was coming to the same conclusion. She almost beat me to it.

"Is that what you want to do, Anna? Manage the barn and stay in Pleasant?"

Is it? Is that what I wanted to do? I COULD make the barn a premier venue. But no, this was a court ordered stop on the way back to civilization. I just didn't like the injustice of being thrown out of a job I wasn't even paid to do. If I could just set the record straight I would be on my merry way, out of Tish's fragile universe.

"I want Duke to understand I was only trying to help. For once in my life I didn't seek the spotlight, and the whole situation backfired on me. I don't want him to think I am an attention whore."

"So talk to him. And Tish. Explain what happened."

"Tish would never listen. And on top of it all, Misty Hart gave *Celebrity* magazine an interview. I have no idea what she might say."

Kit shrugged. "So what? What does that have to do with you? You don't even know her. How did you get her to do that concert, anyway? Did your people contact her people? Do you still have people?" Kit laughed.

"Well, Beau actually got Misty to sign on. He gave up the rights to their songs if she would agree to kick off the Series. He was just trying to help the barn – no danger of them getting back together! But while Misty was here we ended up drinking bourbon in her dressing room, and I can tell you she is no fan of Tish Valentine. Misty never would have agreed to perform if Tish had been the one asking."

The mention of Misty made Kit all twitchy. "Watch your back around that one. So she extorted those songs out of Beau! She always takes advantage of his good nature. Why would he give her anything? That girl just won't go away!"

The last thing I needed was a Kit rant about Misty. "Misty just saw the Series as an opportunity for good press. It was a win/win, good for her and good for the barn."

"It wasn't a win for Beau. What did he get out of it?"

"What did I get out of what."

Kit and I both practically herniated a disk spinning around to find Beau standing at the door. No telling how much he had heard. His eyes were on his mom, and I thought it best to let the two of them hash it out without me in the middle. Maybe I was getting wiser. Kit, however, opted for loud.

"Why did you give Misty Hart those songs? You've been holding them all this time, and now you just hand them over?"

Beau's gaze shifted to me. "Mom, it's none of your business what I do with my music. But I'm curious how you found out. The only people who knew I released those songs to her were me and Misty."

His eyes bored into mine. I could see his jaw clenching; his tone was calm, but fury boiled beneath the surface. He waited. I fidgeted on my bar stool. "Don't blame your mom, Beau. I told her. Misty explained how those songs got buried – she feels badly about what happened! But I shouldn't have said anything. I'm sorry."

He stood there for a few more moments, anger burning in his eyes. Then he turned on his heel and went out the door.

I followed him out onto the porch. "Beau, don't be mad. I didn't mean to cause trouble between you and your mom."

Beau headed towards his truck without looking at me. "What did you mean to do, Anna? How did you end up in a conversation with Misty about my music? Let me guess – your trip down Devil's River? Did you two enjoy dissecting me during your bourbon binge?"

"No! She invited me and Sarah into her dressing room after the concert for a drink. I was curious! Misty obviously broke your heart and I wanted to know what was so intriguing about her. The bourbon might have greased the confessional, I admit. But she only had nice things to say about you!"

Beau spun around and faced me. "I took a risk inviting her here, Anna. You should have left it alone. Who else have you told?"

Ouch. "Nobody. Well, I may have told Duke that the *BACK TO THE MUSIC* series was my idea, but I didn't tell him your part in it. At least I don't think I did. I was mad! He fired me from the barn! And if that music was so important, why did you make a deal with her?"

Beau got in his truck. "Forget it, Anna. Misty has a big mouth. I should have known she couldn't keep anything to herself." He slammed the door closed and sped away. I was left standing on the driveway, his words echoing in my head. I had never seen Beau so agitated. If Misty was a big mouth, I was one too. Good thing he didn't catch me listening through the vent; that would have added eavesdropper to my resume. But the *Celebrity* magazine interview! Hopefully Misty was gracious to Beau in print. I considered calling her to find out. Was it better to be prepared, or ignorant and hope for the best? Ignorant won. I'd had enough drama for one day and retreated to my cottage. After collapsing on the sofa, I realized Beau never answered my question. Why had he made a deal with Misty?

Everything was falling apart, so I jumped on board the train of misery. Solitude inspired a cleansing cry in my little house of sorrows. Weeping makes me tired, so I drifted off into a restless sleep, dreaming that my mug shot was on the cover of *Celebrity.* The headline read "Big Mouth Gets Jail Time." The picture had been photo shopped to make my mouth as big as my whole head, and mascara was dripping down my blotchy face. In the corner was a photo of Beau: "Country Crooner gets married." No mention of the lucky bride. Even my dreams conspired against me.

# CHAPTER 14

Thirst woke me up at 3:00 am, my face imprinted with the tweed pattern of the decorative sofa pillow. The crick in my neck testified to the risks of sleeping on a small couch without benefit of therapeutic support. I stumbled into the kitchen to get a glass of juice. My dream hovered around the fringes of memory, mocking me. Yup, a glance in the mirror revealed puffy eyes encrusted with yesterday's mascara. In a single day I had been booted from the barn, thrown a public tantrum, brokered a fight between Kit and her son, and convinced Beau I wasn't to be trusted. Impressive. And the *Celebrity* interview hadn't even been released yet. I didn't know Misty well enough to guess how that might go, but my gut predicted it would go badly for me. I was on a roll.

I washed my face and collapsed into the comfort of a real bed, but sleep evaded me. At 5:00 am I gave up and made a pot of strong coffee. It's the one thing I do well in the kitchen, and my coffee could give Mable's a run for the money. Lights were already on at Beau's place; not unusual, he often got out in the field early. More surprising was seeing lights on at the main house. Beau appeared, but instead of heading for the ranch he parked his truck in front of his parents' house. Kit and Boone came through their door a few minutes later, travel cases in hand. They were obviously leaving town. That was weird. I knew Sarah and Kit had plans to decorate for the holidays over the coming weekend, and Beau was headlining at The Watering Hole on Saturday night. Ben's house was still dark, so something less than an emergency must have come up. I'd have to probe Millie for information.

The day stretched before me, long and lonely. No barn, no Chorus. No plan for my future. Maybe it was time to call Diane, get some irons in the work fire going. When Frank arrived in Texas for Thanksgiving he told me I looked healthy, which meant I'd gained enough weight to disqualify me for runway jobs. But I had put some distance between me and the Fame Cosmetics debacle. Rachel might be a prophet; the Belle Bridal ad could bridge the gap from diva to humanitarian. I took stock of my assets. A little heavier, yes, but my skin and hair looked good. The slower pace of life in Pleasant had rounded out my features. I looked less hungry (I was less hungry. Go figure). If Fame blackballed me, maybe I should widen my net, do a reality dancing show to get some positive exposure. Even ousted politicians made a comeback after a reality dancing show, and my baggage was much lighter than theirs.

Who said things look better in the morning? I was considering a reality TV show! Time to regroup. What I needed was a talking to by my mom. Perhaps that is the measure of an adult - the realization you need to be talked off the bridge by someone wiser, and the maturity to ask them to do it. Ginger would still be getting her beauty sleep, so our conversation would have to wait. But I could play her tape in my head:

"Anna, you are a gifted woman with many talents! Learn from your mistakes, don't settle for easy just because you are scared or ashamed. You are destined for great things. Now go after it!"

That speech pumped me up more when it wasn't canned, but the hour was early and it would have to do. I needed a job, a paying job. I could not continue to live off the Laurel land now that my assignment at the barn had ended. What are my many talents? Being photogenic seems more like luck than skill, so I scratched that off the list. Sometimes I talk my way into trouble, but I was adept at talking my way out. OK, except yesterday with Duke, that was the exception to the rule. I could think out of the box, problem solve. My competitive nature liked to win; that's why selling concert tickets gave me a thrill. Marketing came easily to me. The success of the *BACK TO THE MUSIC* series proved I had good promotion ideas, and I didn't even do it for the acclaim. Notoriety is overrated, as my run-in with the Pleasant County sheriff taught me, but success is intoxicating. Creating an event that brought people together was fun. Misty could be right, I might have a future in promotion.

What did I have to lose? I sent Misty an email, offering my services. Her reply was brief; "Traveling this weekend. Let's talk Monday. I can use your help setting some things up. Go shopping! Lose the sneakers, get some Nashville clothes, and don't be afraid of a little bling."

Shopping. That I can do. Before I headed downtown I popped my head into the main house. The kitchen was perfumed with cinnamon and nutmeg. Millie presided over a tray of festive gingerbread men, one going into the oven while the other came out.

"Anna! I'm getting a head start on Christmas baking – best to freeze some things, you never know what might come up. We can't celebrate Christmas without our cookies and breads! Would you like to try one?"

Millie's face was so hopeful, I couldn't say no.

"Millie, I saw Kit and Boone leaving early this morning with Beau. Everything OK?"

"My, you were up early! Kit's dad had a fall and they are headed to west Texas. Nothing too serious, but Kit wanted to make sure her mother had some help. Are you OK? Looks like you slept on a waffle iron."

Never fall into a deep sleep with a heavily pattered pillow under your cheek. I assured her I was fine. Fringed jackets and embellished jeans were calling my name so I made a quick exit, an extra cookie in hand. I'm not sure who was happiest about that, Millie or me.

Shopping. My former self had indulged in the hunt like a drug. I even shopped for clothes to wear while shopping. Daily life in LA had this fevered pitch that demanded obsessive attention to detail; the fear of being seen without looking my best had trumped all reasonable boundaries. Grocery store run? A carefully edited outfit of 'old' jeans ($400) and a haphazardly tucked blouse (it took lots of practice to get that just right). Ditch the stilettos and throw on a pair of comfortable booties and you have perfected the 'I look like this all the time and just ran out of the house without thinking' vibe. Beach messy locks completed the illusion. Dressing took longer than the actual shopping, even on stock up day. And a premiere, or an awards show? All day. Hey, all day for 2 days. When your image is your whole life, it demands your full and undivided attention.

My days in Pleasant had broken me of the shopping habit. Two pair of flats and some sneakers had replaced my extensive shoe collection; it's hard to serve snacks to teenagers in spiky heels without looking ridiculous. Now I realize it's hard to buy lettuce and toilet paper in spiky heels without looking ridiculous, but that wisdom was earned after a detour through small town Texas. I did not want to tumble down that rabbit hole again, and the seductive lure of the shopping gods called out to me at the thought of getting Nashville ready. So I tucked a photo of Cassidy Simms in my purse before I left. As the youngest girl in a family of 4 daughters, she had never owned a new dress. Her unmasked joy at wearing the Belle Bridal outfit to the Christmas concert was priceless. Cassidy would be my reminder to make every purchase carefully. This might take practice.

Victory! I found versatile pieces to mix and match, and splurged on only one item – a timeless leather jacket I could wear with jeans or an evening gown alike. Oh, and a far less expensive bedazzled wrap that was just for fun. I stumbled into my cottage, dragging my tissue papered treasures behind me.

What I needed was a refreshing glass of wine and a snack. Shopping with purpose, instead of wild abandon, took a lot more restraint and energy than I'd imagined

I turned on the kitchen light and jumped. A man was lounging in the chair by the fireplace, watching me with a look that can only be described as amused. A man with a gun on his lap. I was too startled to scream. The picture in Millie's kitchen came to mind. Paul. And he appeared to be drunk.

I stared back. My heart threatened to leap from my chest and it took me a moment to catch my breath. The gun had captured my attention so I wasn't about to make any fast moves. Paul seemed to be waiting for me to say something. I finally found my voice.

"Hello. Forgive me for my lack of manners, but I wasn't expecting to find a strange man in my house!" It seemed wise not to draw attention to the gun.

"Hmm. I wasn't expecting to find a stranger in MY house."

"I'm Anna. Let me guess - Paul?" I'd learned from a Dateline episode it was best to connect with a potential captor by giving him your name, becoming their friend. Not that Paul was holding me hostage – yet. But no need to take unnecessary chances. He was the one armed. I had to use what tools I had in my box.

Paul smirked. "Bingo. Let me guess. You must be a struggling musician hoping to study at the feet of the sensitive Beau Laurel. You secretly pine for him and write love songs in hopes of capturing his heart. By the looks of your haul at Nordstrom you have a benefactor, maybe your mother, who also hopes you will land the mysterious country singer and use his charge account instead of hers. Too bad she doesn't realize Beau will never amount to anything because he is too holy to play the games required for success in the music business."

Bitterness practically oozed from Paul. I wasn't sure if I should let him ramble, or distract him. He didn't seem in a hurry to hurt me. Maybe he just needed a listening ear. I slowly sat down in the opposite chair. Paul looked at me with disgust.

"Do you what the name Laurel means? Honor. Beau's name literally means beautiful honor. No wonder he is such a self-righteous bastard. My parents set him up for that. And they probably moved you in here to help Beau forget that tramp Misty. She could never live up to the Laurel name. Just don't let them find out what skeletons you have hidden or you will be out of here in a gunshot."

No wonder Paul was a thorn in everyone's side; he was caustic even when compromised by booze. His smirk made me want to slap him, but again, he had the gun. Humor and hospitality seemed a better approach.

"You get high marks for charm, Paul, but a failing grade for content. I was arrested and sentenced to community service at the Joy Chorus. Sarah offered me a place to live since I am from LA and have no friends or family in Texas. My sentence is complete and I'm moving to Nashville next week, so feel free to move back in once I'm gone. There is no benefactor. I am a successful model with my own income. You should stick to your day job and leave fortune telling to the professionals. I hear you are good with technology. Can I offer you a drink?"

"If you've heard about me you probably know a drink is the last thing you should offer."

"Well, how about you give me the gun and I give you a drink anyway. Seems like a fair trade. But I only have wine – hope that's OK."

"If you only have wine, I may be forced to use the gun."

I didn't know how to respond to that. Paul's deadpan expression erupted into full blown hilarity.

"I'm just kidding! Here, I'll put the gun on the table and pour us both a stiff bourbon. I used to live here, after rehab. Had to hide the good stuff." Paul reached into the TV armoire and pulled out a half empty bottle of Makers Mark, stashed behind a stack of DVDs.

I took the opportunity to retrieve the gun from the table, pointing it towards the wall away from us on the floor. I had never handled a gun before. It was terrifying. Paul handed me a juice glass with a finger of the amber liquid. His glass, I noticed, was considerably more full. He settled back in to his chair, raising his glass to me before taking a gulp. He didn't appear to be going anywhere.

"So, Paul. What are you doing here? It makes a girl a bit nervous to come home to an armed stranger. Since we've never met, I'll assume you mean me no harm. Right?"

"Sure, if you mean ME no harm."

"Of course. Do you need a place to stay? Millie could set you up in the main house. Your parents and Beau are in west Texas. Your grandfather had a fall."

Paul laughed out loud. "Did his super hero cape get tangled in his saddle? Did he fall from his white horse while saving the world? My grandparents are always rescuing someone else while their own grandson is shut out of the family business. Serves him right."

A sharp edge of anger replaced his bantering tone, and I did not want to fuel that. Drunk and angry can make a man do all kinds of terrible things.

"Paul, Millie adores you. She keeps your picture in the kitchen and tells funny stories of you stealing cookies right out of the oven. If you need something, I'm sure she would help. Want me to call over there? At the very least she will feed you a great dinner, and I know she would love to see you."

The mention of Millie seemed to soften the hostility building in Paul. I was looking for an exit strategy; this situation could turn on a moment and I wanted it to turn in the right direction. Paul eventually nodded.

"OK."

I carefully reached for my phone, afraid to take my eyes off Paul while keeping the gun well behind me. I rang the main house, hoping Millie hadn't taken the night off since everyone else was gone. Faithful Millie! She answered on the second ring.

"Laurel residence. May I help you?"

"Millie, it's Anna. I have a guest in my cottage who would like to see you. Can you take a walk over here?"

"Oh Anna. I'm in the middle of baking and the timer will go off in a few minutes. Can you come here?"

I didn't want to take any chances with Paul between here and there. He was considerably more drunk now than when I first arrived.

"It was going to be a surprise, but Paul is here at my house. Can you visit once your timer goes off?"

I could hear Millie gasp through the phone. Her hesitation in responding made me nervous. "Yes, yes of course. Give me a minute or two."

Paul's eyes were closed. Maybe he was going to sleep. I decided to leave him alone. Millie might have some ideas about what to do next, and in the meantime I didn't need to poke the bear.

The front door burst open. Ben filled the doorway, with Millie a few steps behind. He must have been at the house when I called. Relief flooded over me. Ben surveyed the room and saw the gun on the floor behind my chair. He grabbed Paul by the shirt, shaking him awake. "WHAT IS GOING ON HERE!"

Relief turned to panic as Paul took a swing at Ben. Millie scooted into the room, grabbed the gun, and quickly unloaded it, pocketing the bullets. Paul was too drunk to be a match for Ben and he shoved Paul back into the chair. Ben was enraged.

"Anna, are you OK? Millie, call the police!"

"Ben, wait! He did not threaten me! Can't you talk to him? Why call the police – he's drunk!"

Ben did not take his eyes off Paul. "He's always drunk. Trust me, he didn't come here to talk. What were you doing with the gun, Paul? That's MY gun! You stole it from me last time you were here. What were you planning to do?"

Paul glared at Ben with pure hatred in his eyes. His reply was frighteningly calm. "I planned to shoot myself in the head and give you all one last mess to clean up."

Ben glared back. "You are sick. You need help. But you aren't going to take us all down with you. Millie, call the police. He needs to go to detox."

Tears were streaming down Millie's face. Paul turned his eye to her. "Don't ever say you love me again. You are as bad as the rest of them."

Millie's face dissolved into despair. I patted her on the back. "Millie, you go back to the house. I'll make the call." She fled, taking the gun with her. Paul seemed to have lost his bravado and slumped in the chair. Ben raised his eyebrows at me. "Call. We have been through this before. You need to trust me."

I did. Paul didn't fight the officers who led him away. Defeated, he left without another word. Ben breathed a huge sigh of relief as the squad car left the ranch. I discovered I had a pounding headache, probably from clenching my jaw throughout the ordeal.

"Ben, what happens now?"

All of Ben's anger had dissipated. His head dropped into his hands, his body racked with sobs. Ben was always so in charge; I was shocked to see him break down. I waited. After a few minutes he wiped his eyes, looking very tired.

"In the short run, he goes to detox and sobers up. I call his probation officer to report Paul stole a gun, loaded it, and threatened to use it. Those are all probation violations. They will keep him in the county jail until he gets a court date."

"Do you have to call his probation officer? I don't think he meant to hurt anybody. Isn't a suicide threat a cry for help?"

"Anna, everything Paul does is a cry for help. The last thing I want to do is turn my brother in, but you can't give a free pass to an addict who will steal a gun to prove a point. Someone is going to get hurt. At least in jail he is safe. They might sentence him to another rehab program. But his recovery is up to him. The more we try to help, the more hostile he gets. Let me tell you how this incident will play out. You are now part of the evil empire because you called the police. Millie betrayed Paul because she brought me over here when you called the house. I am always enemy number one because I refuse to let him do any more damage to our family. What you won't hear is how Paul is responsible for any of it. He has no chance of recovery until he accepts responsibility for his own crap."

"Why does he hate you and Beau so much? I could read it in his eyes."

Ben splashed cold water on his face from the kitchen sink. "Paul is a slave to addiction. Any success we have rubs his nose in that. You know what? Of the three of us, Paul is the smartest. But he always took short cuts. He refused to work hard or follow the rules. Now his goal is to make us suffer, make us pay for enjoying a life he rejected."

Three kids, all raised in the same family, and one goes way off the rails. How does that happen? My mom isn't one to wallow, but I knew she was disappointed when I quit college for LA. Kit and Boone must be devastated to see their son so lost. No wonder Beau kept his distance.

Sarah appeared at the door with a stricken look on her face. "Ben? Millie told me Paul was here! She is very upset, but insists y'all come eat some dinner. What happened? Where is he?"

I followed them reluctantly to the main house. My appetite had disappeared, but no sense making Millie feel even worse by refusing to eat. She is certain most of what ails you can be fixed with comfort food and chocolate cake. The shortest path to numbing sleep was straight through a meal of pot roast and cornbread. Funny thing – comfort food tees you right up to enjoy the cake. I was learning to appreciate Millie's wisdom. We all went to bed fortified by the knowledge that even during a crisis, some things remain stable.

***

Friday morning announced itself with a deafening silence. The chaos of the past 48 hours almost made Misty's interview a footnote. At this point, nothing she said could make matters worse between me and Tish. Or me and Beau. I could add Paul to the list of Texans happy to see me leave the state. Hopefully nothing in the article would compromise my ability to work in Nashville. As someone new to the music business, I couldn't be too much of a smarty pants. I couldn't come off as a ditz, either. My plan was to lay low, learn what I could, and go from there. Maybe Misty never mentioned my name; artists don't like to share the credit, so the odds were in my favor despite my earlier trepidation.

I was going to miss Sojourner House. In a few short months I felt more at home here than I ever felt in LA. Any desire to live in a sprawling mansion had evaporated. This cozy little haven was peaceful and easy to vacuum. I often teased my mom about her standard for the perfect home – manageable enough to clean yourself if funds or staff disappeared. Now I understood. There was freedom in not depending on other people to wash your delicates. Privacy in this fishbowl age was priceless; no need for non-disclosure agreements, a stable of lawyers, or sophisticated security firewalls just to keep the cameras out. Anna Martin barely recognized a girl known as Anastasia DeMars. In Nashville, I'd have to work hard to create my own quiet space. Working for Misty would throw me back into the public frenzy, but with some effort I could stay behind the curtain.

Most of what I possessed in Texas could squeeze into two large suitcases. Maybe I'd hire Maria to sell or donate most of what filled my storage unit. It seemed silly to move all those clothes cross country. I could send her a list of the things I wanted to keep; there were a few personal items worth shipping, but I was ready to shed the props Anastasia depended on. Fewer possessions made a person nimble! If Nashville wasn't my long term destination, I could pick up and go wherever I wanted.

My respite in Sojourner House taught me that the best blessings fall into your lap unexpectedly. Left to my own devices I would have been isolated in some hotel, marking time until my sentence was over. Enter Sarah, my guardian angel! I needed to find a way to thank her and the Laurels for their kindness. They thought they were offering me short term shelter, when in fact their hospitality changed my life. I now had friends I could depend on.

A firm knock on the door revealed Kit was back in town. She blew into the cottage, carrying a loaded picnic basket topped off with a wedge of last night's cake. Kit couldn't make a quiet entrance if her life depended on it. I was suddenly ravenous. It was after noon and I hadn't found my way past morning coffee.

"Anna! Millie thought you might be hungry. I hear you survived an ordeal last night, and you know her cure for stress is chocolate. Can't say I disagree. Mind if I come in?" She was already in, setting a place at the counter for me. The always chic Kit was slightly disheveled; her shirt was wrinkled, no jewelry adorned her ears or wrists. Dark circles testified to a lack of sleep. I had never seen Kit without lipstick properly in place, but today her face was free of any makeup. The last 24 hours had probably been an ordeal for her as well.

"Thank you, Kit. If I weren't so hungry I'd send you packing. You must be exhausted. How's your dad? Did you just get back?"

"Eat! My dad is tough as shoe leather. He will be back on his feet in no time. I was more concerned that my mother was taking on too much. Beau will stay there for a few days to get the troops organized. Boone and I got back early this morning; Ben phoned us last night about the fiasco with Paul. I'm sorry you got stuck in the middle. Paul has a gift for tipping the apple cart at the worst times."

"Don't worry about me. I'm fine. Sad for all of you, though. Is he still in detox?"

Kit took a deep breath. "Yes. We tried to see him, but he refused our visit. His probation violations are stacking up and I'm sure he blames Ben for calling the police. He's mad! He's been mad for a long time. I wish you could have met him at his best. Paul is so bright and funny. Addiction has handicapped him with anger and self-pity. He doesn't even remember who he is."

"How do you do it? How do you keep reaching out to him when it is so painful?"

The indomitable Kit teared up. This was none of my business, but I had been startled by the man with a gun in my home. A little context seemed fair. Besides, I was intrigued with the Laurel family dynamics. My experience as the only child of adoring parents did not prepare me for unpacking complicated people like the Laurels. My charmed life, I was learning, was the exception, not the rule.

I needed to get an education in mankind where I could, especially if I was headed to the cut throat industry of music. Musicians often fall on the complicated end of the spectrum. Kit was predictably candid; I had never known her to be anything but an open book.

"We survived with faith and a great counselor! Heartbreak over Paul held me hostage for years. Helping him was my focus for a long time, and the stress of it made me sick. Literally. I couldn't sleep, I developed IBS, my hair fell out. I'm a problem solver and I couldn't get any traction. Boone took second place to my obsession with helping Paul. Boone, in turn, put me second place. He found a woman who would give him some attention. It all came to a nasty head and I was left with a choice – get my act together, or lose my marriage. I switched gears, put Boone first, and learned to accept that I can't fix anyone but myself."

"How did you switch gears? I get so stuck! Even when I want to move on from things, my mind won't let me. It's frustrating. I can't tell you how many times that stupid video has played in my head, over and over again. I can't find the OFF button."

Kit nodded. "You give power to whatever you think about, and you CAN change how you think. It just takes practice. One trick I learned? Write things on notecards – funny memories, people I'm thankful for, encouraging scriptures. When sadness threated to hijack my thoughts, I pulled out those cards and read them out loud. We just aren't smart enough to think about one thing and say another, so it's important to say them out loud. Sometimes VERY loud! At first I had to do that MANY times a day. Sounds crazy, right? But it worked. Gratitude is good for the soul! It changes your perspective.

One day I was stopped at a red light with my windows down. I had been battling the depression dragon all morning, so I started listing things I was thankful for. 'Thank you Lord for Boone! And for a car to drive, this sunny day, and chocolate cake!' You know me, I was probably shouting. I hadn't even noticed the guy in his pickup next to me. His window was down too and he chimed in. 'Thank you Lord for a wife who isn't crazy!' and sped off. That cracked me up."

Laughter is great medicine. I could just see Kit, imposing to begin with, yelling affirmations at the windshield.

"I also turned off the news and all sad songs, shows, or movies. Only comedies for me. Frasier and I became fast friends. Then I built in some fun with Boone so we had new things to talk about."

"It must have worked. You two seem like a united front."

Kit laid her hand on her heart. "I'm lucky. Boone is very tender hearted. Losing Paul to addiction was devastating, but losing ME to Paul's addiction was just too much for him. We worked hard to put us back together. I had to learn lessons in forgiveness for him, myself, AND Paul. But don't think I'm a hero! The alternative was letting the stress eat me alive from the inside out. Paul is an adult. I can't control what he does. I love him, but while he is using drugs and alcohol I can't trust him. Boone and I decided we wouldn't let sadness steal the good things left in our life. Loss makes people do one of two things – fall apart, or hold the good things closer. I learned it's a choice. Our response to sorrow defines what comes next. Boone and I hope Paul will recover, and our family needs to be strong when that day comes."

"I'm sure that's easier said than done."

"Loving someone is ALWAYS easier said than done! But once you are a parent you will understand. You never give up on your child, no matter how old they are. Even if they hate you."

"I'm sure Paul doesn't hate you, even if he says that."

Kit fought tears again. "He might. Hate is a choice, and if you feed it long enough, it grows. Everyone has things to be mad about – anger is just a response to a situation. Hate takes root if you don't resolve that anger. Paul seems to be choosing hate, for now anyway."

I had never considered my emotions to be a choice. When I was 15, Frank and I butted heads over a boy. Andy was a year older and had just gotten his driver's license when he invited me to a bonfire party in the woods. This was back in my awkward phase; I was sure no boy would ever look at me without laughing. A whiff of attention was all it took for me to be giddy in a crush. Frank said no to the party, but encouraged me to invite Andy over for dinner any time. I was furious! Here was my big chance to break into the cool ranks and Frank didn't care. I remember yelling "you are not my father!" on my way to slamming the door. A flush of hate consumed me. I fanned that flame for a good week, refusing to talk or make eye contact with Frank. No surprise, all the kids at that bonfire were busted and given tickets for underage drinking, Andy was caught in a compromising position with Abby Harris, and they were the hot gossip for months.

My mom waited patiently for the dust to settle before gently suggesting Frank was on my side.

Admitting that truth was painful, but it opened the door to a deeper trust between me and both my parents. That situation was a tipping point. I could have resented Frank, like many teenagers do, and set us up for a lot of conflict. Instead, we enjoyed my high school years without life altering consequences. It could have gone the other way if I'd dug in my heels. Frank isn't one to back off if he believes his beloved daughter is in danger; he would choose the role of protector over friend every time if I painted him into a corner.

What was Paul's tipping point, when he chose bitterness over the love from his family?

Kit interrupted my thoughts. "That's enough therapy for one day. Thank you for listening! Cake?"

Behind her weary smile was sadness, but not defeat. I couldn't imagine Kit being held hostage to anything. She was strong and purposeful in everything she tackled.

"Kit, I hope you passed those lessons in forgiveness on to Beau. He was really mad at me for opening the Misty Hart can of worms with you. He wouldn't even acknowledge my apology. I'd hate to leave on such bad terms with him."

Kit took a step backwards, surprise displacing the sadness on her face. "You are leaving?"

"I've overstayed my welcome. Community service is complete and Duke fired me from the barn. Modeling gigs are scarce here, especially since I discovered Millie's chocolate cake. I need a job. But I have loved being here! How can I ever thank you for taking me in?"

Kit crossed her arms, staring right through me. "Are you going home to Illinois? Or back to LA?"

I was hoping to avoid this mine field with Kit, especially since the details of my move to Nashville were still up in the air. I hedged. "Not sure where I'm headed yet."

Kit was not fooled. Nor would she play my game. She probably learned that in counseling. "Anna, Beau is a lot like his dad. They are generous and noble, happy to give the shirt off their back if someone needs it. Until they get wounded. Then they lock down like clams. It's how they protect themselves from more hurt. Most men strike back at those who hurt them; Boone and Beau just build a wall around the pain and segregate it. I've seen it with Paul. Boone shuts out the pain to keep from bleeding to death. He almost shut me out too. Regaining his trust was tough, and I was tempted to throw in the towel more than once. Don't let Beau retreat without hearing you out. The longer he digs in, the more rigid his defenses. Climb the wall while you still can."

"I'm not sure he'll let me."

Kit laughed. "So don't ask him! You haven't committed an unpardonable sin. He's had a few days to get off his high horse; make him mad again if that's what it takes to get him talking. Just don't let him bury it. Then you can head off to wherever is next without Beau's funk hanging over your head. And let Millie make you a farewell dinner before you go. Can't have you leaving us hungry."

Kit buried me in a hug. I promised not to let Beau have the last word (or last silence) before I left. Who did he think he was? Kit was right; it's not like I betrayed some deep dark secret! By the time I got in my car to buy a copy of *Celebrity* magazine, I had talked myself into being mad at HIM. Beau was too quick to judge, and too harsh when he did. Nobody was out to get him. Misty's interview was spot on gracious. She thanked Beau for the opportunity to record the songs they had written, and applauded The Watering Hole for giving artists a chance to go back to their first love– The Music. Misty milked the goodwill of giving back to the Chorus, Beau came out smelling like a rose, and I wasn't even mentioned (phew). All that fretting over this interview for nothing. Everybody won. He had no right to be mad at me.

I bought several extra copies – maybe I'd leave one on Beau's doorstep. That ought to get him talking. Kit was right, fighting was better than sweeping conflict under the rug. We'd end up tripping over it if we didn't patch things up before I left. I was gravely at odds with Duke and Tish, no need to keep on Beau on that list. Having Kit in my corner gave me confidence to jump in the ring with him.

I'd regained a spring in my step until I opened the door to Sojourner House. Tish sat in the same chair Paul had occupied the night before. Geez, I needed to start locking the door.

"Tish, what are you doing here? I don't have anything to say to you. You got your wish – I'm out. Now leave me alone."

Tish eyed the pile of *Celebrity* magazines in my hands. "I see you've read the article. Pretty good press for Misty and Beau."

Why did this woman make the hair stand up on my neck?

"Really, Tish? What about the good press for the barn? Oh, that's right, you aren't on the cover so the rest doesn't matter. Here's some advice – you'll never get on the cover by serving brownies at The Watering Hole! And it's not my fault. You can't pin that on me."

Anger flashed in her eyes, but she asked for it. First she gets me fired, then she comes to gloat?

"Anna, I think I owe you an apology."

"There is no THINK in apology, Tish. Either you owe me one or not. Which is it."

"I get it. You think I had my dad kick you out of the barn. And maybe I did. But you must admit, from where I sit it looks like you were using us to kick start your career."

"Tish, you apologize as well as you manage the barn. Which is BADLY. I don't care what you think any more. Go back to your bitter little life and leave me out of it."

Tish looked like I'd delivered a one two punch to her gut. I might have crossed a line with that last comment, but let's not forget I was greeted by an armed stranger less than 24 hours before. I was tired! The relief I felt about the article vanished into frustration at finding Tish in my private space. I needed some peace and quiet.

Tish glared at me in silence. I glared back. This was one showdown I was not going to lose. "Anna, you're right, that was a lousy apology. Let me try again. I'm sorry I let the Belle Bridal ad get to me. My dad explained what happened. And I don't want you to leave town. We need you at the barn."

You could have knocked me down with a feather. I was prepared to tangle with Tish; I was not prepared for her to make nice, or for her to know about my Nashville offer. Kit was the loudmouth now, and I experienced a moment in Beau's shoes. It's maddening when your plans are broadcast without your permission.

"Kit had no right to tell you anything about my plans. But why do you care? You wanted me to leave on day one when you handed me that XXL shirt."

A smile flirted with the corners of Tish's mouth. "OK, guilty as charged. But it wasn't Kit who told me. It was Paul. And if you are headed to Nashville, that means Misty Hart sold you some snake oil to convince you to hitch your wagon to hers."

So many things she just said! My conversation with Paul ran through my head at warp speed, and yup, there it was. I did tell him I was moving to Nashville.

"When did you talk to Paul?"

Tish leaned back into the chair. "I saw him this morning. He said you were very kind last night before Ben came and threw dynamite on the fire. Paul did NOT mention you were pretty, in case you were wondering."

Tish and Paul? She read the question on my face.

"Paul and I go way back. We grew up together. He needed some support, so he called me."

"Paul wouldn't see his own parents this morning, Tish. They were happy to offer him support."

I could see the wheels turning, Tish weighing the cost versus benefit of going down this trail. There was still much to learn about the Laurel family and their entangled small town relationships. But I could see it! Prickly, intriguing Tish, charming Paul. Lots of combustion until the train crashed. Collateral damage everywhere.

"I didn't come here to talk about Paul."

"Oh yea, you came to apologize. Let's go back to that."

"Anna, I admit it. You are a master at managing the business, and I am not. My mom loved it, partly because it gave our family a place to land after Jordan's disabilities took them off the road. But I am more like my dad than my mom. He quit touring because it was the only way to keep our family together. I thought I was supposed to do the same. But my sacrifice hasn't paid off. In fact, I've made a mess of things. I'm sorry I tried to run you off because now I see we need you. Please stay."

That was a lot to process. My mind was stuck in the Tish and Paul chapter: true love or vampire tragedy? Where did Bubba fit it? And what happened between Misty and Tish? Snake oil was a pretty harsh charge. The events of the last few days had compromised my ability to focus. What were we talking about? Oh yes, me staying in Pleasant.

"So let me get this straight, Tish. You are sorry you tried to sabotage me because now you need me? That doesn't sound like an apology; it sounds like you are using me to solve your problem." I wasn't ready to disarm. Sometimes I can hold a grudge.

"Wow Anna, you aren't making this easy. I'm trying to give you some background information. But you want blood? OK! The barn was in trouble before you came. Ticket sales were in the tank. Servers were being paid to wait on a half empty venue. We were hemorrhaging money. Filling the seats the last few months has kept us afloat, and the *BACK TO THE MUSIC* series promises to get us in the black. You did that! All I want to do is go on tour with Bubba. But I can't leave my dad holding the bag without help. You are good at this, and I am begging you to come work at The Watering Hole. We probably can't offer you as much money as Misty, but you won't need anti-venom if you stay here. Move to Nashville and you are likely to be snake bit."

Snake bit. I didn't recall *Celebrity* featuring Misty's serpent side. Looks like I had only witnessed the tip of the Misty iceberg. Or, maybe there was more to her than a 'side.' One 8 second video was all it took to land me in the Spoiled Diva category. Admittedly, I deserved it, but there is more to me than one meltdown. Maybe Misty deserved Tish's disdain, maybe not. I was learning not to jump to quick conclusions about people.

Tish interrupted my musings. "Anna! Listen to me. I said I'm sorry. Will you consider our offer?"

"Our offer? Are Duke and Mo on board? Yesterday Duke showed me the door and was fine with it hitting me on the way out."

"That was my fault. He loves me. Don't hold that against him."

I had Tish on the ropes. It felt good to see her squirm a little. Until I saw desperation creep into her eyes. We were all on edge, and I was in no condition to make a big decision. The emotional roller coaster of the past few days had caught up with me. For once I didn't respond impulsively. If only Judge Goodman could see me now.

"Tish, I'll think about it. My head is spinning. I'm still trying to sort out what happened here last night. Give me a few days."

"Thank you." Her humility disarmed all my snappy remarks. Tish left quietly, and I locked the door behind her. What I needed was solitude. And food. Thankfully Kit's lunch basket was stacked with enough for a few days. It's as if she knew I wasn't leaving any time soon.

# CHAPTER 15

Kit must have alerted the authorities (meaning Millie) because nobody so much as darkened my door that evening. Even the dogs kept their barking to the far side of the main house. I settled into the couch with lasagna and a glass of red wine to get lost in old Audrey Hepburn movies. The model diet would have to begin next week.

*Roman Holiday* delivered swift comfort; at least I didn't have a kingdom riding on my decision to stay in Pleasant. Being a princess is wildly over rated in my opinion. No tiara can compensate for being under a protocol microscope 24/7. Geez, I couldn't even keep it together over a loser like Grant Adams. Gregory Peck would have been the end of my princess career. Good thing nobody was confused about my lack of qualifications to be royal. I dozed off towards the end of *Sabrina,* just when she realizes her true love is cranky Linus, not his dashing playboy brother, David. Why do women always fall for the cad first? Must be their charm and good looks. I wonder if Grant had ever seen *Sabrina.* Never mind, he wouldn't get it. The cads never get it.

The blue screen woke me from my slumber. I turned off my phone, closed the blinds and succumbed to the sweet relief of sleep. Saturday morning came late. After a hot shower, the only cure for my pancake craving was a trip to Mable's. If I lingered at home I risked a visit from Kit or Millie, and no matter how well intended, I needed to clear my head alone. As expected, Mable's was packed. I elbowed my way past a group of guys hanging out in the doorway to see if there was a small table open for one. Fanny caught my eye. She nodded towards the corner where Beau and I had last eaten and sure enough, there he was. Beau must rate a regular table, one where he could see whoever came through the door. He raised his eyebrows before inviting me to join him; his hesitation matched mine. We both seemed to be looking for a pancake feast without company, but since no other seat was available I accepted the chair opposite his.

Beau continued to work his way through Gus' Saturday special. We sat in silence until Fanny filled my coffee cup with a "hrump." Nothing gets by Fanny. "Sorry for crashing your pancake fest, Beau. I didn't know you were back. Kit told me you'd be in west Texas for a few days. I can wait for another table if you want."

"You'll never get another table. Are you eating, or just watching."

"Eating. My coffee rivals Fanny's, but my pancake skills are pathetic. And why couldn't I get another table? Because I don't know the secret Mable's handshake?"

"No. Because all those people gathered in the doorway got here before you did; you don't have the patience to wait your turn. And Fanny isn't looking to give you any favors if you come in here alone." Beau raised his fork to place another order with Fanny. Their sign language was well developed.

"Oh really? Does she have something against models? Or just anyone who violates the unpublished Beau Laurel code of ethics."

Beau's eyes darkened. "Probably both. The model thing will be less of a concern if you can handle your breakfast like a regular. I wouldn't poke the bear by asking for anything low fat."

The tension in the air eased just a bit. "Thanks for the head's up. I'll be sure to use all my butter."

Beau almost smiled. "And they say Hollywood types are slow learners."

"I'm happy to say I am no longer a Hollywood type."

"Best news I've heard all morning. Sounds like you've ditched the high life for bull riding. I heard you got some practice wrangling the Laurel known as Paul. The average model might have panicked when confronted with an armed intruder."

"The average model wouldn't be caught dead in a place where the eggs are fried in last year's bacon grease, either. I fail the model test on both counts."

"Lucky you. Gus' blueberry pancakes are worth surrendering your model card for. Not sure an encounter with an armed intruder is."

"I'm fine. Have you seen him?"

"Paul? No. I can't help Paul. He hates being told what to do. If we all quit talking, maybe he will quit trying to prove he doesn't have to listen."

"Maybe. OK, probably. But you can let him know you care. When I first got home he was drunk, but I got a glimpse of how charming and funny he can be. He never meant to hurt me; he might have been ready to hurt himself, though. You should have seen his face when they took him away, Beau. So defeated. Desperate people do impulsive things. Go see him."

"You're pleading the case for a guy who broke into your house and pointed a loaded gun at you? This is a lot more complicated than you know, Anna. Paul claims to hate our family, but he really hates himself. Until that changes, I have no way in. He wouldn't see my parents, he won't see me."

"He didn't really break in. I left the door unlocked. And he never pointed the gun at me! Just think about visiting him. Getting arrested was so humiliating for me. Smacking a police officer is nothing compared to what Paul has done, but in that moment, the shame made me consider all kinds of stupid things. Imagine how he feels. He might surprise you."

"I don't care why he broke in, Anna. The fact is he got drunk, loaded a stolen gun, and ended up in your house. You could have gotten hurt or killed. Don't you get that? He doesn't care about anyone but himself. It's time he faced the consequences of his choices. And don't kid yourself; remorse is not in Paul's vocabulary. You can't be sorry for something until you admit you were wrong. What Paul understands is revenge. I've had my fill of that."

"What can he do to you now? You are here, he is in there. You have nothing to lose."

"That's where you're wrong. If he's ashamed, me seeing him in jail will only make that worse. It's bad enough Ben saw him hauled away in handcuffs. I hope Paul gets it together some day; if he does, it's better if I never saw him there."

Men are nothing like women. As soon as I got arrested I wanted to call my mom, Maria, and every other friend I could think of to give me sympathy, advice and support. I knew I was wrong pitching that fit at the officer, but I still wanted them to understand WHY. The Why was more important, in my mind, than the offense. True to form, most of my friends let me off the hook once they heard how Grant had treated me. I deserved to be agitated! The officer was practically asking for it, especially when he made me stand in the mud.

If I took a step back, that argument was unwinding. The facts are I let my temper get the best of me, broke the speed limit, and punished a police officer for catching me. I blamed everyone but myself. Maybe if I had apologized to the officer, instead of flipping a biscuit, I could have avoided arrest entirely. He probably wouldn't have made me exit the car if I had been calm. My hysterical ranting about Grant made me look like a crazed idiot. A little remorse can go a long way, and instead I'd flown into a rage.

Hmmm. It's never too late to say you are sorry, right?

"Beau, I made a big mess of things when I blabbed to your mom about those songs. I'm sorry. I should have run when Misty invited me into her dressing room for that drink."

"Then why aren't you running now?"

"From pancakes? I like pancakes."

"From Misty. We live in a small town, Anna."

News travels fast; my anger matched it. "So you accuse me of betraying your secrets, but you are fine with Tish gossiping about me?"

"There's a difference. I never told you about those songs. "

"Well I never told Tish I was moving to Nashville! I mentioned it to Paul because he was mad about me living in his house. He was drunk and armed! Paul told Tish, she confronted me, then she told you, now you are interrogating me! See how that works? Not so different."

I must have been louder than I thought. Fanny delivered my pancakes with a shake of her head. I wasn't sure who she was tsk tsking, me or Beau. No danger of keeping any secrets now; the crowd at Mable's heard about Paul's escapade, my move to Nashville, and our fight in one fell swoop. Who needs cable when small town intrigue plays out in full color over breakfast? The calm, reformed Anna Martin lost her cool in round one with Beau. Nobody seemed to be filming us, but you never know. People think everybody else's business is theirs.

Beau leaned back in his chair. He stared down the nosy diners until they turned their attention back to chicken fried steak. "Point taken. But don't go to Nashville with Misty. She's using you."

I struggled to lower my voice. "And how is that different from everybody else? Tish only wants me to stay so she can go on the road. Duke wants me to stay to sell tickets. Nobody seems to care about what's good for me." I leaned across the table so Beau could hear me whisper and succeeded in dragging my scarf through the pure maple syrup swimming on my plate. Beau handed me his glass of water and a napkin.

"Lots of people care about you, Anna. My parents. Ben and Sarah. Millie. That kid Simon. Duke, believe it or not. Even Judge Goodman. Ever since you landed at The Watering Hole you've had a whole town full of people caring about what happens to you. Take it or leave it – your choice." And with that he picked up his hat and left, leaving me alone with my syrupy mess. Fanny refilled my coffee. "He took care of it."

"Pardon?"

"The bill. Beau took care of it. But feel free to leave me another tip, Hollywood."

One 8 second video, still haunting me months later. It takes more than a slick PR campaign to rehabilitate your image in a small town. I cleaned my plate. Couldn't have Fanny telling Gus I was on a diet, I'd never get a table in here again. I left a huge tip for insurance. Fanny almost smiled when she informed me people were waiting for a table and I should move along. Baby steps.

***

Not even Fanny's robust coffee could stop a carb crash after all that sugar. The last few days had been a roller coaster of drama, comfort food and exhaustion - I was back to phase three of the cycle. Thankfully no uninvited guests awaited me in my living room. Beau's truck was nowhere to be seen. Once I waded through the doggie welcome party, I was alone in my little house. Door locked, blinds drawn, I surrendered to the couch and *Love in the*

*Afternoon.* Audrey Hepburn never loses her cool, even when posing as a man's lover to save him from being murdered by his true mistress' husband. I gave myself an imaginary pat on the back; I had channeled a little bit of Audrey myself when I encountered Paul in this very room. Then a snapshot of me shrieking at Duke flashed before my mind. Pat on the back rescinded. My score was even at best.

Recovery from the crash left me famished for protein. Meat. Preferably a thick, juicy steak. Deli turkey from the fridge would have to do. I wasn't leaving, and the steak wasn't coming to me. *Breakfast at Tiffany's* beckoned. I cobbled together a tapas plate of leftovers and poured myself a glass of wine. Being fired had its advantages. Usually on a Saturday night I'd be working the box office and mingling with the headline artist. Shirley would be getting flustered about now, wondering how to manage last minute ticket requests for the sold out show. Poor Chelsea Mercer. Shirley hadn't mastered the art of selling future seats to tonight's disappointed fans, therefore Chelsea might be singing to a half empty house in a few weeks. Tish was probably bossing everyone around, Jordan and Squawk were making jokes in the booth, and Duke was likely counting his blessings that I was gone so Tish could simmer down. Sigh. Did he know Tish had come to me with hat (and a job offer) in hand? Probably not.

Just as Holly Golightly jumped from the taxi in front of Tiffany's there was a light knocking on the door. I waited, thinking they might go away. "Anna? It's Sarah. Are you home?"

I couldn't ignore Sarah. We parted ways with a hug after Thursday night's fiasco with Paul, but I hadn't seen her since. It suddenly occurred to me she and Ben must have had a difficult few days as well. For all of Ben's bluster, Paul was his brother. It couldn't have been easy to see him dragged off to detox. Millie had served us dinner with a side of tears and heartache that night. Ben was very sweet to take all the heat for calling the police.

"Sarah! Come in. Please excuse the cave. I'm escaping into Audrey Hepburn land."

"It looks like you are trying to escape the Laurels, and here I am interrupting your retreat. I'm sorry! I can come back another time. Just wanted to see how you were doing. Thursday night was pretty crazy."

"Is it possible to escape the Laurels? Kit brought a Millie offering in a picnic basket yesterday. I ran off to Mable's this morning and the only free seat in the place was at Beau's table. Do Laurels time travel? They were all supposed to be in West Texas!"

I handed Sarah a glass of wine. "Anna, there are days when I think the Laurels are superheroes with all kinds of magic powers. I love them! But sometimes they just wear me out."

Sweet Sarah! So quiet, so amiable, thrown into the pressure cooker of the Laurel theatrics.

"You never seem to be flustered, Sarah. How do you manage them all so gracefully? Ten minutes with Beau this morning and I was jumping down his throat!"

Sarah accepted my offer of a seat on the couch. "I have had a lot of practice. Ben and I met in high school, and if you get one Laurel, you get them all. My family is nothing like Ben's! I knew that from our first Homecoming dance. My mom took a picture or two when Ben picked me up. On our way to dinner we stopped at Heritage Park where his ENTIRE family joined us to take photos. I don't think I said a word that night. Ben did all the talking. But when he kissed me good night, my world shifted. I grabbed on and never let go. They have been very good to me."

"You and Ben were high school sweethearts? I thought that only happened in movies from the 1950s."

"And in small towns! I can tell you 2 or three couples who stayed together, and some who started dating long after high school was over. Shared history is a powerful magnet. Bubba is still holding out for Tish all these years later."

"They dated in high school?"

"No, but we all went to high school together. Bubba worshipped Tish from afar. She only had eyes for Paul."

"Paul?" I put Holly Golightly on pause. This was getting interesting.

Sarah nodded. "Paul. You can imagine how volatile that twosome was!"

Tish and Paul. Talk about cage fighting. Paul cynical and sarcastic, Tish pushy and demanding. The attraction was probably intense, just like the crash landing.

"What happened?'

"Paul happened. And Joy was never a fan. Even before Paul's drug use escalated, they brought out the worst in each other. I've never seen a couple enjoy the fight more than Paul and Tish. So many fireworks! It was the source of a lot of conflict between Tish and her mom. Joy wanted Tish to pursue her music; she felt Paul was holding her back."

So Tish finally cut the cord, went on the road, and her mom died. No wonder she couldn't just take the hand Bubba offered – they were all entangled. If that relationship went off the rails, she would lose another pillar of support. The risk was too great. But she wasn't considering the cost of staying in Pleasant. Handcuffed to a job she hated, missing out on the music she loved, and on call to an angry addict was a recipe for misery. And misery was written all over her face most days. I almost felt sorry for her. Almost. She was choosing misery when she could have run towards something a whole lot better. Being a martyr is never a good look.

"What's the story between Beau and Tish? You could catch a cold from the chill between those two."

Sarah sighed. "Tish was the last one to admit that while Paul is using, he's dangerous. She was openly critical of Ben and Beau when they cut Paul out of the ranching business, even though they weren't dating by then. The Laurels didn't appreciate her meddling, but we are like an extended family here in Pleasant and you learn to accept the good, the bad and the ugly of each other."

"Have you and Ben thought of leaving here, Sarah? Does it ever feel too small?"

"The size of a place isn't what makes it small; it's how tight your community is. Chicago has millions of people. How many of those millions were in your circle? You can only interact with a certain number of people no matter where you live. Ben went to a small college in North Texas for Ranch Management, I followed scholarship money to a huge state school. Through the years we learned which friends we could trust, which ones were just passing through. In the end, we had the same number of friends from each college attend our wedding. The size of the pool is irrelevant - it's how deep you are willing to go with people that matters. Have you met Jeff Green?"

"No. Does he live in Pleasant?"

"Yes. He graduated from high school in my class and lives right next door to Honor Ranch in that little blue house by the road. But you probably won't ever meet him. He doesn't hang out at the barn, or grocery shop at regular hours. He works in a manufacturing plant on the night shift and keeps to himself during the day. If he lived in the middle of New York City his life would probably look the same. The down side to living in Pleasant is everyone knows your business. The up side is someone will notice if you don't show up to church, and bring you chicken soup if you have the flu. The up side is worth it to us. Besides, Ben's heart is at Honor ranch. Once we got married it made sense to settle here."

"And you've never regretted it?"

"I did run home to my mother once right after we moved in to Sojourner House. It was a Saturday morning and Ben and I were still honeymooners. Let's just say I'm glad our bedroom door was closed when Kit and Boone surprised us with scones hot from the oven. Ben thought it was funny. I was horrified! I laid down the law after that. If we were going to live on the ranch, HE had to explain the ground rules to his family. No letting themselves in, no open door policy if he ever wanted to see me naked again! It worked. That's how I manage his family; I let Ben do it. He is my buffer and they have given us space. Beau and I are the only introverts in the whole family, so we stick together too. He's always reminding Kit that I don't want to be alone, I just want to be left alone."

"That's an Audrey Hepburn quote!"

"Yes! If she could survive in Hollywood, I can survive the Laurel clan. They always mean well, even if it is at full volume."

"Ben was lucky you said yes, Sarah. Not many women could juggle so many big personalities. Everybody loves you! I tend to take the 'talk before you think' route and get myself in a LOT of trouble. In just one day I ticked off Beau, Kit, Duke, Tish and Paul. And that's probably not even a record for me."

"Anna, you live large! I cultivate a tiny corner of the world. You imagine big ideas like the *BACK TO THE MUSIC* series. That takes guts. I'm happy to be support staff."

"Guts, audacity, you say potato, I say poTAto. Not sure that police officer appreciated my guts, or Judge Goodman for that matter."

"Hmmm. I'd say Judge Goodman saw an opportunity to have a dynamic celebrity bring some much needed energy to a struggling non-profit. Your talents would have been wasted on highway clean up."

"What? You think he sentenced me to community service at the Chorus because he thought I could help?"

"If he did, he's brilliant. Look what you've accomplished in a few short months."

Can a Judge do that? Isn't there a system for community service assignments? Maybe it's less prescribed in a small town. Judges do have a lot of leeway. Maybe Duke and Judge Goodman went to preschool together and share brunch after church on Sunday. The Judge probably knew the Chorus could use some new blood. My mom says times may change, but people stay the same. I guess Small Town America operates much like Hollywood, people trading favors, everyone leveraging information. The only difference is that in Pleasant, your history is documented since before you were born. Hollywood has a shorter attention span.

Sarah hadn't touched her wine. "Anna, mind if I rummage for a snack?"

I jumped up. "Of course not. Cheese and crackers? Leftover lasagna? Millie keeps me well stocked."

"Cheese and crackers sounds great. Or I can just go home if you want to get back to your movie."

No way. Holly Golightly could wait. "Don't you like the wine, Sarah? Can I get you something else?"

Sarah turned bright red. She hesitated, then blurted it out. "Anna, I'm pregnant! But you can't tell anyone. I'm waiting until I get past this first trimester to spill the beans." Joy illuminated Sarah's face.

"Wow! That's so exciting, Sarah! Kit and Boone must be over the moon. First grandchild!"

Sarah grabbed my hand. "Anna, we haven't told them yet. I had a late miscarriage last year and it was horrific. If you could have seen Boone's face when Ben told him we lost the baby – I was sad enough without that. We plan to surprise them at Christmas. Promise you will keep it a secret."

"Cross my heart! Let me get you some milk? Orange juice? Sit down and let me take care of you. A baby! Wow."

"And you can't tell Beau. He'll treat me like I'm fragile and that will set off all kinds of bells. Like you are doing now! Stop! I'm pregnant, not breakable."

"OK, OK. You eat the cheese, I'll double down on the wine!"

Laurel reconnaissance was over. You can't round back to family gossip once you learn a baby is on the way.

Holly Golightly and I eventually finished the evening together. It's easy to get snowed by Audrey's style and beauty but let's face it, Holly was a fortune hunting call girl. Yes, she was rewarded with true love (albeit with a good for nothing novelist who gets paid to have sex with his older benefactor. Eeeewww.) But that's not how it's supposed to work! The shallow are supposed to choose poorly and end up embarrassed on social media. If there was a sequel, *Dinner at Tiffany's* perhaps, we'd discover she got dumped once she got out of that black dress. Glamour is a demanding master; not even Holly could sustain the illusion forever, and no doubt her scoundrel would have moved on. God help me, I saw a little bit of myself in the naïve Miss Golightly. Thankfully Grant moved on before I threw myself at his self-absorbed, Fendi clad feet.

\*\*\*

My late night demanded a late sleep in. Millie texted me that breakfast supplies were on the front porch – bless her. She had declared herself eternally grateful that I called the police instead of her, and was dedicated to thanking me in food. Paul had no idea how much Millie loved him. Or the rest of his family, for that matter. It made sense why Beau wanted to stay away from Paul, but I was determined to bridge a gap if possible. I had witnessed a glimmer of Paul's winsome side, drunk or not. He might listen to me since I had none of his family baggage. Sometimes outsiders have an advantage.

Sunday remained a day of rest for most people in Pleasant, but once the brunch hour was over I texted Clayton: "You kept this troublemaker out of jail, now I need help getting into one. Call me when you have a minute." No harm. He could wait until Monday to reply if he wanted. My teaser worked.

"Clayton! Long time no lecture!"

"Hello, Anna. If keeping you out of jail required a few lectures, well, I can live with that. Do you need a refresher to keep you out?"

I could picture Clayton on the other end, frowning as he pondered the many ways I might have gotten myself back in the soup. "Clayton, I have been a very good girl. Despite being the victim of crimes and injustice, I am the picture of poise and self-control. You should be proud."

"Crimes and injustice! Sounds serious. Maybe you need the sheriff."

Tongue in cheek? Over the phone I couldn't be sure. His serious face leads with a furrowed brow; a faint grin betrays his teasing. I gave him the benefit of the doubt.

"No sheriff required. I need to visit an inmate in the county jail and heard you must get on a list?"

"Yes ma'am. They will run a background check, so with your criminal history I'm not sure you'll qualify. Besides, is it a good idea for you to be cavorting with ruffians? Might tarnish your reputation."

Ruffians? Teasing.

"Clayton! I have paid my debt to society. Surely you can pull some strings to get me in. I am on a mission of mercy."

"Anna, I'm kidding. You just need to fill out an application. The county jail is not Sing Sing. But as your friend, I will advise you to abandon the mission and leave it alone."

"What do you know of my mission, Clayton? Anastasia DeMars might have stirred the pot, but

Anna Martin only wants to build a bridge. I am innocent of all cavorting."

Clayton sighed. "I appreciate your good intentions, Anna. By all accounts you have made the most of your time in Pleasant. But this situation was tragic long before you arrived; you risk upsetting your gracious hosts by butting in. Trust me. Leave it alone."

So he knew about my encounter with Paul. Let's see –did he get the story from the police officers who arrested him? Maybe they all lunched at Jay's Diner. Or maybe Tish filled in Duke, who filled in Clayton? The party line must have been buzzing that night. Information travels at the speed of light in a small town.

"I'll take it under advisement, Clayton. Your wisdom did land me at The Watering Hole instead of on highway cleanup. I'm beginning to think you had a hand in that assignment. And who said I've made the most of my time here? Duke? Beau? Fanny at Mable's?"

"Ah, a smart attorney never reveals his sources. Suffice it to say I'm paying attention. And don't underestimate the sway Fanny has in this community. Best to stay on her good side. I've found a big tip usually does the trick."

"Thanks for the Mayberry education, Clayton. A good lawyer keeps you out of jail, but a good friend keeps you out of trouble."

"All in a day's work, Anna. All in a day's work."

Sterling, my LA attorney, was mainly interested in cashing his retainer checks. We most certainly were not friends.

# CHAPTER 16

Clayton's words echoed in my head. The Laurels had been juggling this situation a long time. I did not want to jeopardize their good will by stepping in where I shouldn't. Beau made it clear he thought it was time to let the cards fall where they may for Paul. The last time I tried to intervene between Laurels I got caught in the crossfire. My time left in Pleasant was short; probably best to listen to Clayton. He hadn't steered me wrong yet.

My phone lit up with a message from Misty: CALL ME. I thought she was busy on the road this weekend. Maybe news about the escapade with Paul had traveled across the country. She answered on the first ring.

"Anna, I want you to come to Nashville. The *Celebrity* magazine interview has started chatter about my *Live at the Watering Hole* record. I'm throwing a party on Friday with the whos who of Nashville to build excitement for its release. It will be a lot of fun."

Friday. I could do that. Best way to hit the ground running in a new job was to jump in the deep end. "How can I help? I've never been to Nashville, but I'm happy to promote the album if you just point me in the right direction."

"Amber, my assistant, is taking care of logistics. She will arrange a hotel once you book your flight. Just show up here in a knock out dress on Friday night. Plan to charm the local DJs so they give my single top billing. Sell the choir story, pull on their heart strings about how I'm donating the proceeds to make the world a better place. We need to milk the good deed thing; DJs love to tell a story. Maybe you should send a picture of those misfit choir kids so Amber can blow it up."

"OK. For the record, it's called the Joy Chorus. If you plan to promote the charitable side of this record you should probably know who benefits from it. And define knock out dress. I might need to get something shipped from my stash in LA."

"Sexy. I want the music bigwigs to be standing in line to talk to you. Think clubbing, not awards ceremony. And it can't be red. I'm wearing red."

"Got it. Will I see you before Friday?"

"If you get here Thursday we can hit Broadway for a night of live music! You can't appreciate Nashville until you are slammed into the shack that is Tootsies. Jeans and boots for that; you might end up with a drink spilled in your lap, but the music is worth it.

"OK. I'll plan to stay for the weekend. Then maybe we can talk specifics about us working together?"

"Sure. Amber will send you the details. Got to run."

Nashville. And a knock out dress. I was out of practice. Maria would have to dig for something in storage. Hopefully she was in town; we hadn't talked in weeks. I could treat her to a spa day for her trouble. I pulled out the notebook listing my wardrobe. Maria's parting gift to me was a detailed summary, with photos, of the clothes I left behind. The black Prada? Or something flashy, like the Versace mini dress? The Stella McCartney was always a hit. So many choices. I needed shoes too; sneakers weren't going to cut it in Nashville. Wow, I had a lot of shoes. Pages and pages of shoes. Pages and pages of dresses, jackets, gowns, jeans, tops, sweaters and handbags. Half of my inventory I'd only worn a few times, and some still had tags attached. How much was I paying to store all this in a climate controlled, monitored space? No idea. How much had I paid for all this stuff to begin with? Afraid to add it up, but I could probably buy a house in Pleasant if I had invested the money instead. I'd have to deal with that reality later; right now, I needed some sassy in the form of an outfit.

Maria was gracious. She would have granted me the favor without the insurance of my blue cashmere sweater, but I was happy to offer it. I could expect a box of designer dresses and shoes by Wednesday. She promised to include several options, complete with accessories. Ah Maria. I don't think I appreciated her as much as I should have. When I called the spa to book her appointment I added a massage and mani/pedi to their usual services. She deserved it. Which reminded me – I hadn't had a manicure in months. My nails testified to all the dishes I had washed at the barn. Time for some beauty maintenance of my own. My hair begged for a trim and I needed to replenish makeup worthy of an event. Good thing I had a few days.

Kit interrupted my planning with a dinner invitation. The family was gathering at the big house for Millie's Sunday night meatloaf and potatoes. Yikes, time to go back to greens and lean chicken. The Versace mini dress didn't leave much wiggle room for mashed potatoes. I declined with a big thank you. Kit said no worries, but she hoped to see me before Boone's big birthday party the following Saturday– dang! I had forgotten. I was tempted to say nothing and cancel at the last minute, but a little voice in my head shook its finger at me. So I confessed I was going out of town. Silence on Kit's end until she simply said they would miss me. Phew. I didn't yet know the full plan with Misty; it seemed better to avoid that conversation for the moment. I'd leave a nice gift and note for Boone. I did hate to miss his party.

Monday morning found me on the spin getting event ready. An album release party was small time compared to the red carpet in LA, but I wanted to make a good impression on Nashville's elite. Networking was important, regardless of the industry. Promoting Misty would require me to develop relationships with wave makers. In between beauty appointments I scoured the internet for information on how the music scene worked in Nashville. Good thing I did some homework. Nashville was nothing like Hollywood! Every DO in LA was a DON'T in Music City; don't toot your own horn, don't promise something you haven't already delivered. Actors and models promote the sizzle, whereas musicians must prove they already have the goods. Paying your dues is a given in Nashville. One "Confessions of a Successful Musician" blog practically screamed the importance of being nice to everyone. Tick off the wrong receptionist and your demo tape might end up in the trash. Or she might end up famous like Faith Hill. Many of Nashville's best and brightest once put food on the table as servers, secretaries and back-up singers. Since everybody embraces a jeans casual uniform, it's hard to know who the top dogs are. Assume everyone can help or hurt you. The caste system rampant in Hollywood, often advertised by the cost of your handbag, was far more transparent. Shallow waters usually are.

By the time Maria's box arrived, I wasn't sure what would play well in Nashville. The Versace, absolutely not. Far too loud and short. One dress was too hoochie, the black Prada too tight. Millie's steady stream of home cooked meals designed to "round out my edges" had done just that. Most of these outfits gushed theatrical, hardly the casual vibe that seemed to define Nashville. I kept digging. Maria sent a collection of favorites along with a few pieces I had forgotten. At the bottom was a soft blue cashmere wrap dress. Simple, elegant, form fitting without being trashy. A pair of brown suede boots were the finishing touch. Maria even included a pouch of jewelry. Perfect. The wrap made room for my softer edges. Rachel sent this dress over the previous year in case I needed something understated in my closet. I intended to send it back – who needed understated? Good thing I didn't. Thank you, Maria!

I avoided the Laurel clan all week, waving from my car when I saw them coming and going. Beau was nowhere to be seen. I did get one short text from Tish: "please consider my offer." It said MY offer. Did Duke know about this, or was Tish planning to ask for his blessing later? Not that it mattered. I replied I was leaving town for the weekend and would talk to her next week. No sense burning a bridge unnecessarily. Tish had swallowed a lot of crow to approach me in the first place; it seemed polite to give her the impression I was considering it. Impulsive responses had gotten me in trouble before. No downside to slow playing things. (I could almost hear Clayton's applause in the background.)

Misty's assistant Amber picked me up at the Nashville airport. She looked to be several weeks overdue with a baby. On our drive to the Union Station Hotel she briefed me on the weekend's activities. First, dinner at Merchants, followed by a stroll on Broadway to take in some music. Great! Misty and I could discuss details about working together. It would be easier to turn Tish down when I had a job already in my pocket. And Friday? Amber was vague. "All the information you need is in this red file folder. Misty promised me you are very capable. As you can see I'm otherwise occupied – I have a C section scheduled for Monday. I plan to spend the next 3 days preparing for my baby's arrival, but if it is an emergency you can call me. Unless the baby decides to make an earlier appearance! In that case, you are on your own."

The file was bulging with instructions. Confirm the vendors for the party, follow up with many A list guests to secure their attendance, make certain Misty's hair and makeup crew arrived at her home on time. Check in with the band, stock the green room with requested supplies, make sure there were plenty of press kits available for DJs and industry moguls. Greet guests as they arrived at the party, making sure to know their names and faces. What? I was a newbie to the country music scene. I had no idea who these people were!

"Amber, I thought Misty invited me to mingle and promote her contribution to the Joy Chorus. Her exact words were "show up here in a knockout dress and charm the local DJs." She never said anything about being her personal assistant."

Amber shrugged. "Welcome to the world of Misty. I hired a replacement – obviously we knew I was going to be leaving – but let's just say she and Misty didn't see eye to eye on her responsibilities. She walked out last weekend. I was under the impression you had done work like this before?"

"Not really. Until a few months ago I had my own Amber. I was under the impression Misty wanted me to help promote her album, not be her girl Friday. No offense! It takes a lot of skill to be a good girl Friday. I had an excellent one. But I paid her well because she can do things I cannot." Like anything administrative, anything that involves paperwork, or keeping people on schedule. I am the idea girl, not the logistics whiz. I sold the tickets, Shirley made sure payment was accounted for. It was awfully nervy for Misty to spring this on me without discussing a job description or compensation!

"Sorry, Anastasia. Not much I can do about this." She pointed to her round belly. "My advice to you? Get everything in writing and fast. Misty has a PR firm, an agent, and a label handling her record sales. What she doesn't have is a personal assistant, or a friend squad for photo ops. Think Taylor Swift and her posse. Misty is missing the girl power factor. You are a great photo prop. And by the way, I will deny ever saying that if you quote me. Just trying to help you out. The restaurant is right down the street; the hotel concierge can direct you. Good luck!"

Amber could not drive away fast enough. I guessed no manner of emergency would compel her to answer the phone, either. Misty and I had quite a few things to discuss over dinner. Good thing I brought my new leather jacket; it was colder in Nashville than I expected. The walk to the restaurant was just long enough to get me vexed about the bait and switch Misty had pulled. Photo prop indeed! That kind of thing works for media spin in LA, but we all knew the score in Hollywood. The Semi-Famous cozy up to the More Famous for help climbing the ladder; the More Famous can play or not, but nobody thinks that makes you friends. The More Famous are cozying up to the Super Famous at the same time for the same reasons. It's how LA works. But Misty led me to believe she valued my promotion ideas and wanted to work TOGETHER. Tish's warning echoed in my head. And Beau's. Kit's would have as well if I'd had the guts to tell her where I was headed. I'd been duped, and they already knew it. Give a girl enough rope to hang herself and she just might do it.

The restaurant was packed. Misty must have rented out the place for her private party. She was surrounded by a bevy of photo props – a slew of almost famous actors, and some musicians I recognized but could not name. Between selfies, a photographer snapped away. Misty waved me over. "Hey everyone, this is my friend Anastasia DeMars. She is a marketing genius! Without Anastasia, the *BACK TO THE MUSIC* series never would have taken off. But some of you might remember her acting debut – hey, someone has to defend the well dressed from law enforcement!"

People often recognize models but they don't always know why, especially when out of context.

But this crowd immediately connected me to that video. The recognition was instant. An undercurrent of giggles traveled across the room. Time seemed to slow down. I had a flashback to my anger when that officer told me to exit the car, reminding me that my impetuous response lead to my arrest. I was on thin ice - this room was crammed with people paid to post photos of the event on social media. Any reaction from me would be trending within the hour. How had I missed it? I was just another player, invited to boost intrigue for Misty's buzz. She hadn't even paid my expenses! Anna Martin was not going to be fodder for their gossip; my days as a video shamed diva were over.

I smiled. I hugged Misty. Then I whispered into her ear, "Beau was right about you, and I am not a sucker. Be a prima donna on someone else's time." I wandered to the bar for a drink before slipping out; no scene, no fit. Misty made such a big deal about giving back to the Chorus, she couldn't afford to burn the bridge with me. I went back to the hotel and texted Amber; 'Turn off your phone! Everything is under control for tomorrow. Have a nice baby." And I threw the red file into the trash. Let Misty figure it out.

I also sent Maria a message. "Maria, I want to thank you for being so gracious as my assistant. If I was ever demanding, or rude, I apologize. I owe a great deal of my success to you." Her reply was swift. 'Thanks, Anastasia. That means a lot to me. Can I have the black swing coat? You never wear it!" True. "Maria, I tell you what. You can have whatever you want in storage. Sell the rest and I'll give you 20% of the proceeds. It's time to unload my LA baggage." I closed my suitcase and called an Uber to the airport. Nashville might be America's favorite new city, but I couldn't wait to get back to Texas.

I stuck it to Misty alright – and myself in the process. The last flight out to Houston was long gone. Maria would have advised me to get a good night's sleep (in the hotel I had already paid for) and take a flight home the next day instead of camping out on an airport bench, but we all know I make a lousy administrator. No problem. I booked a 6 am flight and settled in for the night. This trip was costing me a lot of money, but the education was worth it. I vowed to make this situation a valuable learning experience. At the news stand I stocked up on supplies – neck pillow, blanket, and a book; *RANSOM: The Price of Success*. Perfect. A cautionary tale to remind me to BE CAREFUL WHAT YOU ASK FOR. You just might get it.

My 5:30 am boarding call came quickly. Time flies when you are engrossed in the rise and fall of passionate artists willing to sell their soul to reach the top. If it's the journey that counts, these people in the book had explored quite the route. The Prize – SUCCESS – came with a high price for most of them. The ultimate price for some of them. If they could have foreseen the sad end to their story, would they have embarked on the tour? For many, the struggle paid off in riches and fame. The pressure of riches and fame opened the door to addiction and depression, which led to a loss of riches, or family, or self respect. When you sell a sex tape to keep your name in the public eye, something is very wrong. Why couldn't they see it? The outcome was so predictable I was reading a book about it!

My mother saw the end in sight with Grant Adams before our first date. I poo pooed her concerns, thinking I could handle it. Oh I handled it, right into the clutches of a scandal hungry public. She must be frustrated with me. I am fortunate to have a mom whose faith in me never wavers, even when my actions could fill a chapter in that *Ransom* book. I drank the Hollywood Koolaid, believing success was defined by my Fame contract, or a red carpet date everyone envied. Duke Valentine knew better. Winning a Grammy paled in comparison to creating a life for his family that took care of Jordan. Joy's greatest accomplishment was founding a simple after school chorus where kids could find their footing. Small in the scheme of life, huge to kids like Simon or Cassidy Simms. Joy's legacy was thriving even after her death. Tiny greatness becomes gigantic when it changes people's lives for the better. No chapter like that in this book.

I dozed fitfully on the plane. By the time I pulled into the ranch I was bleary eyed. Desperate for sleep, I turned off my phone and taped a big note to my front door: SLEEPING. I WAS UP ALL NIGHT. PLEASE DO NOT DISTURB! I'LL SEE YOU AT BOONE'S PARTY TOMORROW NIGHT. Hopefully that would deter Kit, or Millie, or anyone else from knocking on my door; they would all be curious as to why my car was back at home instead of in the airport garage. But I was not to be left alone. A nightmare invaded my slumber. In it, Misty and her friends mocked me, my garish mini dress too small in a crowd of jean clad superstars. Grant Adams even made an appearance, his blond tart slung over his arm like a cat. As photographers closed in, I caught a glimpse of my mom and Beau in the background, shaking their heads in disgust. I awoke in a sweat, my heart pounding.

Thank God I made a quick exit out of Nashville. Misty wasn't that different from all the other fame hungry phonies I'd encountered before; in all honesty, I'd been one of them myself. But the veil had lifted and I saw the pettiness of it. Do social media hits make you important? I used to think so. The reality? Most celebrities were paying for those hits, they weren't even spontaneous! And why should I care what some kid in Omaha thinks of my latest shoe purchase, anyway? I can tell Simon he's awesome, and he believes me, because we know each other. Cassidy asks for advice because she trusts me. You can't build trust with people you don't know. You can sell them something, but that's not trust. When did we forget this?

3:00 pm. I needed to eat, shower and pull myself together. I had to go see a man about a horse.

Tish was scurrying around the barn barking orders at the staff, getting ready for the night's concert. The Texas Cattlemen were performing, regulars with a devoted following. They could practically run their own show, but Tish seemed in a tizzy with instructions for their crew. Relief flooded her face when she saw me – that was new – and she handed her checklist to Squawk. "Anna, let's go in the office."

We stood in silence, each waiting for the other to speak. Tish was probably swallowing all kinds of snide remarks. No doubt her bat like ears had heard I was going to Nashville, and yet here I was, back before the weekend even began. Poor Tish, torn between the desire to mock me or woo me, but needing me to deliver a get out of jail free card. She wisely chose wooing.

"Anna. I'm surprised to see you here. I thought we were going to talk next week. What can I do for you?"

I decided not to view her remarks as a fishing expedition about my trip to see Misty. We were both on our best behavior.

"Sorry to drop in unannounced, but my schedule cleared. Let's just get to it, Tish. You mentioned an offer. Does Duke know about this, or are you just exploring your exit options?"

Tish took a very deep breath – relief? Frustration? Resisting the urge to slap me? Hard to tell. "My dad knows I want to tour. He's been urging me to go for a long time; it's obvious I'm better on stage than behind a desk. He's also terrified of being left to manage the barn alone. Mo does a great job with the kids, but he has no interest in the business side of things. His passion is music. I promised I wouldn't leave without a solution. You can be that solution, Anna. Even I must admit our profitability has exploded since you showed up. People like you. They do things for you. I don't have that personality. I think the staff ducks when I enter the room."

Tish had a vulnerable side! She must be desperate to escape the grind here. And the staff did take cover when she showed up. Who could blame them? The worst kind of boss is the one who doesn't want to be there. But she was being transparent; it was only fair I play by the same rules.

"Tish, don't sell yourself short. Your gift is performing, not management. I've seen you come alive on stage, and you should run with that. But you need to understand my gift– ideas! Marketing gets my motor running! I'm brilliant when it comes to casting a vision. I do believe the barn will attract top tier acts with effective promotion. But I'm a blockhead with administration. I want to close the deal and pass the ball to someone else prepared to implement the details. For business at the barn to thrive, you need both skill sets. That means two people wearing different hats."

Tish nodded, processing my assessment. "OK, Anna, I see your point. If we increase our income through profitable bookings, we can afford to hire you and a competent administrator. Shirley tried to help, but her forte is payroll, not sales or management. She's not capable of running this business. I'm no good at it either. I hate it."

Yes, Tish, it shows. I said that only to myself. My mom taught me to count to 10 before firing off a flippant remark. I should make her day and call with that progress report. You CAN teach an old model new tricks.

"So Anna, what do we do? Are you willing to take the marketing reins? I know the barn could never match your pay as a model. And how can we find a good administrator? Pleasant isn't exactly brimming with MBA talent looking to run a music venue. The salary can't match a corporate job."

Tish was asking ME for advice. This just might work. "Tish, you don't need MBA talent! You need someone who is smart, hardworking, and willing to learn. Someone with great executive skills. I might know just the person. If she is open to the opportunity, together we will put The Watering Hole in the music venue Hall of Fame!"

Tish's smile transformed her face, the stress falling away in an instant. If I didn't know better, I'd say she was resisting the urge to hug me. "Really? You think you can pull it off? What am I saying, you can pull off anything."

"Don't get ahead of yourself. This might be tricky, but I'll do my best. In the meantime, keep this discussion between us. Don't book your tour dates just yet!"

"Anna, thank you. I know I didn't make things easy for you here. Frankly, I underestimated you. Paul said you were very kind that night at your cottage, considering the circumstances. He appreciates you not filing the gun charges against him. At least now he might get the help he needs."

"Tish, I don't know what you're talking about. I agreed to let Ben handle all the fallout from that night; he was the one who talked to the DA and Paul's probation officer. I wanted to visit Paul in jail, but Clayton talked me out of it. He advised me not to butt in to a tricky family situation. What kind of help is Paul getting?"

Tish's face registered pure confusion. "I assumed it was you who told the police Paul was just drunk and disorderly. Ben doesn't usually give anyone the benefit of the doubt, especially Paul. The judge in drug court gave him an 18 month labor program combined with treatment. It's very structured with lots of professional help. Graduates have a much lower rate of relapse. Paul has already tried 30 day programs that failed; I think this is his last chance. Any future arrests will land him in the big house.

He never would have gotten this lifeline if the gun charges were in the record."

"Tish, that's great news! Ben loves Paul. They all do. They just feel helpless. Maybe you can deliver the message to Paul that his family wants him well, not locked up. He seems to think they are out to get him."

Tish nodded. "I'll do my best."

Time to let the Laurels sort out their own problems. I had work to do. "I'll get back to you as soon as possible. If I can sell this job to my friend, I'll consider it my first promotion success!"

First rule of thumb, pay someone well. Perks don't hurt. Second rule? Fall on your sword when you need something. That's how I got a box of dresses delivered to my door last week.

"Maria? Hi! Do you have a minute?"

# CHAPTER 17

Maria was skeptical. Last she heard, Nashville was my destination. I had to fill in a few gaps; the newly humble Anna caught her a bit off guard. In the past when something went wrong, I blamed everyone but myself. No escaping the truth any longer – I caught a glimpse of my former self in Misty, and it was ugly. Pleasant and its people had inspired me to want more than notoriety. Anna Martin was happier, and far more likeable, than Anastasia DeMars had ever been. Maria was absent for this transformation, so no surprise she was hesitant to jump back into the fray with me. But I needed her for this proposition to work.

My enthusiasm hooked her. Maria conceded LA was too expensive. She and Leo were looking for a more affordable place to live. They had eloped on their resort vacation – he probably concluded it was the only way to tear her from my clutches. But Pleasant, Texas? To work for me again? NO! Not working for me! Working WITH me. She could be VP of Operations, I would be VP of Marketing, and we would both work for Duke (Kind of. I was confident he would give us free rein once he realized how hand in glove we were.) The cost of living was low and the job would be fun! Leo was a nurse; nurses could always find work.

Then my enthusiasm spooked her – was this a whim? She couldn't uproot her life just to have me chase a different kite somewhere else. Time for rule number two; I fell on my sword. "Maria, I know I've been demanding. I took you for granted, and acted like an entitled brat. I'm so sorry! Community service has given me a new perspective. I've learned the importance of being a team player. I even cleaned up after a girl who barfed all over the bathroom! Maria, I've changed. Please at least consider it?"

My "please" turned the key. In her experience I commanded, I didn't ask with a please. I confess, I boasted about my success selling tickets, and how the *BACK TO THE MUSIC* series promised to catapult the barn into a first-class venue, but I gave credit to Beau where credit was due. Maria caught the fever when I painted a picture of profits climbing on a spreadsheet; nothing makes Maria happier than a spreadsheet. But first things first. "Can I still keep some clothes from storage?" Yes Maria, you can! I wasn't about to burst her bubble with the news everyone wears jeans in Pleasant. Plenty of time to bridge that cultural gap later.

We agreed to a visit the following week, but I already knew she would fall in love with The Watering Hole. Maria had the wherewithal to tolerate Anastasia DeMars; working with Anna

Martin was going to be a breeze. Shirley could go back to her accounting cave, Tish could go AWAY, and Duke could focus on his one true love, the music. It would be hard work. It would be exciting work. I could stay in Pleasant. A huge sense of relief washed over me. Sleep came easy and long that night, free from fashion fail nightmares.

By Saturday morning Tish and I were hammering out the details with Duke, hoping Maria and Leo's visit convinced them to throw their hat into the ring. In the meantime, I had Boone's party to attend. Sarah had introduced me to a local artist who painted a portrait of Boone's favorite dog Ranger, so his gift was taken care of. Part of me felt compelled to surprise Kit at the ranch and help with last minute preparations, but I wasn't quite ready to come clean on the botched trek to Nashville. The Laurels weren't ones to let things go undiscussed, and there was plenty of time for soul baring later. Better to leave party prep in Millie's and Kit's hands.

I wandered into the box office. Shirley practically leapt from her chair. "Anna! You're back. Tell me you are back! I have a slew of unsold tickets piling up! I've been afraid to tell Duke how undersold we are for the next month. I never signed on to do sales! I am a number cruncher. Number crunchers like to be in the back room, not on the phone! Give me better numbers to crunch!"

Poor Shirley. Her tight little bun had come slightly unwound, and her desk was littered with concert schedules. A map of the venue seating for each show was posted on a bulletin board behind her desk. Seats sold were highlighted in green. There were many tickets still available. Shirley looked at me in despair. "Help me, Anna!"

I patted Shirley on the back. "I tell you what. You take a breather while I work the phones for a few hours. Get a coffee, enjoy some fresh air. In fact, why not take the night off? Go see a movie! I have to leave around 5:00, but I'll ask Melissa to staff the ticket office when I go.

Shirley looked ready to kiss me. "Really? Should I talk to Tish?"

"No need. I'll take care of it all. You deserve a break, Shirley. Now get out of here before I change my mind!"

Shirley grabbed her olive green cardigan and bolted for the door. I could not afford to have her burn out just when I was starting as manager. That panicked look in her eye would disappear after a few days in a quiet corner focusing on payroll. The secret to success? Stick with what you do well, and encourage others to do the same. If you want your accountant to quit, make her talk on the phone. Talking is what I do best.

It felt good to be back in the chair, assuring fans that chapter two of the *BACK TO THE MUSIC* series would be announced soon. In the meantime, don't miss Darby Walters, country music's up and coming talent featured at The Watering Hole next week. By 5:00 the seating maps for the following week were neon green. Tish merely nodded when I announced Shirley took the night off. I might have mentioned I sold out future concerts too. Forgive me for gloating just a little. It was for Tish's sake, to reassure her I could handle managing the barn. OK, who am I kidding...it felt good to do something right, and I'm not one to spurn a pat on the back.

By the time I made it back to the ranch, guests were already arriving. Thanks to Maria my blue wrap dress was accessorized, so party prep was fast. I wish I could have been a fly on the wall to witness Misty scrambling as star AND assistant at her own shindig in Nashville. Note to my future manager self – never demand something from staff you aren't willing to do yourself. Never treat people like 'staff' to begin with. Never assume people are lucky to work for you. Misty had taught me a lot in our short association. Maria was going to be blown away by how much I had learned in her absence. Even Ginger would have to acknowledge there are some lessons you can't learn in college. Education comes in many disguises.

Music spilled out of the Laurel's front door. Laughter and conversation greeted me on the porch, as well as a surprised and happy Boone. "Anna! I heard a rumor you were back from an adventure in time for my party! Thank you for coming!"

I made my way through the crowd to the bar in the corner. The house was beautifully decorated for Christmas, wreaths in every window and a huge live tree gracing the foyer. The Laurels had been busy while I was hiding out. Kit declared nothing motivated her to get ready for the holidays more than a party. She wasn't kidding. Gifts were piled under the tree, twinkle lights and garland wrapped the bannister. Fresh magnolia swags draped the mantel amidst candles and heirloom ornaments. Like most things Laurel, no opportunity for 'over the top' was spared. The house had become a Christmas wonderland.

Most of these people, however, were strangers to me. Rocky caught me scanning the crowd for a friendly face. "Hey Anna. Lost?"

"Rocky! Kind of. Who are all these people?"

"Some are friends from church, some are Boone's coworkers from his days in the oil business. A few are neighbors. You will see some familiar faces here and there."

His gaze traveled across the room to Judge Goodman. Yup, everyone knew my business in Pleasant. I smiled at Rocky. "I'll look for Ben and Sarah. Let me guess – the kitchen?"

Rocky nodded. Millie was busy loading up serving platters, Ben and Sarah garnishing per her instructions. Ben let out a whoop when he saw me. "Anna! Welcome home! We were afraid we'd lose you to Nashville's charms, but I see you came to your senses."

Sarah hit Ben in the arm. "Pay no attention to him, Anna. I'm glad you made it."

"Can I help?"

Ben laughed. "I hope so! Beau has been in a rotten mood all week. The last time I saw him this surly was when HE came back from Nashville. What is it about that city?"

Sarah elbowed him again. "Ben! Leave her alone. Anna, forgive my husband. He is cursed with the tact of a Clydesdale."

So Beau had been a wreck since our run in at Mable's. Was it me? Paul? A stubborn bull who wouldn't cooperate with his missus? Ben was easy to read, but Beau was like an encrypted code that nobody bothered to crack. I hadn't seen him at the party.

"Where is Beau? He wouldn't miss his dad's birthday, would he?"

Sarah jumped in before Ben could answer. "He was here helping us set up earlier. If he doesn't show up soon, maybe you could knock on his door? We have a present for Boone and don't want Beau to miss it." Sarah winked.

"I'm on it."

Ben couldn't resist a parting remark. "Tell him to leave the brooding artist in his shack. We're having a party over here!"

I slipped out the back door and headed for Beau's house. No answer to my knock. Maybe he had already gone to the party through the front door and I missed him when I was in the kitchen. If not, I wasn't going to let a moody musician keep me from Sarah's big moment. Just as I was turning away, his door opened.

"Anna? Sorry, I was expecting Ben. He's been hounding me to make an appearance at the party. What are you doing here?"

"Well, I'm certainly not trying to hound you! Sarah sent me on a mission to find you. She and Ben are giving your dad a special gift."

"I'm not much of a gift guy."

Brooding was right. I had little patience for this game when Ben and Sarah were so happy about their announcement.

"Ok Beau. I don't think you'll want to miss this one, but do what you want. Did it ever occur to you it might be important to THEM? Even if YOU aren't a gift guy? This party is for your dad! What is your problem?"

Beau looked ready to fire back, but reconsidered. "No problem here. Message received. Let's go." Beau and I arrived just as Kit gathered everyone for a birthday toast. Ben scanned the crowd, looking for Beau. Never one to be subtle, Ben called him out to join the family by the piano. Beau reluctantly left the back of the room and accepted a glass of champagne from Sarah.

Kit raised the first glass. "Thank you friends and family for coming to celebrate Boone with us. Boone, it's been a great ride together so far. I love you. Here's to MANY more celebrations together!" Boone landed a big kiss on Kit. Amazing that after more than 30 years together the sparks still flew. Kit laughed, and Boone looked at her with unmasked adoration. To think it could have all disappeared if they hadn't fought for each other. I had seen Frank look at my mom the same way – had they ever been on the brink of disaster? When I was in high school, my psychology teacher gave us an assignment to draw a diagram of our family dynamics. I had drawn a circle, with me in the middle. I hadn't given much thought to Frank and my mom as a couple, separate from me. I just took it for granted they would always be there, ready with a safety net if I needed it.

Ben handed Boone a box. "Dad, you gave us a very special gift once, and Sarah and I want to return the favor." Boone lifted the lid to reveal the tiniest pair of cowboy boots I'd ever seen. Kit threw her arms around Sarah. Boone looked confused until Ben yelled "You are going to be a grandpa!" The room erupted in cheers. Kit called for cake and champagne. Sarah was glowing. I worked my way to the front of the room to see those cute little boots. Sarah grabbed my hand and gave it a squeeze.

"Thanks for keeping our secret, Anna. Boone bought those for us when we were expecting the first time. If this kid is going to be a rancher, he or she needs to be properly outfitted!"

"Sarah, I am so happy for all of you! What inspired you to announce the good news before Christmas?"

"We wanted today to be special for Boone. Besides, it's time to celebrate the blessings instead of living in fear! Life is full of risks. At some point, you just have to jump in and swim."

I snuck up on Beau. He owed me an apology. What if he had missed this great moment?

"Well, Uncle Beau, are you a gift guy now?"

Beau turned to face me, a smile replacing the furrowed brow that greeted me back at his cottage.

"As far as gifts go, that's hard to beat. Thank you for getting me here. But I thought you were headed to Nashville for the weekend?"

I was tempted to spin a tale. Nobody wants to hear 'I told you so,' and Beau tried to tell me so. Ignoring his question seemed easier for the moment.

"Remember our breakfast at Mable's last week? When you said a whole town cared about me, and I could take it or leave it?"

"Yes." As usual, he was a man of few words. Or word.

"Well, you mentioned your family, and the Chorus kids, and even Judge Goodman. But you failed to mention one person."

"And who would that be?"

"It's a mystery, Beau. Enlighten me."

Yes, I was going to make him say it. He wanted answers from me, he needed some skin in the game. He leaned in to whisper in my ear.

"Me?"

"Is that a question, Beau? Or are you saying you should be on that list?"

No more retreating into the silent artist routine. He'd been snared and he knew it.

"Then yes, add me to the list. Put me at the top of the list."

At last! A declaration from the tight lipped cowboy!

"Then I'll take it."

Relief flooded Beau's eyes. Kit descended on us with cake and hugs, leaving his questions hanging in the air. Good, let him sweat it for a while. No better way to get a cowboy talking than to give him something to stew about. Kit had taught me a thing or two. Maturity is the fruit of experience, and it is earned, not given. I was just getting my feet wet. Best to listen to those who were further down the road than I.

Kit and Boone's friends knew how to celebrate! Ben rolled up the living room rug, dimmed the lights, and everybody danced. Beau grabbed me for a two-step lesson but I surprised him with my expertise. Mo had been teaching me on the side between Chorus practice and kitchen duty. After four months at the barn I recognized most country artists, even the oldies, and matched Beau's lead to George Strait's "I Just Want To Dance With You." Ben and Sarah spun by us, teasing Beau, "Hey Beau, don't let George do all the talking!" Beau swung me away from Ben and I swear he was blushing.

"I must be a pretty good dance instructor. You'd never know you were from Hollywood."

"Sorry Beau, you can't take the credit – that's all Mo. And I am NOT from Hollywood."

George serenaded us; 'I gotta feelin you have a heart like mine, so let it show, let it shine, if we have a chance to make one heart of two, I just want to dance with you.'

My skill in dancing the Cotton Eyed Joe left Beau astonished. "Anna, I believe you have been Texified. Be careful! People might assume you are a Texan."

I took Ben's advice; it was time for Beau to do some talking. We'd spent four months building a friendship, and I'd just been given the first hint he might miss me if I left. Once the party began to disperse we helped Sarah clean up. Millie was a guest tonight and Kit demanded she relax. When the guests were gone, Boone insisted we abandon the dishes for a nightcap by the fire. The Laurel family all raised their glasses to Boone and I felt right at home. And to think this all started because I got arrested for pitching a fit. Clearly I had a guardian angel who guided me to The Watering Hole; his name might be Judge Goodman. I vowed to say an extra prayer for him that night.

It was well after midnight when Kit declared the mess could wait for another day. Sarah and Ben headed home, Kit and Boone went to bed, and Beau invited me to linger by the fire. The dogs flopped down on the rug, basking in the warmth after their party exile. I kicked off my boots, happy to put my feet up. Between the fire and the Christmas tree lights, the room glowed. A sense of deep peace settled over me like a blanket. My Nashville experiment seemed like a distant memory. Why had I ever considered leaving Texas to work with a self-centered narcissist?

Beau and I sat in silence, mesmerized by the fire, each waiting for the other to speak. I was uncharacteristically patient. The ball was in Beau's court this time. He finally lobbed it my way.

"So, no Nashville?"

"Nope." Silence. "Aren't you going to ask me what happened?"

"If you aren't going, that's all I need to know. Staying here?"

"In Texas? I think so. I got a job offer."

More silence. If he wanted to know, he would have to ask.

"Where?"

I let him squirm before I answered. "At The Watering Hole."

He was caught off guard by that. "You and Tish, working together? Really?"

"The details are still in the works, but it looks like Tish might be going on tour. I'll give her credit – she humbled herself and came to me with heart in hand. I've invited Maria to come help on the Operations side, and I will work on promotion. Don't tell anyone. It's still up in the air. But I think it will all work out."

Beau sat back, more relaxed now. A smile made its way to his face. "Tish humbled herself! I hope you were civil in return. That couldn't have been easy for her."

"Hey, this is supposed to be about me! I'm the one you're concerned about, remember?"

Beau sipped his bourbon. "When did I say that?"

"Earlier tonight. I believe your words were "put me at the top of the list" of people who cared about me."

"Hmmm. Must have been drinking."

Two could play this game. "The Watering Hole job is just one option. If it doesn't pan out, no problem. My mom would LOVE for me to go back to Chicago. Lots of work there."

Beau squinted at me, trying to figure out if I was serious.

"Let's say you take this job at the barn. Would you stay here at the ranch?"

"I've probably over stayed my welcome. Your parents have been more than gracious and I know they'd never kick me out, but if I stay in Pleasant long term I need to find my own place."

"Why. Sojourner House is your own place."

"No, I mean my OWN place."

Beau looked away. The grandfather clock in the foyer chimed 1:00. Neither of us moved. The house was quiet except for music playing softly in the background. Miranda Lambert sang about her childhood home and suddenly I was homesick for my mom. We should plan to share Christmas together here, with the Laurels, before I moved out. It was magical on the ranch, even without the snow of my childhood memories. Big families make every celebration more festive.

Beau shifted in his chair. "Or…"

I waited. "Or what, Beau?"

"Or, we could get married and make Sojourner House OUR own place."

I can count the number of times I have been speechless in my life on one hand, and they all happened since being arrested in Pleasant. It took me a few moments to process. Did he just say we could get married? Was he drunk? Last summer I was living the Hollywood dream, flitting around town with Grant Adams and posing for paparazzi. Now Beau Laurel, a cowboy who hated publicity, was suggesting we get married? After knowing me four months? Was he joking? His face read serious.

"Beau, did you just ask me to marry you?"

"Sorry, I made a mess of that. I'm not good at romantic gestures. That's why I write things down in song. Want me to try again?"

He wasn't kidding. His eyes never left my face, trying to read my reaction. I had to back track.

"Beau, why did you let me run off to Nashville if you felt this way?"

"Because I am never leaving Pleasant, or Honor Ranch. This is where I am happy. If you don't love it here, if you wouldn't choose to be here, it could never work with us. But I love you, Anna. If you love me, and you love it here, marry me."

I did love it here. If I had to pick one person to sit by a fire with, it would be Beau. But this was crazy! We hadn't even been on a date. He read the uncertainty on my face.

"Anna, this is not an impulsive proposal. I've been thinking about it a lot. Don't forget I met you at your worst. I already know the most annoying things about you, and I can live with them." His grin dared me to answer back..

"Really! Well, you can be annoying yourself, Beau Laurel! Who springs a proposal on a girl before he even kisses her? What if you are a lousy kisser?"

"That is easily fixed." Beau pulled me out of my chair and kissed me in front of that fire. He was not a lousy kisser – quite the opposite. But he wasn't getting off that easy. I sat back down in my chair.

"People spend years getting to know each other before they get married, Beau. Do you even know what my favorite color is? Or my favorite movie? Maybe I have habits you can't live with, but haven't discovered yet!"

Beau laughed. "Your favorite color is red. Nobody buys red cowboy boots by accident. Your favorite movie is anything with Audrey Hepburn in it. You quote her on a regular basis, and tell everyone who she is, as if nobody outside of Hollywood has ever seen a classic movie. You are a messy eater, you can't hold your bourbon, and you look like death with a hangover. You devour brownies, but won't eat anything fried. That's the annoying stuff. It's small compared to the best of you."

"Which is...?"

"You buy clothes, wash them a few times, then give them to underfunded Chorus kids because 'they don't fit anymore.' You stand your ground against Tish, but are kind to old Shirley. You make ticket sales a game, you can keep a secret, and you'd rather see the Chorus kids in the spotlight than yourself. You abandoned your silly high heels for boots at the ranch, and have shown nothing but gratitude for living here. You even had compassion for Paul, and he deserves a swift kick in the ass. Plus Millie likes you. That sealed the deal."

He HAD been paying attention. How did he know about the give away clothes? Millie, of course. She caught me in the laundry room, washing and rewashing the same new clothes to make them look slightly second hand. No kid wants to be a charity case.

"And what makes you think I love you, Beau Laurel?"

"For starters, you are still here talking to me when I just delivered the world's worst proposal. Besides that, you take an interest in things that matter to me. Unglamorous things, like grazing methods and breeding stock. You got to know me without trying to impress me. You don't finish my sentences. You hum my songs when you think you are alone. And I overheard you tell your mom I was the finest man you'd ever met; that gave me hope. That kiss just filled in the rest. Marry me."

"When did I say you were the finest man I ever met?"

"At the barn, during the Chorus concert. That's the thing about great acoustics – even whispers travel across the room. Marry me, Anna."

He was very pleased with himself. And rightly so. Beau was the first person I looked for, the one I hoped to see on my porch for late night coffee. I trusted him, and I wanted to kiss him again.

"Yes." Our roles had reversed; I was the one defaulting to one word responses. "When?"

"Christmas. Right here, in front of the fire. Just our family and closest friends."

This Christmas? In a few weeks Christmas?

"Perfect." And I kissed him again.

*** 

Since becoming a model, I had pictured my wedding in terms of magazine cover shots; a beautifully produced set, imported flowers, scores of high profile guests in designer outfits ducking the paparazzi. The food would be exquisite, my dress one of a kind. Funny, I never pictured the groom.

I happily traded that fantasy for a cowboy in jeans. My mom and I dragged Beau and Frank to Nordstrom to buy some wedding worthy denim. Beau was shocked at the price tag of men's dress jeans. Why would a reasonable man pay almost $200 for a pair when he can buy Levis on sale for $40? Because if he didn't, he would have to pay $300 to rent, and wear, a tuxedo. Given that choice,

Beau waved a white flag in surrender. Overpriced jeans it was. Happy wife, happy life. He was learning. Frank met my friend Blake at Cavender's and scored a handsome pair of ostrich boots for the big day.

My dress? Plucked from the sample rack at Uptown Bridal (short notice alterations were more expensive than the gown!) I retrieved my sparkly Jimmy Choos from storage, still damaged from the walk through the mud the night of my arrest. It seemed apropos to commemorate the events that landed me at The Watering Hole. At the time, being sentenced to community service in Texas was my worst nightmare. Now I couldn't imagine my life without Beau, or Sarah, or the Chorus kids. How many times have I missed out on life's greatest gifts by focusing on what I didn't get, or complaining about what I did? Treasures often lay buried in the most inopportune places if we will just look a little closer.

Beau and I wanted our ceremony to be intimate and simple. Red Christmas roses graced my bouquet, Millie made the chocolate cake, and Beau surprised me with a diamond band to make up for his ring free proposal. Surrounded by those who loved us the most, we exchanged vows on December 26th in front of the fire and Christmas tree. I then ditched my heels, grabbed my red boots, and we headed to the barn for a jubilant reception. The Chorus kids and barn staff joined us in dancing the night away. It took just one boot stomping turn dancing the Copperhead Road for Maria and Leo to become part of The Watering Hole family. Clayton toasted our health, and even Tish wished us well. The photographer captured Ginger and Frank learning to two-step; my mom is much better at following than I am. At one point in the evening I sat down to catch my breath, overwhelmed by my good fortune. All the people I loved most were celebrating together in this room.

When the party wrapped, Beau threw me over his shoulder, dropped me into his truck, and we spent our wedding night at Sojourner House. Ben and Sarah had filled the cottage with candles and promised to leave breakfast at our front door in the morning.

Our wedding was perfect. No stress, no overpriced food or favors, just joyful fun with our people from Pleasant. An anti-Hollywood event. That's probably what caught Kelly Roger's attention. Dylan Worth was home for Christmas and surprised us at the post-ceremony dance party. Some of the Chorus kids took selfies with him and posted them online. Somehow, in the weird world of social media, Kelly found photos from our reception. She wanted an exclusive, promising a feature in *Celebrity* magazine. To sweeten the deal she offered a sidebar for the Joy Chorus, The Watering Hole, anything we wanted to nail down the interview. I could see it now: MODEL GOES COUNTRY. THE TRUE STORY OF ANASTASIA DeMARS AND HER TEXAS CROONER. I sent her a very nice message.

"Kelly, this is Anna Laurel. You cannot persuade me to publish our wedding story – it is not for sale. If you ever want to run a non-gossipy feature on the good work happening at the Joy Chorus, let me know. Have a GREAT Day!"

Beau grinned at me sideways. "That was a tiny bit snarky, Mrs. Laurel. Is Anastasia DeMars in the house?"

"Hey, Kelly Rogers lit the spark that torched my career. Our first encounter kicked off my demise at Fame Cosmetics. All things considered, I was very nice. But be warned, Beau! Anastasia took years to cultivate, it may take more than a few months to completely bury her. In the meantime, tell me everything you love about Anna Laurel. I hear she is fabulous."

\*\*\*

Kelly Rogers laughed. "I deserved that snarky remark! I had you pegged as an attention hungry bimbo willing to do anything – include date that skank Grant Adams – to get yourself in *Celebrity.* But to be honest, I was desperately trying to move away from gossip into real journalism. I thought if I highlighted pertinent issues, like the sexism rampant in those movies, I could move up the ladder. You were just collateral damage. Sorry. I misjudged you."

We were enjoying lunch at my favorite LA bistro. Beau had been nominated for a Grammy Award and after much arm twisting, he agreed to attend the event. Kelly Rogers had moved on from *Celebrity* to the online publication *No Stone Press.* Instead of tracking fashion trends and high profile breakups, Kelly was exposing the dirty underside of the entertainment business. When we first met four years before, stars threw themselves at her feet for a mention in *Celebrity* magazine. Now, Hollywood bigwigs bolted when they saw her coming. Kelly had made her fair share of enemies as she pulled back the veil shrouding corruption and misogyny in Tinsel Town. I had underestimated HER.

"Kelly, what made you leave the limelight for investigative reporting? You scored a lot of perks at *Celebrity.* Sounds like you traded the red carpet for the penalty box."

"So true! The penalty box might not be very well appointed, but I can sleep at night. Soon after my daughter Eden was born, I was bemoaning the condition of the world to my mom. Her take on it was direct. 'Change it. You have talent, access to information, and a following. Use it for something more important than fluff.' That struck a nerve."

"You have a wise mother! So do I. But I'm confused. *No Stone Press* unmasks the dark side of the entertainment industry. Beau and I remain in the light, tucked away in Pleasant. No story here."

Kelly nodded. "One way to initiate change is to expose the ugly side of things. But even the scandal hungry public tires of misdeeds if you never introduce some hope! People want to be inspired. I want to be inspired. Reporting nothing but exploitation is depressing, so I vowed to balance the distressing with the beautiful. I think you have a beautiful story that would encourage people to invest in others."

"I agree! But Beau shuns publicity. I doubt you could convince him to share his story, much less put it in print."

"I'm interested in YOUR story. It's the transformation from Anastasia DeMars, notorious model in the news, to Anna Laurel that fascinates me. You are committed to things that matter – kids in your community, a viable business, your marriage. Everything about your life breathes authenticity; this generation craves authenticity in their shallow social media lives. I have a publisher interested, and you get final approval of the manuscript. This could be a bestselling book! Trust me. I know that sounds crazy in light of our history, but I want to do this right."

"I do trust you, Kelly. Your *No Stone Press* features are well researched and professional. I did my homework! But the public has only seen the Hallmark version of the past four years. Once the *BACK TO THE MUSIC* series took off, business at The Watering Hole exploded. That success triggered growing pains, professionally and personally! Beau is determined to keep his world small, while I'm paid to invite the world in. Our competing priorities often clash. Conflict is sometimes the main course for dinner at our house."

"That's exactly what intrigues me! Success never comes without cost. You must have discovered a way to bridge the gap because love radiates from every photo taken of the two of you."

"Thank you! The more obstacles we overcome, the deeper our connection. But it hasn't been easy.

Beau deserves a lot of the credit. He encourages me to put pedal to the metal, even when promoting the barn infringes on our time together; the music business isn't exactly a 9 to 5 gig! And we've both learned to temper our ambition when it threatens to harm our marriage. That means delegating, which is not easy for either of us."

Kelly was furiously taking notes. "If Beau's passion is songwriting and ranching, and yours is marketing at The Watering Hole, where do your aspirations intersect? The Joy Chorus?"

She remembered the name of the Joy Chorus! The sting of Misty Hart calling it a choir for misfit kids was still sharp.

"Yes, the Joy Chorus. We bring different skills to the table, but our hearts are one in continuing the great work Joy began. When Tish left the barn to tour, Beau stepped in as music director. I herd the cats! Mentoring 50 teenagers always gives us something new to talk about. We've expanded the mission to include summer internships in marketing, music production, and business. And our commitment to the Chorus gives The Blue Valentines freedom to tour again. They have enjoyed something of a national comeback. Tish even joins them on stage periodically."

Kelly clapped. "That's amazing! I saw them interviewed on *Entertainment Now*. Mo and Duke credited an angel for with holding down the fort so they could chase chapter two of their youth. I'm guessing that's you! What's the key to making it all work? You have so many kites in the air!"

"Lots of support! Beau and I are blessed to have family and business partners who share our vision. The old adage is true - it takes a village to achieve success in any venture. Nobody gets there alone. If anyone tells you otherwise, they are either lying or deluded!"

Kelly was very persuasive. She was confident we had a compelling story to tell. Joy's legacy inspired me, I knew it could inspire others, but I wasn't comfortable making Anastasia DeMars the only star of the narrative. Kelly agreed. The book would explore the importance of community, how we become our best selves in the company of other good people. Everyone from Clayton, to Judge Goodman, to Tish, to Beau would get their due. The best tales unveil the full truth, warts and all. Was I game?

Beau would take some convincing, but I was in.

"Kelly, I have one condition before I sign on a dotted line."

"Beyond final approval of the manuscript?"

"Yes. Once the book is published, all references to me become Anna Laurel. This book needs to be the final chapter for Anastasia DeMars."

"We have a deal! I look forward to working with you, Anna."

"OK, well a deal should be celebrated! Dessert? The best part of being an ex-model is dessert!"

"Of course! Champagne too?"

Kelly promised to keep my pregnancy a secret as we toasted our new project with crème brulee instead of bubbly. We parted as friends, two women determined to live a more purpose driven life than what we imagined years ago.

Beau was surprisingly open to the project. "I trust you, Anna. And we DO have a great story. Tell it well."

I called Ginger, but got her voicemail. She and Frank were busy packing up their house in Chicago. Jeff Green sold them his little blue house down the road from Honor Ranch, and remodeling was complete. They would have time to get settled before Baby Laurel arrived. "Mom? Call me back – and buckle your seat belt for this one! I love you."